Christmas in Crisis

PAUL CUDE

DEDICATION

Two names... Polkinghorne and Vimes. The first, my favourite teacher at school and one I owe a great deal to because he, of all people, introduced me to the sport that I love and which defines me absolutely, and in that moment, changed my life forever.

Second and quite possibly instantly recognisable to a great many of you, a character's name out of the books of my favourite author... Terry Pratchett. I never got to tell him how much his work meant to me, simply because I was never brave enough. If I could go back, I would in a heartbeat.

This story is dedicated to both of you. Enjoy!

PROLOGUE

Hope is a powerful thing. As powerful as love? Maybe, maybe not some would argue. Both are potent forces, generally for good and have the potential to spur every being on the planet on to something more, to better themselves, to transform and empower, to change lives, to throw off the shackles of darkness and come back into the light. If the most formidable festival of hope is extinguished by unrelenting dark forces, how will the world cope with the profound consequences? Can a group of unbelievers thrown together at the last minute battle shadows and despair, win against all odds, and restore that much needed optimism and expectation? How far would you be prepared to go to save Christmas itself?

CHRISTMAS IN CRISIS

White, frosty mist surrounded his face as he exhaled, the chilly, wintery cold leaving its mark, as was its wont at this time of year. Maintaining his grip on the pushchair with one hand, whilst holding onto his elder daughter Megan's tiny gloved appendage with the other, Michael attempted to weave his way along the cracked and bumpy pavement, all the time avoiding pedestrians stalking past him in the opposite direction, their silhouetted frames backlit against the darkness by the dazzlingly bright car headlights that fought their way towards the centre of the city.

Ducking off to one side of the path, in a conveniently located space, the children's father circled around the buggy to make sure that Rhianne, the younger of the two tucked up warmly within, was as content as she could be. She was, her smiling and curious expression just visible above the layers of blankets that were there to keep her warm, fighting off the typical December temperatures, eyes all the time locked on the numerous Christmas decorations that hung securely above the Salisbridge street.

"I'm hungry," announced Megan from off to one side, still holding her father's hand even though they were a little way from the busy main road.

"We're nearly home sweetheart," replied Michael, pulling a face at the tucked up Rhianne in an effort to make her smile and take her mind off the biting cold. "Five more minutes and then we'll be there."

"Will mummy be in when we get home?" enquired the inquisitive toddler.

"I should think so."

"Great... I'm going to tell her all about our shopping trip."

"I'm sure she can't wait to hear all about that," replied Michael, wondering whether he'd just stitched his wife up, knowing exactly how much of a chatterbox his eldest was.

Checking that the numerous bags above, below and attached to the handles of the buggy were still all okay, he checked the path was clear and they resumed the short journey, all the time relishing the cold battering the light stubble covering his chin and cheeks, through what remained visible of his face poking through the hood of his bright blue winter coat. He loved this time of year, and had for as far back as he could remember. Of course the fact that it was Christmas and his birthday all in the same month had played a huge part when he was younger, spoiled senseless by both sets of grandparents, who were the love of his life up until, that is, he met his gorgeous, intelligent, kind and caring wife Caroline, who completed him absolutely, someone he now thought of as not only his best friend but his soul mate as well. The main reason that he loved this particular part of the calendar, and had done since at least the start of his teenage years, was because of his chosen sport... HOCKEY! Although played nearly all year round now, the main leagues and games always came thick and fast during the autumn and winter periods, along with training on those nippy nights that on occasion got cancelled because of the build up of ice on the Astroturf pitch, the only weather condition that could do that. It didn't happen often though, with the cold only really spurring him on to run harder and faster, bringing out the best in his competitive nature, the sport that he loved so very much defining him as a person.

Arriving at the zebra crossing, Megan reached up to press the button as she always did, fascinated to see how long it would take for the red man to turn green and the traffic to stop. Nothing if not consistent, it took what seemed like an age for them to be able to cross. Eventually though, the colours changed and the harsh beeping drowned out running engines momentarily.

Having made it to the other side, Megan's hand was released, allowing her to walk of her own accord on the inside of the pushchair now that they were away from the main road, something that delighted her no end and allowed her to take in numerous festive lights in the windows of the houses that they passed. Scooting up the narrow pavement past all the terraced houses and the multitude of parked cars, the toddler walking as fast as her little legs would carry her, occasionally poking her head around the front of the buggy in an attempt to smile at her sister, the three of them and their assortment of presents covered the last part of their journey in only a few minutes. Grabbing the black metal gate, Megan expertly opened it, provoking the usual harsh sounding squeak as she did so. Michael slipped into the tiny front garden, with the pushchair, which was mainly concrete with a few surrounding plants, the toddler closing the gate behind him. Searching for his keys amongst the jumble of stuff in his pocket, eventually he pulled them out and, selecting the correct one, slid it into the light blue front door, with a semi circle of glass at the top. Immediately, the need to push it open disappeared as the stunningly beautiful, blonde haired Caroline appeared at the entrance and made enough room for them all. Megan rushed in first, keen to get out of the cold and tear off all her layers. Michael followed on with his precious cargo of tiny baby and shed load of presents, kissing his wife fully on the lips on the way past. Securing the door and pulling the dark blue velvet curtain back behind her to help keep out the cold, Caroline expertly extracted Rhianne from the comfort of the buggy, holding her tightly in her arms, much to the child's delight.

"Shopping I see," remarked the doting mother in the direction of her husband, before he'd even had a chance to unzip his coat. "Did you have lots of success?"

"I... I mean, we, picked up a few bits and bobs," he said, knowingly and with a subtle wink that neither of the children would have picked up on.

"Mummy, mummy, mummy... we saw Santa. He was sat at the entrance to a huge grotto," babbled Megan excitedly, her rosy red cheeks bobbling around as she did so.

"That sounds exciting," observed Caroline.

"And there was snow, and icicles, and a huge reindeer."

"Wow... I wish I'd been there. Perhaps we could go back at the weekend?"

"That would be fantastic mummy," the keyed up toddler replied.

"Megan," asked her father. "Do you think you could switch on the Christmas tree lights after you've taken off your coat?"

Pulling off her jacket and tossing it wildly on the floor, the enthusiastic youngster bounded over to the brightly decorated tree, slipped down onto the dark blue carpet and with a simple flick of her fingers, switched on the lights. Abruptly, a multitude of ever changing colours enveloped the small rectangular living room, bathing them all in greens, blues, reds, whites and pinks, much to the delight of Rhianne, prompting something of a dribbling giggle.

Not quite perfect, more like a contented bliss, the four of them, all in their loving bubble, remained happy and relaxed, each in their own way looking forward to the festive season that was all but upon them. Little did they know that their near perfect world and love for everything festive was about to be turned upside down because, unbeknown to them, this year, Christmas was cancelled.

Christmas is a lie! There, I've said it. But not the one you're thinking of. Which bit then, I hear you ask? Most of it, but not all, and especially not the magic, because there's plenty of that, only it's based solely on ancient, timeworn, dragon magic.

The exaggerations that have built up include Santa's workshop in the North Pole, packed full of elves making toys all year round for the children, a stable full of reindeer and the beloved Mrs Claus, fussing over her husband. Such things do not exist I'm afraid, but the rumours surrounding them have served their purpose for a very long time, much as any good distraction should, compelling you to look in one direction, when everything is really going on in the other. It really is that simple. And the beginnings, some thousand or so years ago, went something like this...

A tinkerer would best describe his true nature. Of course there was some scientist thrown in, along with accomplished magic user, a fascination for the natural world, a kind and caring heart, the need to do what was right and an exquisite imagination. All wrapped up in an outstanding dragon body, around fifteen metres in height. Sumptuous red scales stuck out from nearly every part of him, varying in shades a little, but not a lot. Dark, inky black covered his knees down to the razor sharp talons on his gigantic feet, making it look as though he wore dark, shiny boots, something regarded as unusual by others of his kind. Around his wrists, knees and neckline most of the burnished scales flushed a pristine white, setting off the primary red no end. As if that wasn't fantastical enough, long, wispy white hairs draped from beneath his prehistoric jaw line, surviving the regular bouts of flame that burst forth from his mouth and nostrils by the skin of their teeth. All in all he was an astounding looking creature, one that had come to live and call home the middle of a large forest in what would now be classed as Malaysia, somewhere just south of Pahang.

That gentle giant of a dragon who went by the name Strawberry Snow, accredited to him during his stint in the nursery ring by not only the *tors,* but also his fellow pupils, due mainly to the colours of his scales, had discovered a labyrinth of connected caves quite by accident, whilst out exploring one day. Right there and then he decided to set up home inside one of the caverns, having fallen in love with not only the country, but the entire continent as well. In the middle of the lush, green jungle, a huge, dark hole almost fifty metres across, carved out of stone by rainwater through the ages, the sides of which were as smooth as a well crafted plastered wall, outlined his nearest entrance and exit. And he was sure just the apparent danger from its gaping maw was enough to deter any would be adventurers. Months went by, with all being well, his sneaky hideaway many miles from the nearest human villages. Keen to avoid any sort of interaction, he knew first hand just how badly any contact with their species could go and just how quickly things could spiral out of control. Of course they didn't represent a real threat, not to him or any other dragon for that matter. But under orders from the dragon council and the king himself, they were to be protected, nurtured and guided, in line with what the prophecy that they were all bound to had stipulated all those years ago. It was a shame it didn't work both ways, he thought, having often glimpsed potential in their ape-like charges. If they could unveil themselves, work together and get over that initial shock, then who knows just what could be achieved. Of course that hadn't happened, and on every occasion that a human encountered a dragon, fear, hatred and violence had predictably reared their ugly heads. Not so much a surprise, rather a misguided hope that one or two of them at least could attempt some form of communication before their baser instincts compelled them to attack, he did wonder whether or not that boded well for the future of both their races currently hiding side by side in plain sight.

Being the consummate loner that he was, he continued happily with his experiments, having moved all his laboratory equipment here from his home in the dragon domain, occasionally using magic to probe and prod insects and creatures from the surrounding wilderness, a fascination for butterflies and birds nearly always prevalent, constantly amazed at the beating of their tiny wings in relation to his, keen to try and capture, alter and understand the miniscule amounts of time related to their flight and whether or not it somehow correlated to that of his own race.

Caught up in his experiments, brilliant blazing sunlight piercing the darkness of the hole that he thought of as the entrance to his home, his enhanced supernatural senses failed to recognise the tiniest of noises, as something unusual crept quietly into his mysterious lair.

His huge, beach ball sized eyes focused fully on the interior of the huge glass container, watching two humungous butterflies interact with a bright pink orchid, using a smidgen of the ethereal energy that was his birthright to zoom right in and almost slow down time in an effort to gain a true appreciation of what was going on, it was only the startling shattering of glass on the cold rocky floor behind him that alerted him to his uninvited visitor.

Moving faster than the eye could see, well... the human eye anyway, Strawberry was up off the floor in an instant, and almost on top of the dark skinned human that stood carrying a primitive spear, in the entranceway to what he considered his private realm. Waiting patiently for the typical response, either flight or fight, having a little bet with himself deep within his mind to see exactly which one it would be, (he'd opted for flight, given the size of the lithe little human, who he assumed must have been somewhere in his teenage years,) he was more than a little surprised when the young man stood his ground, kept his weapon pointing away, and with only the tiniest amount of trepidation, ventured a question.

"C... c... can you understand me?" he ventured, shaking just a little.

Caught off guard to say the least, his prehistoric opposite pondered how to proceed, having never come across a human either brave or inquisitive enough to stand their ground against one of his kind. Feeling that this one was more than a little special, and hoping to build some kind of bridge between their races, Strawberry lowered his guard, pulled himself back a little, and whilst attempting as much of a smile as he could, which given his massive primeval skull was tricky at best, replied in his most kind and considerate voice.

"I most certainly can understand you, child, thank you for asking."

Nicolaus, as that was his name, was absolutely awe

struck and had never seen anything like it. Discovering the gigantic hole in the middle of the jungle had seemed enough of an adventure in itself, but to shimmy down here, guided by the brightly lit beams of the sun and then to discover this, was nothing short of magnificent, and everything that he'd ever dreamed of. On being caught, he knew there was no way he could retrace his steps in time to escape. And so the only logical thing for him to do, in his mind at least, was to stand his ground and try to communicate. Against what he considered all the odds, it had worked, and here they were, talking as equals.

Strangely, after that one unique encounter, they became the best of friends, with Nicolaus keeping Strawberry's secret safe, never revealing his existence or the location of the cave to any of the villagers, the dragon tinkerer always looking out for his friend, making sure he was fed, as well as using his magical gift to heal any wounds or injuries that he sustained. Not only did their camaraderie grow, but they complemented each other as well as could be. Scouting the humid jungle together when they were able to, Nicolaus could access places Strawberry couldn't, and vice versa, with each doing their own part in collecting animal and plant species used in the tinkerer's experiments. Along the way, they made sure to collect enough fruit, fish and small rodents to justify the young boy's supposed hunting trips into the forest and away from his neighbours.

At least five days a week saw them trampling side by side beneath the evergreen canopy of the bountiful forest, exploring and hunting, fishing and collecting, all the while their bond of friendship getting ever stronger, the two of them becoming as close as any human and dragon could. To the point that, as the sun started to set against the bright blue sky on one of the warmest days of the year so far, Strawberry did the unthinkable, at least it would have been only a short while ago, and offered to take Nicolaus up into the darkening evening skies, on his back. Stunned, at least momentarily, the excited young man quickly gobbled up the opportunity and slid into place just behind the dragon's thickly scaled neck. With almost no effort at all, Strawberry bounded into the air, and with two strong flaps of his enormous wings, had them cutting through the warm wind, much to the delight of the young human. Soaring across the all encompassing canopy in the dark was no problem for the dragon, due in no small part to the magic that coursed through his body, allowing him access to a number of different types of vision, one of which, if you like, could be called infrared; he had little trouble seeing in the dark, quite the opposite in fact. Swooping through the air, Strawberry swished his tail, banking this way and that, provoking whoops and cheers from the boy as the heavy breeze washed over his barely clothed body. Long, powerful legs folded away against the rest of his prehistoric form, the dragon continued with his astounding aerial acrobatics, circling, spinning, pitching this way and that, lurching one way and then the other, slingshotting around huge rocky outcrops, forcing Nicolaus to hang on for dear life, corkscrewing through canyons, whipping through deserted valleys, plunging down waterfalls, soaking themselves in the cool, refreshing spray, and generally having the time of their lives. Catching the mother of all updrafts, Strawberry glided some way up above the canopy, both friends looking down on the world through strange new eyes, with a much better appreciation of everything around them.

"What do you think?" asked the relatively young dragon, only a couple of years out from the nursery ring.

"Wow!" exclaimed the young man, barely able to gather his thoughts, an unparalleled view of his land making him quiver with excitement, all the time contemplating the opportunities to come. "This is how you spend your time travelling about when I'm not with you?"

Rolling his giant shoulders and suppressing something of a laugh, the mighty flying beast tried not to offend his friend.

"Not during the day... there's too much of a risk that

someone might see me. But at night, under the cover of darkness, I quite often take flight, sometimes remaining within the boundaries of the forest, occasionally skipping off out to sea. On a hot day like this, feeling the salty spray from the ocean tickling your scales is a sensation almost second to none."

"What about the fishing fleet? Aren't you worried that they'll see you?"

"My vision in the dark extends far beyond theirs, and I'm easily able to avoid detection by any of the boats. It's really only the jungle that causes me concern in that regard. With the variety and abundance of life within its confines, it would be easy for me to overlook a concealed human or two. I do try and be as vigilant as possible, but still the likelihood of that remains an ever present risk."

"I'm sorry that you have to hide away and not reveal yourself. If only the other villagers knew you like I do, then there really would be no problem. We could all live together as one happy family."

"It's a great sentiment Nicolaus, but something that's unlikely to occur any time soon. You are, in my experience at least, unique when it comes to your kind. I haven't met, or don't know of any other dragon and human encounter that hasn't been riddled by fear and violence. To some degree it's understandable from a human point of view. Just look at us. Sometimes I startle myself when I'm looking at my reflection, so heaven only knows how I would present to another of your kind. In their position I would be afraid and tempted to lash out. It's only natural."

"But surely something can be done?"

"Maybe... in the future, at least, that's what I gather the hope is from the dragon king and his council. But that will be some way off to say the least, probably hundreds of years, if rumours are to be believed."

"That's so sad."

"I couldn't agree more," replied the brilliant red dragon, streaking through the air, having circled back in the direction they'd come from. "But I think for now at least we need to keep our friendship to ourselves. Alerting anybody else could put both of our lives in danger."

"Understood," replied Nicolaus over the whipping of the wind washing over rider and mount.

"Anyhow, I think it's about time you got back to the village, otherwise your disappearance might start to attract unwarranted attention. I'll drop you off close to the edge of the forest if that's okay."

"Thanks... that's great."

With that, Strawberry found a tightly knit clearing that his prehistoric frame only just managed to fit into, and like a feather drifting to the floor, landed without even the softest of sounds. Slipping silently down into the knee high grass, the young human garnered everything he'd gathered, along with his spear, and sped off in the direction of the village, waving a muted farewell to his friend over his shoulder. As Nicolaus disappeared into shadows of the tree line, inhaling deeply, the dinosaur-like beast, only with wings, threw himself vertically into the air, before casually circling around and then heading back in the direction of his underground warren that he thought of as home, paying scant attention to his surroundings or the beings within them. It was a shame really, because if he'd allowed the magic within him to amplify his senses, something that normally happened when he journeyed throughout the forest, either above or on the ground, then he would have discovered that one more human had uncovered his secret, one that perhaps didn't have quite the empathy or positive attitude of the youngster he considered his friend.

With the next two days of the calendar being spent in the village, Nicolaus helping out in various ways, from reconstruction and boat building to menial chores for his parents and extended family, the two friends both knew that they'd have to wait until the third day to see each other again, as that's when the young lad's next hunting trip had been prearranged for. And so life went on, with both friends in their separate little bubbles going about their business, Strawberry continuing with his experiments, his young human comrade being as helpful as he could to those in his own community. Little did they know that a plan had been enacted, and that their short-lived slice of contentment was about to come to a rather abrupt end.

Up with the dawn chorus, marvelling at the chattering birds and bickering insects, Nicolaus grabbed his carry sack and spear and, not wanting to disturb the rest of his family, snuck quietly out of the house, marching stoically through the deep grass and into the jungle with as little fuss as possible. Across the village, doors slid silently open, the men within slipping effortlessly across the thresholds, all armed to the teeth, all in pursuit of one of their own in an attempt to correct his grave mistake.

Without a care in the world, looking forward to seeing his dragon pal, the young villager trod the well worn path that only he knew, careful not to leave any sign of his presence for fear of anyone else discovering what he'd been up to and just where he had been going during his supposed hunting excursions. Reaching the tiny clearing that opened out into the rocky outcrop that surrounded the fifty metre hole that was the entrance to Strawberry's home, abruptly people he recognised from his village and those surrounding it appeared out of nowhere, mostly men, all heavily armed, some with swords, others with pitchforks, catapults and spears just like the one he carried. Breath taken away, he couldn't believe what he was seeing, and had to shake his head vigorously to make sure that it wasn't a dream. It wasn't! About to rush ahead and warn his friend, from out of the long grass in front of him, a familiar figure appeared... HIS FATHER!

"H... h... h... how did you find out?" he stammered, his heart beating faster than the hooves on the fastest of runaway stallions.

"That is not your concern now, son. Only that it is done, and that your mistake will be atoned for."

"Mistake?"

"Not telling us of its existence was an error of quite some magnitude. Whatever influence it has over you will be quelled once it has been dealt with, rest assured of that."

"What, what, what...?" ranted Nicolaus, trying to get his head around the implications of his father's words.

"Shush," uttered his dad, trying to calm him down, not wanting to make any more noise than they already had, for very obvious reasons. But it was already too late for that, because supernaturally enhanced senses had already heard what had gone on, from some way off.

Shaking off the strong grip his father had on his slim, dark wrist, the brave young man and fearless dragon protector backed up towards the shadow filled hole, putting himself between that and what must have been about one hundred or so angry and crazed looking villagers.

"What is it you think you're doing, son?" asked his father softly, hoping to calm down the boy he'd helped develop into a man.

"You... you... you can't hurt him. He means you no harm."

"You can't possibly know that," whispered the leader of one of the other villages from off to one side.

"But I do..."

And then it happened!

A barrage of glistening red scales, lined with soft white and black shot up and out of the darkness, landing with the tiniest THUD in the world on the dew soaked grass beside Nicolaus.

Collectively, the villagers gasped, astounded to see the fifteen metre dragon in all its glory, absolutely amazed, despite having already been assured of its existence. It took a moment or two for the multitude of humans to get their heads around what had just happened, but when they did, instinctively they raised their weapons, much to the two friends' dismay.

"Stop, stop, please," begged the young human, sliding

out in front of Strawberry, holding out his hands, palms showing, in an effort to calm the situation down.

But fear and human conditioning had come to the fore amongst all the villagers, with none of them willing to listen or even contemplate the idea that the monstrous prehistoric beast before them could be anything but a threat. And so ignoring all common sense and any smidgen of intelligence that they might have had, giving into the basest of instincts, and with Nicolaus still in the line of fire, as one, with the exception of the young lad's father, they attacked.

"NO, PLEASE, HE MEANS NO..." screamed the frantic young man.

Unusual for him to be caught in two minds about what to do, the surprise and realisation of what was happening slowed his dragon reflexes and was about to cost him dearly. Had he been just a little quicker of thought, then he would have been able to ignite his magically powered shield into existence and extend it out in front of him to encompass his friend, the young human, but as it was he'd been just a little too late in reacting. As the silvery tips of the first dozen or so spears rattled against the scales adorning his huge red chest, an anguished cry of extraordinary pain echoed out from their position, the voice tearing apart two of those there, as the onslaught continued.

Looking on, absolutely horrified, the hand holding his rudimentary sword shaking like a tree in the wind, Nicolaus' father could only stand frozen to the spot and watch as some of the attacks meant for the dreaded beast pierced his son's body, over and over again.

Wits regained, full of absolute fear, not for himself but for his friend, Strawberry reacted, catching the boy's body before it could hit the ground with one hand, before casting out a devastating mantra that unleashed a semicircle of charged invisible air out along the ground, tearing up the grass and plants in its way across a distance of one hundred metres, throwing every being there into the air, the tang of the supernatural almost palpable, at least to one who knew what to look for. Not stopping to see the results, sheltering his friend's body with his own, Strawberry started weaving his magic like never before, giving all of himself over to it, determined to make up for his slight hesitation. Casting mantra after mantra, spears were removed, pitchforks disintegrated, and projectiles disappeared. Awash with ethereal energy, the broken hearted dragon flooded his friend's ruined body with as much of it as he could, knitting together major organs, repairing arteries, stopping the flow of blood, rebuilding lungs, ignoring muscle and sinew in an attempt to keep the youngster alive long enough to triage. As much as he tried, and he did, with everything he had, in the end there was only every going to be one outcome. The damage incurred had been too extreme, with two of the tiny projectiles fired from crude looking catapults, having nicked either side of his heart. Head slumped over his friend, huge teardrops the size of tennis balls dropping across the shattered form, his magic of absolutely no use, all Strawberry could do was look down at the torn and twisted shape that he'd spent so much time with, reliving all their adventures. Exactly then though, his enhanced hearing picked up the sounds of the villagers getting back to their feet amongst the tattered ruins of the clearing that they all found themselves in. Normally kind and carefree, with not a wicked thought of any sort ever entering his head, here and now a vicious anger the likes of which he'd never felt before started to consume him, the pleasant and cheerful expression that was nearly always plastered across his primeval face turning into the most malevolent of snarls as he readied himself to exact revenge on those humans remaining alive, determined to hunt every single one down and end their days on this planet in the most horrific of ways, the ancient urge to fight buried deep down in his DNA bursting to the surface. Only then did he hear it, and only then because of his magically enhanced hearing.

"Please... my friend. Don't do it. They're just afraid... that's all. It's part of their nature. They know no other way.

Give them a chance, some sort of hope and optimism...
please, for me," Nicolaus sighed, before closing his eyes one
last time.

Heart well and truly crushed, anger and fury raging
within him, the prehistoric monster rose to his feet, just in
time to see the humans fleeing for their lives.

'Hope, optimism, fear,' he thought, confused as hell, the
corpse at his feet sucking all the anger and rage out of him.
'What on earth am I supposed to do with that?'

Bending down to pick up his pal's body, it was then that
he spotted him, peering out from behind the tree line in the
direction of the village... the boy's father. As their gazes
locked, unspoken words passed between them, despite
them not even being the same race. Fear, anger, sorrow and
regret at having attempted such a thing were just a few of
them, the heartbreaking loss abundant in both sets of eyes.
As swiftly as their glances had come together, the human
disappeared, leaving his son in the arms of something he
considered an abomination. Confused, scared and unsure of
what to do, Strawberry gathered up the boy's body and leapt
back down into the cave, landing gently on the rock some
three hundred or so metres down below. Placing the cold,
pale cadaver on what he thought of as his bed, the distraught
dragon tried desperately to order his thoughts, with one
thing at the top of his mind... to give his friend the most
respectful send off that he could. Wondering just how to do
that, knowing that burial was of course what the humans
favoured, something inside screamed at him to do more.

It took him three hours to come up with what he
regarded as an appropriate course of action. Flicking
through a few of his rare, dusty old tomes from what was,
in essence, a rather pathetic excuse for a library here
underground, he just about managed to cobble together the
words that he needed to set the magic required alight. And
so gathering up his friend's corpse, he bounded into the air
and using all his might, powered his wings high up into the
bright blue sky, finding temporary solace in the baking

sunlight that bathed the both of them. Ignoring the ever demanding tug of gravity, Strawberry climbed higher and higher, heart pumping faster and faster due to the lack of oxygen, a thin layer of frost slowly developing on the outer edges of both wings. Deciding he couldn't go any further, momentarily he levelled out, took a breath and eyed the ground down below. Sure enough, his trajectory had taken him up and over the villages of those who had deigned to attack him. Knowing that they couldn't have failed to notice his ascent, and silently wishing his friend goodbye, he cast the mantra that he'd hurriedly put together, let go of the corpse, and as it started its descent, pulled in one big breath, and using the supernatural that resided deep within his body, ignited the flame within, savouring its touch as it rattled around his stomach before racing up his throat, delightfully licking his monstrous tongue and tickling his shiny, sharp, bright white teeth on the way past, in the form of one humungous fireball. Exiting his jaws, a roiling, boiling, blazing sphere of flame shot off after the cadaver that was now cutting through the atmosphere at quite a rate, the magic holding it together, forcing it back down to earth head first.

Much commotion in the community below had all the villagers out of their houses, their heads turned skywards, compelled to look at the human shape plunging towards them at quite some rate, a colossal rampant, yellow, orange and red ball of death in its wake, gaining on what remained of the boy's body, ever so slowly.

Sorry that it had come to this, feeling no small measure of guilt, through enhanced dragon eyes the stunning red, white and black bedecked dragon looked on in as much sadness as he'd ever known, not really ever having made many friends before, even during his time at the nursery ring, what could better be described as the school environment for their kind. Renowned as a loner, he'd always thought that it was just his thing, but right here and now, a huge part of him decided it was better that way, if for no other reason than to save him from the hurt that he was now experiencing. Forcing himself to watch, sure he knew what was about to happen, the tennis ball sized teardrops reared their ugly heads once again, immediately turning into giant balls of hail upon leaving the dragon's scaly chin.

With his friend, the villagers and the world watching on, something of a pivotal point in history was reached, none of them there realising just what had, or would happen in the future.

In one fell swoop, the blazing ball of supernatural flame caught up with the speeding corpse, not blowing it away, but catching light to the poor boy's body. And so in one hell of an extraordinary display that looked very much like a phoenix being reborn from the flames, Nicolaus' body burnt out as it continued to get ever closer to the ground, scattering his ashes across the whole village as it did so, something his friend, the dragon, thought the most appropriate thing of all. All together, the villagers wept for one of their own, none more so than the grieving father.

Immediately returning to his home, he moved everything that he regarded as his in the underground dwelling, deeper into the cave system, making it all but impossible to be discovered by the humans. Hopefully, if they came looking for him again, they would assume that he'd moved on to somewhere far, far away. After that, he spent all his time, with the exception of one hour a day sleeping, working on something that would honour and do justice to his friend's memory. It took nearly nine months. Throughout all of that, he'd had to use his magical ability in all sorts of different ways, the most unusual of which was to transform into human form and interact with the villagers who'd despised him so much. As you can probably imagine, for him that was the hardest part of all, especially when on occasion he'd caught a glimpse of his friend's father in the distance, provoking a strong sense of anger, regret and sadness throughout the prehistoric monster's body. But it didn't matter and he pushed on, determined to follow through on his plan and enact the legacy he thought only fitting for his deceased friend.

When not disguised as a human, learning more about the villagers that he'd almost gone on a rampage and killed, he spent his time in his lair, tinkering with and building magical constructs beyond the imagination of even the most gifted dragon mind. It had to be this way if he was going to achieve his goal. Mantras, spells and written hexes were torn apart piece by piece, something that in itself was incredibly dangerous, and about to be outlawed by the dragon council any day now, or so it was rumoured. However, that didn't dissuade him, only really powering him on.

Now at the point where he spent days at a time staying in the village, ironically swapping fish, fruit and small animals for board, the same things his friend had pretended to gather, he listened to those around him, trying to garner any information that would help him, only ever coming up short. So with little choice, a decision was made, one that would present a risk not only to him, but to the surrounding humans as well. Deciding to wait until the early hours of the morning, when everybody but the fishermen were fast asleep, he maintained the ruse of slumber and applying all his magic and will, reached out telepathically on the hunt for something very specific.

At first there was nothing, well... not quite nothing, merely random images, objects and words floating in the ether, a jumbled up mess. Deterred, but only a little, he pushed on, inching ever closer to what he was looking to do. Strangely, it was the last person he would have wanted that provided him with the breakthrough... Nicolaus' father. The tentative telepathic touch that he'd sent out had broken through into the consciousness of the human mired in misery, and had granted the dragon a view into not only his thoughts, but his wishes as well. And at the top of this man's yearnings was, of course, to have his son back. Choking back tears in the bizarre human form that he found himself in, it was all Strawberry could do not to cry out from his ragged cot in one corner of a guest house on the harsh, hard ground that he'd been assigned to. Holding his nerve, he extended his ethereal touch to incorporate more of the human minds, slowly, one by one. On doing so, he was afforded a glimpse into their psyches, allowing him to acquire a vague understanding of their hopes and dreams, his eventual goal all but achieved.

Three nights, that's how long it took him to delve into the minds of all the humans from each of the villages there, by the end becoming quite adept at using his empathic and supernatural powers that way. With his primary goal achieved and saying goodbye, at least for now, in his human guise, he hightailed it back to the system of caves, making sure not to be followed, and pondered his next move.

It didn't take him long to realise exactly what he had to do. It would, however, require all his magic, and then some.

Disappearing back off into the underground domain of his kind for about a week, he set about purchasing as many powerful magical artefacts as he could find within his budget in an effort to bolster the ethereal energy available to him. Once done, he returned to his cave system via the vast array of flying tunnels below ground, in the hope that he could fulfil his dying friend's last wish.

And so in the early hours of one cloudless morning, he snuck into the village, having taken on human appearance once again, but not the same one as last time. Having come up with the idea whilst staring at his reflection in the small lake that he regularly bathed in, this time he really did look the part. Black boots mirroring his dragon identity set off his bright red suit, lined with white, while a fluffy beard in the same colour disguised the vast majority of his face. Bulbous belly, resembling that of his dragon form, wobbling as he walked, carrying a huge sack made from the same colours as his clothes, which could be considered the forerunner to the 'Traveller's Bag of Capacity' that a certain master mantra maker had locked away deep inside his secret vault below his Emporium (see 'The White Dragon Saga' for details) silently he weaved his way throughout the village, careful not to wake any of the sleeping humans, all the time using his magic to focus in on what they... not needed, but wished for... anything that would add to their contentment, make them happy even for the briefest of moments. And so tapping into the powerful artefacts that he'd managed to procure, the tinkering dragon let rip with all his supernatural power, letting it flood through his prehistoric body disguised as it was, bringing to life all the dreams and wishes around him. Houses were noiselessly repaired and reinforced, becoming all that they could be. Food was replenished to the point of there being bountiful supplies filling almost all the dwellings. Crude toys and clothes appeared out of nothing for children, along with all sorts of exotic fruits and treats. Weapons were sharpened, made good and in some cases brand new ones lined up amongst their kind. The finest blankets and bedding blinked into existence all around in piles that measured higher than the tallest of men. And just when you would have thought that would be enough, Strawberry gave himself fully over to what remained of his ethereal energy in a feat that surprised even him. On the shoreline, amongst the villages, six brand new fishing vessels, perfectly constructed, shimmered into existence right there on the sand, fitting right in as though they'd always been there, brand new nets and sails topping them off. Dreams, at least for the residents of all the villages, didn't get better than that.

Inspecting the ships from afar, pleased with his work, it only then really occurred to him to leave some sort of message. But what, that was the puzzler. Tired beyond belief, desperately needing some sleep, all he could think to do was mention his friend, after all, that was why he'd gone to all this trouble. And so writing his name in the sand, after the words, 'in honour of', a tiny titbit of information that he'd remembered from the nursery ring came back to him. Some of the cultures, and he wasn't sure that it was this one, worshipped Saints, of all different names. And with that in mind, he rubbed out the words he'd already written in the sand and started again. This is what was left there on the beach, beside the brand new boats.

FROM SAINT NICOLAUS

Turning to head back into the forest, it was then that Strawberry noticed the tiny pair of eyes peeking out from under a raggedy set of covers, watching his every move. Breaking into the biggest smile that he could, just about showing through the mass of tangled white hair that enveloped the lower part of his face, the ridiculously bright and cheerful human lookalike waved briefly at the young girl who could have been no more than six years old, and feeling absolutely spent, turned and headed back out into the forest, hoping that he had enough energy left to retake his natural form and return to the cave system that had become his home. He had, making it back before exhaustion overcame him, his exertions leaving him so drained that he slept for three days solid.

As you'd expect, there was quite a commotion in the villages at about sunrise, just as the fishing fleet pulled up onto the beach, unable to believe their eyes. Rushing into all the huts and shacks in the village, waking everybody up, momentary confusion set in about exactly what had happened and where all the fantastic gifts had come from. That is, until a bellowing shout alerted all of them to something on the beach. As one, all the residents from each of the villages sprinted over to a section of sand out of reach of the waves, directly in the midst of all their homes, only for the writing to be revealed. To a man, woman and child, they dropped to their knees in wonder, thanking whatever divine entity had bestowed such luxuries upon them. It was then that one of them spoke up assuring them all that only the spirit of the boy that had befriended the dragon would do such a thing. From there on in, they worshipped that spirit, rightly or wrongly, every day thereafter. As well, that one encounter opened their minds, broadened their horizons and helped expand their visions. And as you might expect, on the same day, every year after that, those special villages continued to receive everything that their residents dreamed and wished for.

Something so simple (well... not necessarily magically so, but you know what I mean) but something so straightforward has, as you can probably guess, changed the world beyond belief. That, ladies and gentlemen, was the very first Christmas, inspired by the will to honour a friend, powered by dragon magic, and... more importantly, handed down from generation to generation. Dragon father to dragon... I was going to say son, but that's not the case at all, as many a dragon daughter has adopted the persona of what can now be called Santa Claus and everything supernatural that it entails. With magic being what it is, and constantly being adapted, constrained, experimented on, over the years, the whole... well, not necessarily lie, but the whole venture, let's call it that, had grown exponentially, and now, as you're well aware, covers the entire planet. How, I hear you ask? All might be revealed later, but rest assured, dragon magic is still at the heart of it. But that's not what's important. What's absolutely imperative is that the current incumbent, a dragon known as Henrietta Polkinghorne, right at this very moment, was in a whole load of trouble, with Christmas as we now know it, very much resting on a knife edge.

Setting up the classroom, prepping experiments before finishing off some last minute marking, Vincent Vimes or Vinnie, as most of his dragon students had come to think of him, found himself with fifteen or so free minutes, something unusual in the chaos of the nursery ring, and totally by chance decided to download the latest edition of his favourite telepathic paper and catch up on the news headlines from across the domain. With the local storage facility for everything telepathic being only a short distance away in the centre of Purbeck Peninsula itself, the *tor* (that's dragon teacher, to you and me) unleashed his conscious will and let it whistle off into the wind of its own volition. Shooting high up over the playing fields, the warm touch of a breeze sent shivers down his tail, despite the fact that he was sitting at his desk, in the huge leather chair with the perfectly positioned hole in the back that his appendage currently hung through, the tip of which nearly touched the floor. His mind raced up over the mighty outer wall that encapsulated the entire facility, ducked back down along one of the well traversed walkways, lined with huge cracks, filled to the brim with boiling hot orange, yellow and red lava, and zipping in and out of what few pedestrians there were at this time in the morning, continued to seek out its target.

Reflection, that was his current choice of telepathic paper, something of a change since his youth, the main reason for which was the in depth reporting on all the laminium ball matches. Of course there were other parts of the news sheet that he enjoyed, the quizzes about magic, which were easy for him given his job and experience, the political intrigue and gossip which always caught his eye, as well as the overview of what was happening on the surface that it gave.

Mid-season, with the leagues as close as it was possible to be, only fifteen or so points separating the top two from the relegation contenders, this particular time of the season was the part that he loved the best, scanning the stats, perusing the analytics, looking for the slightest oddity that might have been overlooked by the laminium ball pundits in an effort to predict a winner or indeed a loser. Not supporting any one team, instead he just loved watching the sport that he favoured, as many dragons do, knowing as much about all the different teams as any single fan could. And that's the main reason that he wanted the paper now, to lose himself in that which he enjoyed for those few valuable minutes.

Zipping down one side of a cobbled plaza, his psyche swerved a sharp left, before turning immediately right, delving straight into a dead end, or at least it appeared that way in the physical world. Passing half a dozen darkened shop entrances on either side, the highlight of which was one of the finest cape makers in the land, approaching a mouldy rock wall at speed, heading for a hexagonal spot of moss about the size of a fifty pence piece, just like every other time he'd ever attempted this, he rallied against his involuntary reflexes and gave everything he had in an attempt not to close his eyes back in his physical form in the classroom. He failed miserably once again, screwing them tightly shut, so much so that tiny squirts of flame dribbled out of his huge scaled nostrils. Berating himself for having not succeeded once more, he caught up with his consciousness which was now pleasantly floating around a huge open air arena filled with shelves, filing cabinets, cupboards and even tables, something he would recognise anywhere. Avoiding all the other minds there, not wanting to fly right through them, which wouldn't have been any sort of problem at all but just felt 'icky' to him, he twirled and twisted, darted and dropped, all the time heading in the direction of the antique dresser that he knew stored the past and present collection of the Reflection telepathic newspapers. About halfway across, cheerily enjoying the journey, abruptly he sensed something corporeal grab him from what felt like behind but who actually knew, and pull him off course. On the verge of panic, at least back in the classroom, it was then that he remembered one of the peculiarities of this particular storage site was the way that it prompted you to perform a specialised action of any sort. So letting the mysterious grip on his mind take him, he waited patiently to see just what it had in store. And it didn't take long to find out.

Dragged through the metaphysical air, he was slammed inelegantly against a tiny little dark wooden drawer that had the words 'Personal Mail' written across it in tiny yellow letters. Slightly perturbed, and shaking his huge prehistoric head back in the nursery ring, he racked his brains in an effort to understand exactly what was going on.

'Ahhh... that's right,' he thought, vaguely remembering now. When he'd moved here, almost eight years ago, he'd had to register a private mailbox at the storage site to maintain access to all the papers there, something he hadn't used in all that time, and something that had totally slipped his mind.

But here he was, well... at least his mind was, hovering right beside it, the yellow letters emblazoned into the wood flashing ever so slightly, he was only now noticing. It could only mean one thing... there was a message, but from who he thought, unable to recall giving anyone the means to contact him that way. More intrigued than ever, he burrowed his mind straight into the drawer, wondering exactly what he would find.

Brilliant, bright white light burst into being, disorientating him ever so slightly. But that didn't stop him from immediately recognising not only what the message was, but who it was from. As a pristine cream coloured envelope drifted softly around the room, the giveaway for him was the sparkling trail of emerald green that it left in its wake, a telltale sign and one that the two pals had developed decades ago, during their flourishing friendship across the final few years of their nursery ring stints. It could only be from one other being on the whole planet... Polkinghorne! Having spent the best part of two decades as best buddies, he hadn't seen or heard from his friend in over eight years. In some ways it was understandable, especially given the secret that had been confided in him. While he'd gone on to become one of the youngest nursery ring *tors* in all of Europe, first at an ever improving academy in a very multicultural part of Liverpool in the north west of the United Kingdom, after which he'd had quite a choice, and had of course opted for the famed Purbeck Peninsula, his friend had been coy at graduation, alluding little to what awaited her. It was only on their last night together, after the consumption of some, quite literally, magical cocktails, that young Polkinghorne had let him in on her secret. And WOW, what a secret it was... the next in line to be SANTA CLAUS! Imagine that, he was friends with Father Christmas, or at least the next dragon to be incarnated as such, handed down from family member to family member. Unsurprisingly, he'd had to swear to a binding supernatural oath not to tell a living soul about what he knew, on pain of some very disturbing consequences, which he never wanted to materialise. And so they'd gone their separate ways, well... at first keeping in touch telepathically, using all the new fangled messaging attachments normally once a week, which quickly became once a month, and then you know how it is, that becomes once every three, etc, etc. After that, there was no more. He'd sent messages off into the ether, and on not receiving a reply, had just assumed that his companion had moved on and either got tangled up with other beings, something he didn't think too likely given her secret, or had got caught up in her mysterious new job. But to see a message from her here and now was uplifting and delightful, if not something of a surprise. Instinctively, he delved right in, diving head first into the envelope with his consciousness, eager to hear what his mischievous mate had been up to across all this time. Unfortunately fate and Santa Claus had other ideas. In an eruption of bright, sparkling, emerald green letters, the emboldened words stood out like a wildfire in the dark, both tempting and dangerous at the same time.

COME QUICK. I'VE BEEN TAKEN. SECRET AT RISK.

Panic! Full blown, unadulterated panic was his first reaction. Followed swiftly by uncontrollable hilarity, back in his body anyhow, because of course it just had to be a prank, a jolly jape, one of Polkinghorne's many, many great wheezes. And then reality returned and the dust, or more likely, the emerald green glitter, settled, which it had to be said, was everywhere in the ethereal world that his mind currently inhabited, the letters having exploded out in every direction after he'd read them.

Forgetting and foregoing the paper, the reason his will had gone off of its own accord, instantly the troubled *tor* commanded his psyche to return, something it did in only a matter of seconds, sliding seamlessly back into his huge prehistoric body. Exhaling sharply, all thoughts of today's lessons shoved to the back of his brain, tens of questions filled the inquisitive part of him that had got him so far in such a short period during his relatively fleeting time so far on the planet. What had gone on? Taken? Taken by who? And why? Who the hell would want to kidnap Father Christmas? Come quick? Come where? All Polkinghorne had really revealed was the extent of the secret, and that it was something of a family thing, handed down from generation to generation and she was imminently about to be next. There was no where it was all taking place, no location for a magical grotto, no explanation as to how the event even worked. Of course the timing was obvious... duh! But apart from that, that's all that he knew. And... SECRET AT RISK? What the hell was that all about? Could it mean that others knew she was Santa, or something more ominous? Did it mean that the whole event, something a good deal of the human population up above them all relied upon to spread goodwill and hope, particularly when they were in short supply, was in jeopardy? Could Christmas be cancelled?

Head spinning, he lounged back in his chair, the tip of his tail this time scraping across the shiny tiles of the almost mirrored floor behind him, wondering what on earth he was going to do. Something... that was for certain. Of one thing he was sure. He'd need help. There was no way that he could accomplish this, whatever this looked like, on his own. Where that could come from, and just how he'd achieve it without breaking his secretive vow was anyone's guess. Right at that very moment, the shrill sound of two dozen or so humongous bells going off throughout the facility jolted him back to reality and the jostling of feet that signalled his class of young dragon students arriving.

They'd only gone and made it... FORTY! What an achievement, and pretty much all together. Okay, Tank hadn't been there quite from the start, but still, forty years together, who would have thought?

Pulling in a deep breath, Richie, the perfect dragon female of the three added a twinge of her ethereal energy deep down inside her stomach, and whispering the words inside her head, allowed the mantra to take hold as a satisfied rumble traversed her throat. Opening her mouth directly in front of her two friends, she watched with absolute amusement as a dizzying array of tiny fireballs, about the size of table tennis balls, shot out of her delicate prehistoric jaws and assaulted the two of them, splattering against the scales of their faces and upper bodies with a sickening squelch, leaving huge orange and red sticky marks that smelt of sulphur and something acidic.

"Oh very funny," smirked Peter, a little irked, while the third of the trio, Tank, took it all with the good grace that summed him up perfectly.

Attempting to remove the splattered spots of fire using a little of his own magic, without, it had to be said, much luck, Peter, or Bentwhistle as he was sometimes known, put into words what they were all thinking.

"So what are we going to do tonight? Forty years is quite some milestone, so we really should do something to celebrate."

"What about venturing into Purbeck for a night out?" offered up the young female dragon, a glint in her eye.

"You know full well that you can only do that if you're year 45 and above," replied Tank, a knowing look on his face, having heard all this before.

"I won't tell if you won't," was her answer.

"There's a sandskimming race broadcast tonight that we could go and listen to in the common room if you like," offered up Bentwhistle, much to the other two's disdain.

"That sounds... fascinating," replied Richie sarcastically.

"I was just saying."

"Looks like we'll be falling back on the usual," observed Tank, a smile lighting up the intelligence behind his huge primordial face.

"A picnic at Lava Falls... who'd have thought we'd be doing that, and something different for a change."

"It's not that bad Rich... is it?" asked Peter, concerned by his friend's continual caustic comments.

"It's not, but it would be nice to do something different for once, especially since we do all have something quite significant to celebrate."

The two of them couldn't argue with that, but no other options really came to mind for any of them.

"I'll tell you what," continued the young female. "I'll grab the drink, you two bring the food, and we'll make a real evening of it. How does that sound?"

"Sounds great."

"Sure thing."

"And maybe," she continued, "we can dive bomb some of those year twenty students who gave us so much lip the last time we were there. They deserve to be handed out a lesson or two."

They all smiled at that.

"Sounds like a plan," agreed the massive dragon form of Tank.

"Uhhh... guys, I think we'd better get a move on. We don't want to be late for Tor Vimes' class," announced Peter, as a matter of urgency.

"Relax," replied Richie. "Who cares if we're a few minutes behind all the others? Enjoy the day and finish up your food," she said, swallowing down half a dozen fried eggs on three humungous pieces of toast, the food itself barely touching the inside of her prehistoric jaws. "After all, breakfast is the most important meal of the day."

Taking the register, almost on autopilot, his mind calling out the names as his spindly little fingers ticked off the boxes on the sheet with the flaming red pen, going through the motions almost as if nothing had happened. But it had, and he was at a huge loss as to what to do, and who to go to for help. Polkinghorne had been his only real friend, not having known his parents, with the *tors* of his home nursery ring of Newcastle guiding him on his journey to adulthood. After that, well... it had just been work, work, work, the students under his care coming before anything else, even, it appeared, a life. Filtering through his vast eidetic memory, he just couldn't see who he could trust and rope in to help him out. Just then, a laughing, playful ball of commotion in the form of three dragon friends, students that had been under him for some time now, came jostling through the door, altering his thinking, igniting the first spark of an idea within his cunning and creative mind.

She was brilliant he knew, in almost every aspect. Across every nursery ring, those in charge and the *tors* themselves were always on the lookout for that once in a generation student who would in some way, shape or form go on to stamp their mark on the course of history and somehow reflect the tutoring they'd been given on their way up the ladder. In the staff room, talk would often centre around Richie Rump as being Purbeck Peninsula's answer to that. Most of the *tors* agreed that she certainly seemed the most likely, but her wilful attitude and occasional arrogance deterred any kind of favouritism from those higher up, with their support and sway very much behind some of the forty seventh year male dragons from much more prosperous backgrounds.

Tank he knew was all kinds of smart. Huge, for a nursery ring student, Vimes wondered briefly if the young dragon had considered applying for a laminium ball scholarship, he certainly had the build for it. Intelligent as well, with him knowing almost everything there was about anything plant or animal related. Always with a smile on his face and a kind and caring demeanour, nothing ever seemed to deter him from whatever goal he focused on... a handy dragon to have on your side.

And that just left the Bentwhistle youngster. Unsure really what to make of the shy and retiring male, he'd heard all the talk from his colleagues of wicked bullying in his younger years by some of his classmates. Speculation derived that's why he hung about with the other two. But on the outside looking in, Vimes considered that to be... what? Certainly wrong, but also... unfair! Although not seemingly bringing quite as much to the table as his friends, it appeared to him, at least, that Peter was the glue that held the three of them together. Without that, there would be nothing and that, he granted, was as important as anything his friends had to offer. In all, a strong and well rounded collective, one whose help he could very much do with.

"Sorry," uttered Bentwhistle, on stumbling through the door, almost pushed out in front of the other two.

"We were just finishing up our breakfast," added Tank apologetically.

"Won't happen again," observed Richie, munching on yet another piece of toast, Vimes barely able to understand her.

All of this, much to the amusement of the rest of the class.

Forgetting all about the register and, to be quite frank, the lesson that he had planned out for them, he knew this was the opportunity that he'd been waiting for, one that might be the only chance he had. And so grasping it with both his metaphorical, tiny hands, he continued.

"Your tardiness is noted. Make sure all three of you join me here after lessons have ended today, so that we can... discuss the issue. Now, please take your seats."

"But it's the fortieth anniversary of..."

"I don't care. I want you in here at the end of the day,

without delay. Do all three of you understand?"

"Yes."

"Yes."

"Yes."

"Good, now sit down, we have a lesson to get on with."

And that was that, at least for now, with the *tor* and the young students all going about their business. But it wouldn't be long before all that would change.

Staying in their own social bubble, the three friends moved from classroom to classroom over the course of the day, taking in Astrophysics, Supernatural Construction Techniques and Human Geo Political Posturing, something each of them hated, having to do their utmost to stay awake.

Finishing at six o'clock, all three of the close knit pals plodded, disappointed, down one of the cool stone corridors that made up the outside loop of the facility, desperately wanting to go back to their rooms and then head off to Lava Falls for some fun, each in their own way worried about what Vimes had in store for them.

"I bet it's cleaning," mouthed Peter, as miserable as ever. "He's renowned for that, and for making misbehaving students do every last bit of the classroom, even the ceilings."

"It had better not be," stated Richie, a look of absolute thunder inundating her face at just the thought of her night out ruined.

"It'll probably be a private dressing down," declared Tank sensibly. "I'm sure he just wants us to set more of an example to the rest of the class. And you all know, that as *tors* go, he's probably the best of the lot. Give him the benefit of the doubt until we see what he has in store for us."

Wise words indeed.

Consciously wiping the disappointment of being kept back from their faces, the three of them walked into the classroom to see Vimes sitting at his desk with, unusually, three chairs set right at the front of the class, clearly meant for them.

"Close the door please," he announced, not looking up from what he was working on.

They did just that.

"Please... have a seat."

'Odd,' they all thought simultaneously, without saying a word. Effortlessly, they slid into the chairs, Richie in the middle with the two males either side of her. Silently they waited to see exactly what their punishment would be. Little did they know what was about to be asked of them.

Dropping the pen and pushing the paperwork aside, Vimes sat back in his chair and for the first time since entering the room, looked all of them in the face, unsure of what he expected to see. For two of the three, it was obvious. Defiance from the young girl dragon, which was no surprise, because that was embedded into her very nature, something he knew only too well. Bentwhistle had submission rolling off him, so much so that it was almost visible, with the third of the three, the kind and caring heart of the trio, giving absolutely nothing away with his neutral blank stare and his relaxed body language... incredible really. And so with everything left unsaid, the *tor's* time was up. It was now or never.

Clearing his throat, which for any dragon presents an ever present danger to the surroundings and those everyday things of value, normally involving at least a dribble of flame from one orifice or another, the nursery ring employee started off as best he could, determined to test the depth of the water if you like.

"First, let me say two things. One... you most certainly aren't in any trouble, and two, thank you for coming here this evening. I know you had little choice in the matter, but still, I wanted you to hear me say it."

'WOW!' they all thought as one. 'What on earth is going on?'

"And now on to the TRUE reason that I've brought you here," the *tor* continued.

"It's hard for me to say this to anyone, least of all three of my students, but I need your help, and wouldn't be asking unless it was of the utmost importance."

That changed the dynamic of the room, and not just a little.

"I... I... I... I don't understand," stammered Peter, relieved not to be in trouble, but confused at their current predicament.

Gone was the raw anger from Richie's beautiful dragon face, replaced by something more like wonderment, keen to hear just how one of their teachers, their guardians, needed their assistance.

Tank marvelled at the situation and the turnaround of events, at least on the inside, like his female friend, eager to understand exactly what was being asked of them. In the end, it was him that spoke first.

"What is it we can all do for you?"

Closing his huge dinner plate sized eyes, rubbing both of them and his forehead with the spindly little hands that looked totally out of place, the dragon *tor* tried to lay it out for them.

"There's a problem that I have to deal with, one of a delicate kind of nature and one which involves, at the heart of it, a magical vow."

None of the three youngsters saw that coming.

"Magical vow," spat Richie, unable to believe what she was hearing. "Is this some kind of test, one to determine our moral aptitude or something, because if it is, it sucks!"

"No, no, not at all, I promise you. It's just that... hmmm. Let me try and start from the beginning," reflected their tutor, sweat dribbling down his forehead, the scales on his cheeks glistening in the artificial light of the classroom. "I've always been pretty much of a loner, from as far back as I can remember, finding it hard to make friends, and even harder to keep them, and this applies to all my time in the nursery ring. During the last two decades or so though, surprisingly I found myself spending more and more time with one of my classmates, someone I very much considered another loner, almost my mirror image. Looking back on it, the only real surprise and regret is that we hadn't discovered our compatibility sooner and that we missed out on many more years of companionship. Anyhow, Henrietta Polkinghorne, as that's her name, was, and still is, I hope, my one and only best friend. I would do anything for her, including laying down my life in a heartbeat."

'Curious,' thought the female sitting in the middle of the three youngsters.

"As you can imagine, much like yourselves, we were thick as thieves, getting into everything, including a variable amount of trouble, but nothing too serious. It was, and still is, up to this day, the most enjoyable part of my life. On graduating, it had become time to go our separate ways, me on the nursery ring fast track, Polkinghorne, surprisingly reserved about what the future had in store for her. That is, until our very last night together, after having imbibed more than a little alcohol, probably in fact, more than enough to sail quite a reasonably sized ship in. And that brings us to the first of the magical vows... mine in fact."

Hooked, all three were unable to tear themselves away from the tale each wondering what the hell it had to do with whatever help was required.

Letting out a long deep breath, Vimes continued.

"My friend, the one that I desperately didn't want to part with, told me that she could only reveal what was in store for her, if I took a supernatural vow, one imbued with magic from both of us. Understandably, and given just how merry we were, of course I thought it was a joke. But in that moment, she'd become more serious, more solemn and earnest than I'd ever seen her. Of one thing I was sure of... she wasn't kidding. And let me tell you that sobered me up mighty quickly."

Unbeknown to them, all three friends leant in just a little further.

"And that was as far as we got, with her unwilling to go

any further until I'd taken the vow. As decisions go, it was a tough one, with me having absolutely no idea what I was getting myself into."

"What did you do?" asked Peter, almost a little too eagerly.

Smiling for the first time since they'd entered the room, their teacher and guardian looked all three of them in the face.

"What do you think I did? The only possible thing I could."

"You took the vow," stated Tank, never one to knowingly miss anything.

"Yes I did. And the surprise hit me like one of the humans' freight trains that we talked about the other day, with an impact like nothing else I've ever experienced."

"Was it worth it?" asked Richie, having listened intently, not at all drawn in to asking the most obvious of all the questions.

Thinking long and hard before answering, Vimes considered his answer.

"I believe it was. I did then, and I still do now. An unbreakable bond was formed between us, and a secret shared, an important one at that."

"What did she tell you?" asked Peter, falling into the trap any year twelve dragon would easily have seen coming.

"Of course he can't tell us," Richie scolded her friend, "because if he did, no doubt he'd be breaking the vow."

"Exactly!" declared Vimes.

"Then why are we here, and exactly how do you need our help?" enquired Tank, still thinking things through.

Shaking his head, tapping his fingers against the dark shaded brown scales on the top of his skull, the conflict within the *tor* was there for all to see.

Aware of reaching a crucial moment, all three friends remained absolutely silent and still, giving their teacher the time he needed.

"Polkinghorne's gone missing, and from the message I

received, it looks as though she could be in deep trouble. I need help in not only finding her, but rescuing her as well."

"What?!" exclaimed Richie, nearly leaping out of her chair. "You're MAD! What on earth do you think we're supposed to do?"

Attempting to get up in an effort to leave not only her chair, but the room as well, one of Tank's two huge muscular wings stopped her from doing just that. Turning to face her friend, angry at having her path blocked, his good tempered and smiling face was almost impossible to be furious with for any length of time.

"Let's just hear him out," urged the strapping dragon, aware of not only his friend's discomfort, but of how upset their *tor* had become.

With Richie reluctantly sitting back down, Tank turned to Vimes.

"What exactly is it you'd like us to do?" he asked, nice and calmly.

A seriously troubled look embedded into his dinosaur-like face, the *tor* lifted his head up to face the youngster.

"You see, that's the very first problem to be overcome. To help Polkinghorne, I need to tell you all about her, which is something I can't do, because... it would break my vow to her, and cause me considerable, well, let's just say... INCONVENIENCE, which doesn't quite do it justice, but we'll stick with that."

"Then how the hell are we supposed to help?" fumed Richie, her mood steadily deteriorating.

"Well... here's the thing. There is a way, or at least I think there is, but you're not going to like it, and I probably shouldn't even be suggesting it, not given my position here within the nursery ring."

"Go on," urged Richie, the anger within her transforming immediately into inquisitiveness.

Vimes stayed silent, unable in the interim to bring himself to say it. That frightened Peter more than a little.

"You want to share your vow with us," suggested Tank,

his quick thinking brain and immense knowledge of all things magical having put all the pieces of the puzzle together.

The *tor* just sat there and nodded, now unable to look all three of them in the eyes.

"What else can you tell us?" enquired Richie.

"Nothing."

"What about the consequences of the vow, at least let us know that much."

"You're not actually considering doing this, are you?" asked Peter, now almost terrified and wanting nothing more than to just storm out of the classroom, but unwilling to leave without his friends.

"Let him answer Richie's question," proposed Tank, putting a calming hand on his friend's scaled shoulder.

"Well...?" ventured the female youngster.

Not wanting to... really not wanting to, but unable to come up with any other alternative, Vimes, as conflicted as he'd ever been, and not just about the whole Christmas thing, reached the only conclusion that he could and spelled it out for them.

"The vow pertains to Polkinghorne's job, as no doubt you've already surmised. If, and it's a big if, I were to reveal to anyone, exactly what she does, then my memory would be wiped... permanently."

"That doesn't sound too bad," ventured Peter, perking right up.

"You, you, don't understand," the *tor* continued, "I don't just mean about Polkinghorne's job. I mean the whole of my memory would be wiped, and everything I'd ever known would cease to exist."

"Oh..." sighed Bentwhistle.

"Yikes!" whispered Richie.

Tank remained totally still, in quiet contemplation, at least for a while. Silence ensued, making the classroom feel more than a little eerie. When it was broken, sometime later, it was the largest of the three friends, Tank that spoke up.

"It must be something important then," he enquired, "her job?"

All Vimes could do was nod, knowing that he'd already said too much.

"What about if we all tried to guess what it was?" suggested Peter. "That way, it wouldn't be you telling us."

"No," said Tank, beating his tutor to it. "It won't work that way. Even the slightest confirmation will enact the magic. Even the most basic supernatural bond will recognise that."

"Then what do we do?"

"What do you think Rich?" asked Tank.

"I say it beats an evening at Lava Falls, and I think we should do it."

"REALLY?" exclaimed Peter mortified.

"If the job's that important, then yes, we should go ahead and help out. As well, you can see just how torn up Vinnie is about all of this. Of all the *tors* we study under, have you ever known anyone more calm, dependable, reasonable and trustworthy than him?"

Simultaneously the other two both answered no.

Turning to Vimes, the bold young female looked him firmly in the eyes and said the words he'd hoped to hear.

"I'm in."

In much the same way that she lived most of her life, what she'd just done was reckless, but her gut feeling told her it was the right thing to do and on that, she relied an awful lot. She just hoped the gamble she'd taken would pay off, and that both of her friends would follow suit, desperately not wanting to do it without either of them.

A quandary, a pickle, a conundrum, that's what both of the other two found themselves trapped in. That is, until the biggest and brightest spoke up.

"I think she's right, Pete. We should help out. From the outside looking in, and not even knowing any of the details, it does seem of great consequence. If that's the case, then I think we all need to step up. Not only are we stronger together, but I wouldn't want Rich going in all alone. What do you say?"

Scared and unable to believe that his friends were about to throw their weight behind this chain of events, this one young dragon wanted nothing to do with things, with just the word adventure turning his stomach, making his legs feel weak and useless, and forcing any bravery that he had into the darkest recesses of his being. But the one thing above all else that defined him down to a tee, was his regard for the other two of their tight knit trio, knowing full well that he'd do anything for either of them. And with that in mind, and as anxious as hell, reluctantly he stepped up.

"Okay."

A huge smile, that to any human would have looked like their total and utter downfall, spread out across the *tor's* face, the tiniest of victories and the very start of what would no doubt be something of a challenge.

"Do you know how to share the vow?" Tank asked seriously.

"I checked it out earlier and I believe I do, youngster. Shall we get started?"

With all of them agreeing, albeit not quite wholeheartedly, Vimes explained exactly what they had to do. Moments later, having all moved over to an empty workbench off to one side, all three of them squeezed around it together and, one by one, laid their hands atop each other. With all three of the students having been told to open their minds and not resist even in the slightest the magic that would be flooding over them, because that would definitely be enough to cause some serious side effects, the *tor,* all the time worried for his friend, expanded his supernatural power, focused his will, and in his mind at least, spoke the words.

"Memoria damnum et inanis est infernus, erit ex hoc potens carmine. Revelare secretum tuum periculum."

Ringing in their psyches, the young dragons tried to keep up with the phrases and expressions, which shouldn't have been that hard given their language training. Two of them had little trouble, but as you've already probably guessed, it was Peter who struggled the most. If his friends could have translated for him, then they probably would have, letting him know it meant something along the lines of:

'Memory loss and empty hell will be the result of this powerful spell. Reveal the secret at your peril.'

Without any ado, Vimes' magic vanished in an instant, leaving all three of the youngsters with but a single thought. 'SANTA CLAUS!'

"What?" uttered Peter.

"Wow!" ventured Richie.

"Unbelievable," voiced Tank.

"And now you know what was so important, my young friends, and just why I feel compelled to help."

They didn't know all of it, of course, because that one last secret was his and his alone.

"Where do we go from here?" asked Tank eagerly, ready and willing to get on with things now he knew what was at stake.

"A good question, youngster, a good question."

"You mean you don't know?" interjected Richie.

"I'm afraid not. I wasn't privy to where she was going, where the set up for the whole thing was, and especially not how things worked."

"Not even a clue?"

"The one overall impression I got when we parted was that she was going somewhere... hot! But I've racked my brains and that's it, there's simply nothing else."

"That's not a whole lot to go on," ventured Richie, stating not only what they all thought, but the obvious as well.

"Surely it would be somewhere cold like one of the Poles," suggested Peter, knowing all about Father Christmas, "after all that's where the story says he lives."

"Where HE lives?" pointed out the female among his two best friends. "And I'm pretty sure that won't be the only lie in the whole thing. Think it through Pete, for a dragon, any dragon, even one powerful enough to pull off the whole Santa act, they still would not be able to survive in polar conditions. Cold, particularly on that kind of scale, would decimate any of us in only a matter of minutes, and all the magic in the world couldn't curtail those relentless temperatures. I can see the appeal to the humans about the North Pole and the snow and reindeers, etc. It is very much a cunning ruse, but that's all."

"What if it's filled with irony?" butted in Tank, his mind whirring away like a child's windmill in the breeze.

"What do you mean?" asked the *tor*.

"Think about it. A tall tale to spread joy, peace and happiness across the world amongst those up above, all based around a fictional character situated in one of the coldest and most unforgiving environments on the planet. If you were setting all this up and you could do it from anywhere on earth, what kind of surroundings would you choose?"

"Somewhere hot!" announced Richie, slapping herself on the forehead with the palm of one of her cute little hands.

"Somewhere hot," mused Vimes, pleased that the youngsters seemed to be working as a group.

"But where and how do we find Polkinghorne's particular spot?" pondered Peter, out loud.

"Assuming what she was doing required a huge amount of not only magical capacity, but power as well, I wonder if there's any way to track that much ethereal energy," quipped Tank.

"One of my past pupils, a favourite of mine, has recently started work at the 'Misuse of Mana' department in the council building in Buckingham, London. Perhaps he'll be able to help. I'll reach out later tonight and get in touch."

"You have favourites?" observed Richie cheekily.

"Every *tor* has favourites," replied the tutor, looking much more cheerful now than he had at any point since all

43

three of them had entered the room. "Despite them telling you otherwise and the rules saying you can't."

"Good to know," replied the young female.

"Where do we go from here?" asked Peter, feeling a little left out.

"I would suggest you go away and think about the problem, ideally together, as that's how you seem to work best. Even if we can narrow down an area in which we think magic might be working overtime during the December period, finding any sign of where Polkinghorne has been holed up will be no easy feat. Anything we can do in advance to speed things up will help a great deal. And don't forget, it's that big anniversary, something that should most certainly be celebrated. So let me say congratulations now on hitting the big 40! Chill out for the evening, spoil your bodies and let your minds ponder the issues before us. I'll get in touch with my boy at the council, and then we'll regroup this time tomorrow. Is that okay?"

All of them affirmed their response with a nod.

"Good, good," said the *tor*. "One last thing though. Do not, and I mean not, under any circumstance, reveal what you know about Polkinghorne. That vow was undertaken for a reason, and will turn your memory to jelly, from which there might well be no recovering."

Nodding, all three of them picked up their stuff and made their way out of the classroom, minds blown, their perception of everything totally rewritten.

In a dark, lightless room, scattered chunks of dull white enamel littered the dirty floor, along with puddles of thick, chocolatey brown, from which huge rodent footprints could just be seen scurrying about every surface. Across the walls, which were no cleaner, broken arrow shafts remained embedded in the middle of thick, gooey redness that dripped and ran, the smell of which was both sweet and disturbing at exactly the same time.

Knees hugging her chest, sitting on the floor in the corner, taking in this bizarre and extraordinary sight, sat a filthy young woman, battered and bruised, mucky white gag pulling at her face tied firmly behind the back of her head, wrists bound, her once pristine suit covered in blood, filth, the sickly sweet gooey redness and unbelievably... CHOCOLATE! Scared, alone and as bereft of hope as any being had ever been, she looked a sorry mess and far short of the fantastical and famous myth that she actually was. Taken and tortured from out of nowhere, the opportunity to fight back had never really presented itself, so quickly had she been ambushed, and in her own home at that. Over and over again, she continued to ask herself why. Why her? Why now? What could she possibly have done to deserve such a thing? Nothing rational or even crazy mad presented itself as any kind of answer in her psyche. As far as she knew she'd never harmed, berated, even had a cross word with any other being on the planet, with her life selflessly devoted to the wishes of others. What possible reason could there be for her abduction and the cowardly way in which she'd been treated? She just didn't understand, and once it had become obvious to her what was happening, which took a little while, her mind struggling to grasp the reality of the situation, both thinking and wishing it were a dream instead of her worst nightmare, she had of course tried what all of us would in that situation, and fought back. But it was over before it had begun, the worst part being that her underlying magic had been expunged, taken, whether temporarily or permanently, she just didn't know, not to be seen again but not before she'd managed to get off an S.O.S., or at least, thought she had. It was too much of a blur to remember in any great detail, and had happened just as she'd been badly beaten about the head. Maybe it had been something, or perhaps it was just a figment of her rather vivid imagination. Either way, she couldn't be sure. And so shivering against the cold, tears running down her eyes from below dark, beautiful, curled eyelashes, she cowered in the corner, crushed and dispirited, the abundance of hope that once a year she unselfishly shared with others gone for good. Remaining in her human shaped shell, nothing like the magnificent dragon she should have been. Santa Claus looked, for all intents and purposes, absolutely done for.

Instead of heading off to Lava Falls to celebrate their fortieth anniversary, the three friends, on leaving Vimes, decided immediately to head to the library instead, in an effort to see if they could make some headway in tracking down the famed doer of good, Father Christmas, or as they now knew, Polkinghorne.

Plodding past the ever present guardian of the magical repository, Ella Echoheart, a dragon renowned for her kind and caring stewardship, not only of her books but the pupils as well, each of the three gave a nod in her direction. In return she offered up a smile, well aware of the friendship all three dragons shared, and the mischief they had on occasion got into. Reaching the hexagonal wooden table that they almost considered their own in the far reaches of the library, they put all their stuff on the floor, slumped into the well worn seats, the tips of their tails brushing against the bright green carpet of that particular section, and took a moment to reflect on everything that had happened.

"Who could have seen any of that coming?" announced Peter, his mind spinning with all the possibilities, mainly things that could go wrong.

"Imagine being friends with someone so historically important," added Tank. "It hardly bears thinking about."

"Much as this is all very nice, given everything that's on the line, I think we should get down to doing some research," suggested Richie, keen to get on and help, now at least having some idea as to what was at stake.

"Where do you think we should start?" asked Peter, unsure of exactly what they were looking for.

Before Tank had a chance to answer, his female friend

jumped in.

"Anything historically unusual about that time of year."

"What do you mean Rich?" asked the biggest of them all.

"I was wondering whether or not Santa, or that particular family line, has stayed in the same place ever since all this started. We might not know how it all kicked off, but perhaps if things were on a much smaller, more local scale originally then maybe we can work our way back in the hope of finding that site. It might prove to be what we're looking for, or at least offer a clue as to where they moved on to."

"So are we looking at human or dragon books?" put in Bentwhistle, wanting to be sure of what they were doing.

"Both," urged Tank eagerly, approving fully of Richie's idea. "I hope that there would be something from either side of the veil. For the humans, it must have been a shock of epic proportions. From the dragon point of view, maybe just the tiniest of ripples, but there must be a mention of something relating to it, no matter how small. Rumours of wishes fulfilled, joy and happiness spreading out across a certain land, unexplained miracles happening with absolute regularity at that one time of year, if we can nail any of that, it might just prove to be the breadcrumb at the start of the trail."

Richie nodded approvingly.

"How about you guys scan everything human in an effort to track back as far as you can go with the whole Christmas thing and see where it leads, and I'll delve into the dragon history books and see if I can find any mention," ventured the young female.

"Sure," Peter and Tank replied simultaneously.

"And don't forget," added Richie. "We're looking for a place, no matter how big or small. A continent would be okay to start with, or even one of the larger countries. That will at least help us narrow it down. If you find anything, let me know."

And with that, she shot off down one of the adjacent

fifty foot tall aisles, heading deep into the dragon history section that spanned almost a quarter of the library itself, and sat in the diagonally opposite corner of the giant labyrinth.

For the two males, what they required was much closer to the table they'd chosen to sit at, with the human section being only a quick flap of the wings away. Starting at opposite ends of one massive wall-like shelf, both the young dragons gathered in as many relevant tomes as they could find, and then staggered back to the table under their weight, plonking the books down onto the floor, before slipping effortlessly back into their chairs. It was time to get to work, and unlike the homework from all their lessons, this didn't seem either a chore or a bother, with the excitement in both of them at the thought of exactly what they were doing and the adventure to come, bubbling just beneath the surface.

Gliding smoothly to a halt in the midst of the dragon history section, the cool, calm and collected young female took a moment or two to scan the huge shelves that towered above her, used to working in this environment and knowing that taking some time to look at everything now in an unruffled manner would pay dividends a little later on. Taking everything in, her above average intelligence and eidetic dragon memory started making decisions about every book, tome and set of parchments she could see, categorising all of them. Instantly dismissing some that she was certain would be of no use at all, the rest she broke down into two different groups: Maybe and Useful. After spending ten minutes going along all the huge ledges, she returned to the start and began rifling through each and every one in the second category.

Hours passed with sleep all but forgotten. Occasionally the youngsters would convene back at the table and discuss what they'd found, but as at precisely one in the morning, nothing of any value at all had been discovered. So far, it was a bust, with the thrill and enthusiasm they'd started out with all but vanished, replaced by disappointment and frustration, something that was playing out right in front of them.

"I can't believe you haven't found anything," stated Richie, the annoyance in her voice aimed towards her friends, but more indicative of the fact that she herself hadn't come across something of use.

"We've tried Rich, we really have, but there's nothing, not even a hint of anything that we've discussed," replied Tank, weary and more than a little fed up.

Abruptly, out from behind one of the nearest gigantic rows of shelves, a huge prehistoric head, the scales around her neck and face bathed in lightly shaded pink, an inquisitive look engrained on her face, belonging to the chief librarian, shot out and surprised all three young dragons.

"You all seem to be working very late," announced Ella Echoheart, "especially on a school night."

Peter sank back into his chair, hoping not to catch her attention, knowing that his two pals would deal with the situation much better than he would.

"It's just a project that we're all involved in," ventured Tank, "something we'd hoped to get a head start on, but alas we seem to be coming up short."

That got the magical repository guardian's attention.

"What seems to be the problem?" she asked, the rest of her body joining her head and neck, before plodding on over to the three of them.

Richie gave Tank a look, reminding him of the magical vow that bound all three of them not only to Vimes, but via him to Polkinghorne as well. In his own way, the strapping male dragon ignored her glare, and continued on talking to the archive specialist.

"We're... trying to get to grips with the origin of what the humans call Christmas, in an attempt to see how far back it goes. It would be just our luck to be assigned something so difficult," he huffed, nonchalantly.

Inside, Peter waited for something bad to happen, whilst Richie cringed, but their friend, the hulking great dragon known as Tank, the one that had almost become a laminium ball player, was nothing if not genuine, something that dragon Echoheart had totally picked up upon.

Pausing for thought, the well rounded and experienced librarian pondered the problem, having never come across any other students being set work like this. For a moment, she wondered if it was a ruse, a prank, or something that would see the youngsters in humungous amounts of trouble. But that was quickly dismissed, because she just couldn't see how, and after all, they had been diligently studying for many hours now, when realistically they should have been getting some rest. There and then she decided to help as best she could.

"If I were looking into that, and you all know I'm not supposed to do your work for you, especially all of you, then I might start off with some of the humans' religious books, tomes and scrolls, given just how intrinsically linked Santa, Father Christmas, St Nick, whatever you like to call him, is to the festival of Christmas. And in doing so, I'd scan for anything unusual, any offshoots, or a particular faith popping up somewhere unexpected. But that's just me."

"Thanks," said Tank. "You've been a great help."

"I'm not sure about that youngster, but you're all very welcome. And please try and get at least some sleep, otherwise I'll have your head of year in here berating me for letting you study all night."

Nodding vigorously, they all mumbled a "will do" in the direction of the retreating dragon's back.

Three hours later, they at least had something. It wasn't much, but it did offer a miniscule amount of hope. In a tattered old scroll bound up by a raggedy piece of string, that out of the three of them, surprisingly Peter had found, an astonishing tale of the death of a boy from a thousand years ago was recounted, one who unbelievably had, it was thought, befriended a dragon. The fable from far in the past suggested that the dragon revisited the village in Malaysia at the same time every year after his friend's death, bestowing wonders the likes of which the villagers could hardly imagine. Not only did all of this occur during December, but sketchy accounts from exceptionally young children spoke about a man dressed primarily in red and white, with a huge fluffy beard, carrying a sack full of goodies. This might very well be the clue that would lead them to the start of the hunt.

Exhausted but happy, the three of them headed off to their separate dorms in search of a couple of hours of quality sleep before their lessons resumed, determined to mull over what that they'd found, eagerly anticipating their next encounter with Vimes at the end of the day.

Staring into the tiniest mirror in the world in the entrance to a clothes shop on a cold and drizzly Princes Street in Edinburgh, Scotland, a heavy set man with cropped blonde hair, wearing dark blue jeans, black shoes and a thick blue and white skiing jacket, gradually turned the carousel display of umbrellas and scarves, doing his best to feign interest, despite shivering from cold on the inside, and I'm not just talking about below his coat.

'Unbelievable,' he thought to himself, not for one moment taking his eyes off his target, who stood about one hundred metres further up the street on the opposite side of the road, talking on his phone outside a brightly lit jewellers. Strands of long dark hair poking out from beneath a woolly blue beanie hat, a dark brown leather jacket and black trousers completed the man's ensemble, making him look like someone trying to appear half their age. Not bothered at all about that, currently, his concern was more about the temperature than anything else, something that exhaling and watching his breath freeze in front of him, brought home now, more than ever. Austria, Denmark before that, with an excursion into the wilds of Canada for his trouble previously. Why on earth always him? Logically he knew, well... a little. Given just who he was, and his reputation for getting the job done probably accounted for the reason he'd been selected rather than it being any sort of punishment, but yet one more chilling undertaking was almost more than he could cope with. Suddenly, deep within his psyche, a small, almost methodical and professional mentality, that seemed to have its own voice, berated him for his lack of concentration.

"Eyes on the prize," it reprimanded, startling him back to reality, forcing him to run his right hand down yet another scarf, finally holding the tip up against his neck to see how good it looked against his pale white skin. Ignoring the icy wet drops of drizzle dripping from his matted hair, surging across his neck and then down his back, causing an amount of pain that might well have felled another of his kind, he adapted his eyes, magically zooming into the minute mirror, and attempted to see if he could garner anything else about his target.

Nothing! Not a damn thing. He supposed it would be too much to hope for that the scum sucking piece of filth wouldn't be covering his mouth while he talked, or that the display on his phone would at least be facing this way, but no. With time of the essence, and that tiny niggling feeling that something bad was about to happen wriggling away in the pit of his stomach, Dendrik Ridge, or Flash as his comrades were given to calling him, decided that he had to take a chance and try and get that much closer. Letting go of the end of the scarf, he whirled swiftly around, flicking droplets of rain off his waterproof coat, sending them spiralling out in all directions, and ever so slowly and as casually as possible continued up this side of the street, glancing this way and that, pretending all the time to be on the lookout for a bargain. Weaving in and out of precariously balanced shoppers coming the other way, and ignoring the howling wind playing havoc with the hood of his jacket, Flash continued, very quickly closing the gap to thirty metres or so. Aware of just how near he was now, the Crimson Guard, as that's what he was, a highly valued member of the dragon king's secret force, only answerable to the monarch himself, ducked into a newsagent in an effort to maintain anonymity. It worked, only just, with his objective lowering his phone before turning fully three hundred and sixty degrees, just as the blue and white of his jacket disappeared from sight.

'He knows,' was all that the brave, cold battered agent could think... 'but how?' Perusing the papers on the shelves in front of him, his vast intellect considered the problem, immediately coming up with the only solution available. There had to be two of them. If that were the case, both he and the city he was trying to protect were in an awful lot of trouble. Contemplating everything he knew about what was going on, the thought of calling for back up crossed his mind, albeit briefly. It was then that the stark realisation that they wouldn't get here in time hit him like a sledgehammer. Sure that he could take down two of his own kind, because there was no way in hell they would have the kind of training, magical adaptability and experience that only resided in him, it was the human element involved that had him more worried. How many of them were there? Were they working alone, or in their dedicated cells? Either way it presented issues, ones that he might not be able to deal with on his own. Not only that, but the city centre was getting mighty busy, something they were no doubt counting on, to spread as much terror, chaos, carnage and death as possible. Knowing that he had to act soon, with his target spooked, calmly he took a breath and used his intellect to reach down into his very being, reassured by what he found... the powerful and potent magic that was his by birthright. Vowing there and then not to let anything bad happen to the humans surrounding him on his watch, he let go of the paper he'd been holding and, living up to his name, decided to take the most direct approach possible.

Newspaper rustling and flapping in the thin air beside

the front window of the newsagent, a thick, slightly blurred breeze was all that any of the humans in the surrounding area felt, their minds so inconsequential and primitive in comparison, they simply had no way to comprehend what was going on around them. And what was that? It was a bold and daring dragon agent, moving at speed, trying to prevent a terrorist atrocity that had been set in motion by a vicious dragon who'd been up to no good for over two years now, and whose modus operandi involved using humans as the delivery system for the evil that he spread. But while the humans hadn't seen him coming, his prey had, and also being a dragon, responded in kind, taking off into the Princes Street gardens in the direction of the renowned castle.

'Phew!' was the overriding thought crashing around Flash's mind, glad that his opponent had chosen to go in the opposite direction to the throng of unknowing shoppers. But his relief didn't last as he tore after the monster behind so many of these attacks, gaining all the time, but not enough to stop the beast from tearing into a group of visiting school children and their teachers.

BOOM! The saturated sound of breaking bones reverberated across the air along with the harsh cries of the victim's pain.

'DAMN!' he cursed, within his mind anyhow, but there wasn't time for that, not if he wanted to capture the fiend that had evaded his colleagues for so long. With part of him wanting desperately to stop and heal the injured, something no doubt his quarry knew he would be tempted to do, he did the only other thing possible in the situation and with a few carefully chosen words, a magnificent amount of willpower, and more than a splurge of his supernatural power, he inundated the whole group of humans, young and old, with the most potent healing magic that he possessed. Few other beings on the planet could pull off what he'd just done, with the king perhaps being one of only a handful. Unsurprisingly, and because it was him, it worked, most of those injured being instantaneously restored back to full health, with the exception of some mild bruising.

Glancing back over his shoulder, sure that his ploy would have worked and that whatever dumbass they'd sent after him this time would no doubt have stopped and be helping heal the sick and wounded, of which there would soon be many more should he have his way, Lenorous, as that was his name, was utterly astounded to see a crazed look in the eyes of the dragon that was... still chasing him. More astonishing than that was the fact that in the distance, he could just make out all the children and adults that he'd careered into, getting to their feet, pretty much all intact.

'IMPOSSIBLE!' he thought, wondering what the hell was going on, zipping around the bandstand, tearing up grass in his wake, for once a very forceful fear coursing through the veins of the falsehood of a form that he found himself in, by necessity. Deciding that now was the time not to hold back, Lenorous, constantly on the move, thrust out his right hand behind him and let rip with everything he had, colourful magic missiles, wicked zigzagging bolts of fluorescent green, blue and red lightning homing in on his enemy's position, splitting the air as they did so.

Fast didn't do him justice, and that was in dragon terms, let alone human ones, with the Crimson Guard gaining on the terrorist leader with every second that passed. Sadly, right at that moment, it didn't look as though it would be enough, with roughly the amount of magic to level a small town being spat back in his direction.

If they were out in the open, thought his psyche, then none of this would be a problem. But the main issue here and now was the safety of the humans and the surrounding landscape, given exactly where they were. All of which limited his options considerably. However, he wasn't held in such high regard by the dragon monarch for no apparent reason, but because he was the best of the best and so once again searching deep down inside him, he used his conscious will to grab everything thrown his way and adapting the ethereal energy within with just a few choice words, reversed what he would normally regard as a personal shield into one gigantic invisible box and then proceeded to capture everything offensive in it. Slamming the supernatural lid closed, so to speak, by joining up the enchanted forces that had created it, all the time on the move, muscles burning, legs a blur, giving everything he had in an effort to catch up, he looked on, satisfied, as the magic of every different kind contained within, exploded.

Horrified at seeing the most potent magic he had gobbled up by the dragon chasing him down, it hit Lenorous smack bang head on, right at that very moment. There was no way he was getting out of this, his fate almost certainly a return to the dragon domain to be incarcerated for a very long time. Death, of course was an option, but not one that he truly considered, especially being the coward that he almost always was, apart from on those first two occasions, ever since having got others to do the dirty work on his behalf. NO! He wasn't getting out of this, and he wasn't dying, not here, not today.

Skidding to a halt on the rain slicked grass, causing two muddy looking trails, one from each foot, both parallel, resembling railway lines, the dastardly dragon in his human guise turned to face his stalker, hands by his sides, looking as benign as possible.

Pleased that his target had given in to the inevitable, and still seething with rage at the attack on the school children and their teachers, Flash pulled up short, taking a deep breath to calm himself, just as he'd been taught to do, letting at least part of the anger built up inside him simply melt away into the ether.

"Give it up," he said calmly, wanting nothing more than to get this over with, "you've got nowhere else to go."

Willing and able to comply, Lenorous nodded solemnly, accepting that he'd lost after all this time on the run. And that was when it happened, much to the shock of both dragons, in the middle of the park, in the centre of

Edinburgh.

Flash's guess had been right, and the wickedly evil dragon hadn't been working alone. Not only had he been brainwashing the weak willed humans into thinking his cause just, but all along he'd had the help of another of his kind, one that instead of running away on being discovered, had just turned up here, determined to keep their run of malevolent deeds going, unwavering in the belief that he could destroy the latest prehistoric runt to pick up their scent.

Lighting up the park in a rainbow litany of colours, the air crackled, popped, fizzed and ignited as an ordinary human runner, dressed in white shorts, trainers, and tee shirt rippled and abruptly became all but a blur. In a wild magical reaction that shredded the branches off trees over two hundred metres away, tore a hole straight through the middle of the bandstand and blew all the doors from the public toilet blocks to smithereens, the tiny wrinkle in the air where the jogger had been, suddenly became much, much larger, still a smear, slowly thinking about resolving itself.

Flash swallowed hard. A small but very noticeable smile crept across the conceited and haughty face of Lenorous, his mind having just understood what had happened. With things going to straight to hell all around him, this was enough to cause the Crimson Guard to lose his temper, and knowing that he didn't have time to split his concentration and deal with two threats, as quick as his name implied, faster than even a magically enhanced eye could see, he ploughed straight into Lenorous, knocking him flat to the floor, unconscious. Still acutely aware of the danger from whatever supernatural transformation was taking place behind him, with just a handful of words the Crimson Guard did two things. First, he placed a series of magical binders on his captive's arms and legs, making sure that if he did wake up, in no way, shape or form would he be joining back in. Then, he did something that tore him up inside, something no Crimson Guard in their right mind would choose to do. But there and then, especially given exactly where they were, deep inside him, he knew it was the correct thing to do. Telepathically, he called for help, letting it be known that he needed it... NOW!

Whirling around to face the threat, utterly astounded at the sheer amount of supernatural residue given off by whatever kind of change was happening in front of him, suddenly, through a haze of exploding ethereal energy and a mind blowing light show, the raging wind died down, the colours and the ear splitting noise disappeared and leaving just the sickly smell of spent magic hanging in the air, Flash's worst nightmare swam into focus, making him, for the only time in his life, reconsider his choice of employment.

Nearly twenty five metres tall, dwarfing the remaining trees in the park and what remained of the bandstand, looking more Godzilla-like than anything else, a mighty brown and green dragon with huge spikes protruding out at every angle from across his tail, head and back, turned its gigantic head around to face him, murder in its eyes.

Not much had ever induced absolute terror in the Crimson Guard, but here and now, this mammoth fiend did.

'Oh crap!' was all that Flash could think, not solely for himself but because there were so many humans so close by. If he couldn't contain the monstrous beast, and he wasn't sure that he could, he knew without a doubt that many of their number would die here today. And that would be on him.

Tapping into the inherent confidence that his instructors had instilled in him during his training, bringing his supernatural gift to the fore, Flash licked his lips, took two steps forwards and addressed the crazed looking dragon, hoping against hope that it would refrain from this disastrous course of action and resolve things peacefully. That was never going to happen.

"You need to..."

That was as far as he got before a huge yellow, orange,

red and blue tinged streak of flame five metres wide assaulted his position. Cat-like reflexes exploding into action, Flash backflipped three times in a row and then bounced off to his right, tumbling head over heels before jumping to his feet. The prehistoric beast stomped forward, extending his shower of flame out into an arc, scorching grass, shrubbery and trees despite the rain and damp, his sole focus on putting his opponent in the ground.

'What to do, what to do, what to do?' thought the Crimson Guard, his mind whirring, taking in all the considerations, only wanting to buy himself and everyone in the immediate vicinity more time, so that help could arrive and all this could be over.

Unexpectedly, the enraged creature jumped up into the air. Now, when I say this, I don't mean took off, flapped his wings, or launched himself skywards. It was a jump, and that was unusual in itself, as was the fact that it surprised Flash. Never in all his battle hardened life had he seen the like. Now that he had though, his admiration for his adversary and the caution with which he regarded him almost doubled immediately, because you see, it might well have only been a small jump, but it shook the ground violently, felling most of the remaining trees, shattering what was left of the bandstand, destroying windows of shops on the nearest streets, sending roof tiles from buildings all around crashing to the ground, and of course knocking the Crimson Guard off his feet, which I suppose was the point. Panic ensued throughout the city centre, shoppers screamed in fear, running blindly in almost every direction as drivers honked their horns against the headache inducing shop alarms whistling through the air creating even more terror, as if that were at all possible.

Watching his adversary fall unceremoniously to the ground on his front, Xero, as that was the monstrosity's name, plodded forward, his huge tail swinging out behind him, the massive bony protrusions dragging through the mud, creating random sludge filled canals in their wake.

Slow to react, having banged his head on one of the concrete pavements as he'd fallen, Flash stumbled to his feet and tried to get his bearings. Before he had a chance to wrap his mind around what had happened, the next wave of assaults came zinging his way.

With a wave of his tiny right hand and a dollop of willpower, Xero let rip with a ferocious storm of crackling lightning bolts, that instead of cutting through the air as was their normal wont, came rippling across the ground, hugging the earth, closing in from all sides on the pesky human shaped dragon that had tried to put a dent in their plans, the damp rain soaked grass ramping up the intensity.

'Well,' thought the deranged and demented dragon with a penchant for all things terror related, 'let's see how much you like that.'

Instinctively his first thought was to transform back into his original form and fly up into the air, but he knew without a doubt that there simply wouldn't be enough time to pull it off. Even at its quickest, the change would take just over a second, and by that time he'd be well and truly electrocuted. Having done the maths in his head in but a split second, the only likely conclusion that played out was that of his imminent death, the attacker escaping and going on a rampage at the same time, causing a multitude of human casualties in the process, and putting a huge question mark over not only his legacy, but of his time in the Crimson Guards as a whole. No doubt his detractors, of which there were many, would love all that. As a microsecond of self pity threatened to overwhelm him, his very nature rallied against it all, determined to not only live but prevail, protect the humans and take down the group of terrorists he'd set out after, including this monster who'd had the audacity to turn into his dragon form, here on the surface of the planet, something that was totally and utterly forbidden under dragon law. NO! He would not be put down, not here, not now, not... EVER! Well, that was a little optimistic, but you know what I mean. And so with desperate times needing desperate measures and knowing just what a mess this would cause, and just how much trouble he'd be in not only with the rest of the Crimson Guards, but with the monarch as well, he did the only thing he could... prepared himself for the pain, and hoped it would be enough.

COLD! It's a dragon's greatest weakness, very much like Kryptonite to Superman and although mid-December in Scotland was not a particularly warm place, it wasn't quite the depths of the Arctic, well... not yet at least. But that's all that Flash could come up with to try to contain the chaos and mounting danger all around him. Gathering every last ounce of ethereal energy, or mana as dragons like to refer to it as, deep within all his dragon cells, in his mind he found the words to the mantra that he'd hoped never to use. His instructor, the mean and grumpy dragon that had punished him so hard, had torn away all self doubt, had pushed him to within an inch of his life, had in many ways forged him into the being he'd become, had warned him about ever using this particular magical endeavour. 'Pain and suffering on an unimaginable scale,' he'd said, and that was just what lay in store for the caster. That stark and inconceivable warning from one of the singular toughest dragons he'd ever had the misfortune to meet made him, here and now, fear the consequences of his actions, but with the seriousness of the situation this rash and reckless path seemed the only way forward. As the words drifted lazily across his mind, the brave and faithful dragon focused all his considerable willpower on them and without further ado unleashed every dragon's worst nightmare.

Oddly, it started in his smartly booted feet, spreading out in a concentric circle on the grass and concrete surrounding him, as well as up his false human shaped body. Tiny intricate flakes of frost sprang magically into being from nothing, expanding out exponentially in every direction at an unblinkingly rapid rate, freezing everything in their path, Flash first, followed quickly by the entirety of the park.

Mind numbing pain quite literally encompassed every

part of his phony form, from the smooth fingernails that reminded him of the strong, sharp talons of his original form, to the delicate little ears that looked nothing like their dragon counterparts. The hairs on his arms screamed in pain as they froze in place, every molecule resisting with everything it had, only to find there was no defence from an enemy of this magnitude and power. Eyes wide open, the crystalline cold spread out across the tiny lashes surrounding them, pricking and piercing, before thousandths of a second later attacking the protective watery layer of the eyeball itself, obscuring at least part of Flash's vision. It didn't matter though, because he could just make out what was going on in front of him, and despite the unwavering agony that hammered every single one of the atoms he was made of, he knew there and then that his gamble had paid off.

Xero's lightning was good... powerful, strong, clearly the result of a magic user incorporating a great deal of his will. But as it zigzagged across the ground, it came up against the kind of unmoveable magic that only comes along once in a generation, and I'm not talking about a human generation. Dragons usually live for hundreds of years, normally at least two hundred, sometimes three. Rumours abound throughout the underground domain that they rightfully call theirs, about one particular individual that has managed to extend their life beyond five centuries... a shopkeeper of all things, with the most extensive knowledge of everything magical and supernatural on the planet. Whether it was true or not was difficult to prove, with the magical mantra maker in question, as that's what he was, the only being really able to confirm or deny. And so a generation in these terms would most certainly refer to someone special, and that's exactly what Dendrik Ridge and his ethereal energy was.

You might think that supernatural lightning travelling at such a rate would conduct across the bonds of water that made up the ice and frost circling out from the dragon agent in his fictitious human guise, but part of the spell cast by the ingenious Crimson Guard had skewed the makeup of the atoms pertaining to the ice, making them not only unbreakable, at least by another's magic, but also giving them all but the resistance of wood, essentially stopping the electrical bombardment in its tracks.

With Xero's spell overwhelmed and truly surpassed by Flash's magic, the wondrous mantra continued on its way, freezing whole swathes of grass, mud, plant life, as well as an ornate pond and fountain, spreading out as it had been ordered to do in a radius of five hundred metres.

On the ground, magically bound and shackled, still rendered unconscious, luckily for him, the inert body of Lenorous transformed in a split second into a huge frozen mound, the cold white shimmering and shiny surface thick enough not to give away any secrets as to what lay beneath. And still the frosty freezing behemoth of a spell continued unerringly on its way, tackling the surrounding gorgeous trees, the ones that looked almost naked at this time of year without all the intricately coloured leaves that had so abruptly left them only a matter of weeks earlier. Weaving up the coarse harsh trunks, infiltrating the lairs of the tiniest of creatures, startling birds into flight, the extra weight from the ice bowing even the strongest of branches, the Crimson Guard's powerful paranormal enchantment finally caught up with its intended victim... Xero!

Pleased at having unleashed such scathing magic, knowing that the newcomer, just like all those before him that had tried to hunt them down, was destined to die a meaningless death, leaving absolutely no legacy, the mammoth terrorist leader in the natural form that he'd entered this world in, threw back his head towards the sky, and in much the same way as he'd released his magic, with all his might let out the biggest, longest, cruellest chuckle that he could, taunting Fate herself. Given the circumstances, it looked as though she might well have the last laugh. Only when he'd finished guffawing, dying flame licking his teeth and nostrils, did he have the presence of mind to take in what was going on all around him. In that moment, he received the biggest shock of his eighty year old life. GONE was his rainbow coloured lightning, ably replaced by a blanket of soul destroying white covering everything in its path, unstoppable, moving at a dizzying rate, making a snowman out of his adversary and an inexplicable ornament out of his former partner on the way. Too slow, that's what he was. Not so much body, more his intelligence. Had he acted sooner and leapt skyward, there was every chance that he could have avoided his frosty fate. Unfortunately, it just took him too long to process what he was seeing, his very first thought being whether or not his supernatural ability had set all this in motion. Of course it hadn't, but he couldn't know that for sure. And that hesitation and confusion drew him straight into Flash's trap.

Talons, those were first, his bright white nails assaulted by the crystalline cold, pinning him to the ground, causing outrageous amounts of agonising pain to surge up into his body, clouding his thoughts, torturing what was left of his mind, his capture now all but assured. Spreading swiftly up his powerful, tree trunk-like legs, the searing cold battered his scales, easily slipping into the most minute of gaps between them, tearing into the soft, delicate skin beneath, rendering him not only inert, but by now, unconscious as well. A second later, it was done, with his gigantic eighty foot frame now resembling the biggest and best looking ice sculpture in the world, and something, had the chaos and the potential terrorist threat not been present, to marvel at.

Heart slowed to practically nothing, something dragons can cope with for some time, Flash smiled, at least inside, his frozen false human face unable to move in any way, shape or form, knowing that he'd captured not only the main player that he'd been tracking, but the ringleader as well. He just hoped that help, in the form of the dragon 'clean up' squad he'd called for, would be here soon, able to dissipate the chilly mantra holding them all in place, find and take into custody the human terrorists that had to be somewhere nearby, and perfectly wipe the minds of all those humans affected by the epically evil events of the day. They should be able to do just that, he thought, knowing that they were the best of the best. Briefly, he wondered what fate lay in store for him, and whether or not he'd be punished for how events had unfolded and gotten out of hand. That soon passed as the frost continued to multiply, affording him more pain than he could handle. Unsurprisingly, darkness took him.

Bright, harsh, white light burned his eyes, momentarily blinding him. Instinctively he tried to sit up, only to find he wasn't able to.

"It's all right Dendrik, you're safe and in good hands," whispered a familiar voice.

"Doc?" enquired the brave dragon agent from his prone position on the hospital bed.

"Of course, who else would have the time and patience to treat your casually inflicted wounds, originating from something so unbelievably stupid, that it could only have been you?"

"Ahhh... now I know it's you."

"Hmmm..."

And then he remembered.

"Did... did... did they get them... the terrorists?" he asked, in a blind panic.

"Slow down agent, slow down," urged the experienced healer stationed to their particular unit. "They got both of them and all the humans involved, all of which remain in custody on the surface, I believe."

"And what about the two dragons?"

"They're residing somewhere special at the king's pleasure. Speaking of which..."

"What's going on, Doc?"

"Majesty," observed the healer.

"Doctor," replied the king, having strolled purposefully through the two, giant swing doors of the private room that

Flash found himself in.

Swallowing hard, the dragon agent tried once again to sit up, this time a mite more successfully, his eyes now accustomed to the intense light shining down on him from above his bed.

"Sire," he observed croakily, his mouth drier than the most infamous of sandskimming courses.

"Ahhh... if it isn't one of my most dedicated, loyal and intelligent agents," observed the dragon monarch, with more than a hint of sarcasm, "Or, as your fellow Crimson Guards are calling you, 'The Winter Storm'."

Flash tried to gulp, but his mouth was just too dry.

"I'm sorry Majesty, I really am. But I wouldn't have done it unless I'd totally run out of options. It was very much a last resort."

"Hmmm... as we'd surmised, my young warrior. And while I in no way, shape or form encourage the kind of reckless act that created so much chaos, over thirty, yes THIRTY dragons had to make it right, with mind wiping not having been seen on that type of scale for nearly one hundred years, I do commend your original and out of the box thinking. But Flash, my boy... that particular mantra? I'm assured you were warned vigorously about what it would do should you ever ignite it."

"I was, Sire."

"And yet you still went ahead?"

"There truly was no other choice."

"You really are one of a kind," ventured the king, all the time shaking his head.

Leaning in, so that only the two of them could hear, George, the dragon monarch and effectively ruler of the entire planet, unbeknown of course to the humans on the surface, offered up some praise to one of his chief protectors.

"If you repeat any of this, not only will I deny it, but you'll be washing the outside the council building for the next two years. Do I make myself clear?"

Flash nodded, which was about all he could do, and enough to satisfy the king.

"Good work. The council would not only have me not say it, but to reprimand and demote you as well, given the mayhem caused. But I know your character and am totally sure that, as you've already said, you were in a tight spot. We have the two main protagonists in custody, one of which we've been after for years, the other whom we didn't even know existed. As well, those doers of evil on the surface will be spending a long time incarcerated, all thanks to you. Your actions were, as usual, both brave and selfless. Please though, don't go making a habit of that kind of thing. There's only so much protection I can afford you."

"Thank you," replied the Crimson Guard.

"You are, as always, very welcome."

Once again, Flash nodded.

"If you feel up to it, I have some other urgent business that I need help with," mused the monarch, wondering if the young agent had already been through enough for now, but knowing that perhaps after an event like that, the best course of action might be to get straight back on the horse. Also it might take him away from his colleagues, who he knew first hand could sometimes go a little too far with their ribbing and teasing, almost to the point of bullying.

"I'm at your disposal, Your Majesty."

"Excellent. There is at least one piece of good news for you, Flash."

"And what's that, Sire?"

"You're not going anywhere cold."

'That is good news,' thought the Crimson Guard, absolutely delighted.

"Actually it's somewhere quite the opposite... Malaysia in fact."

"Really?"

"Oh yes. We've gotten word that a group of fairy tale legends have gone rogue in some vain attempt to big themselves up and disrupt the human holidays. We're not sure who's behind it, but you can see the whistleblower transcripts and the notes on the case before you go. If what we're led to believe is true, then this poses an epic threat to humans across the globe. Not so much life or limb, but more to their mental and spiritual wellbeing. You need to be on your A game Flash. Can I count on you?"

Bounding out of bed, standing tall and proud, ready to go, the cunning, courageous and sometimes ruthless Crimson Guard gave his answer.

"I'm just the dragon for the job, Majesty."

Watching the lights of the Christmas tree twinkle beneath the shiny silver and gold tinsel that weaved in and around the dull dark green of the branches, a sprinkling of fake snow adding to the illusion, making both children feel special, despite their very young age, Michael, sat at his desk next to the iconic object, wondering just how it had come to this.

Things had been tight over the last few years that was for sure, but as a family, he, Caroline his wife and the two children, Megan and Rhianne were at least all happy and loved. However, with only one income supporting all four of them, money was in short supply and at this time of year that was something of a disappointment. With it already having been agreed that he would once again forego any Christmas present, his wife doing the same, what little spare money they had was showered on the two youngsters in the form of presents.

Glancing away from the decorative tree, he gazed lovingly across at Rhianne, fast asleep on the sofa, her perfect angelic face not betraying even a hint of the sometimes fiery temper that rose out of nowhere when things didn't go her way. Not being fed quickly enough, or changed too slowly, even the simple lack of attention from her sister could provoke much irritation. Wishing her sweet dreams, Michael's gaze transferred to the dark blue patterned carpet, where his elder daughter Megan sat with a colouring book and some crayons, happily scribbling away, trying desperately to keep within the lines of the pictures but not quite succeeding, lacking the fine motor skills because of her age, but not once getting frustrated. Memories of her birth flooded his mind, one of the best days of his life and one engrained within him forever. Gowned up and waiting to be brought into the operating theatre, he could remember sitting on a bench outside, around about 7 am, just as the sun started to rise over the horizon. It was almost a perfect moment. And then it happened, all very quickly. Rushed in, he was put on a stool next to his wife's head. Briefly they shared a smile, and then... BOOM! Their world changed forever. For a moment, and that's all it was, she panicked, not a sound coming out of the almost alien creature that had just vacated her body. Unfortunately she couldn't see what Michael could. And what was that I hear you ask? Utter professionalism and calm from those doctors and nurses working within the operating theatre. And so absolutely fascinated and thrilled in equal amounts at his daughter's arrival into the world, he watched as they gave her some oxygen and a hearty pat on the back, the reward for which was some reassuring noise. After that, much to his delight, she was wrapped up and placed in his arms. A perfect moment this most certainly was, one that he would often reflect back on throughout his life.

Turning away from his gorgeous kids, he thought about returning to the monitor and continuing with his work. Before he did so though, he stood up, and from the shelf on the wall above his desk, retrieved the box to a computer game that had long since been thrown away, but sat there in the midst of many others. Sitting back down, he opened it up and pulled out the contents... twenty five pounds in screwed up, wrinkled notes. DAMN! He thought. That still wasn't enough. For the past few months, he'd endeavoured to scrimp and save what he could. Only a little here and there as that's all that was possible, and that was the grand total he was now looking at. And the reason for his frustration was that it simply wasn't enough. Although both parents had agreed some time ago not to get each other any sort of Christmas present, Michael had his eyes on a pair of boots from an outlet at a shopping village a few miles out of Salisbridge itself, something he knew his wife coveted. But so far, with only a short while to go, he hadn't even reached the halfway mark, with absolutely no idea as to how he was going to get the rest. What he needed was a miracle, should such a thing exist. Slipping the crumpled notes back into the box, and putting it back onto the shelf, he supposed at least it was the right time of year for something like that.

Once, a long time ago, on Christmas Eve, or more accurately the early hours of Christmas morning, he'd been lying in bed, pondering the important questions in life, as most of us do. Did Santa truly exist? If so, where did he live? Flying reindeers? What was that all about? How on earth did the presents really get inside the house? What happened to all the sherry, mince pies and carrots? And how did it all occur in only one night? Surely that wasn't possible, was it?

And then it happened. In the total and utter silence, due to the early hour and the location of the house, from out of absolutely nowhere, a sound that can only really be described as jingling cut through the air, startling him fully awake from the dreamy doze that he'd been in.

'Nah...' he thought. 'I must have been mistaken.' Shattering the stillness once more, the sound echoed around, not at all eerie, more optimistic and cheerful, but this time topped off by something that would make sure this particular incident was well and truly cemented into his memory until his dying day. A distant, "HO, HO, HO," could just be made out against the backdrop of the jingling. Only at this point did he have the presence of mind to leap up, pull the curtains back and look out of the window, into the housing estate itself. As you'll have probably guessed, there was nothing, only the reflection of the dull orange electric streetlights playing out over the frost bitten row of parked cars on the street below. If you'd had asked him whether or not he believed in Father Christmas before that night, he would have been sceptical to say the least. It probably wouldn't have been an outright NO, as he'd always had a fantastic imagination and loved anything to do with science fiction and fantasy, but now, after what had happened, and he was one hundred percent sure that it had happened, his mind was well and truly changed, even years later as an adult, sure that Santa did roam the skies on that one particular night of the year. And he would go on to tell each of his children about that night across the course of both of their lives.

As schooldays went, this one, for the three friends at least, seemed to drag on (get it?!) and on and on. Finally though, they reached the end, and in search of one particular *tor,* raced off through the huge stone corridors, heading for his classroom. If the day had seemed never ending to Richie, Tank and Peter, that was nothing to what it felt like for Vimes, who'd barely been able to concentrate on any of his lessons, so great was his concern for Polkinghorne. At least he'd heard back from his friend at the 'Misuse of Mana' department. Keen to tell the three youngsters exactly what he'd found out, he waited patiently for them to arrive. It didn't take long.

Bounding through the doorway at speed, or at least trying to, their three dragon bodies momentarily all attempting to take up the same limited space, it was of course Richie who fought her way past the other two first, a small smile creeping across her face at beating her friends to it, with Tank next, and Peter as usual last, but by no means least.

"Glad you could make it," stated the *tor,* pleased to see all three of his young charges. But before he could go any further, the female of the trio, who he'd always very much thought of as their leader, butted in.

"We were up in the library most of the night, and we found something that might just be of interest."

"Go on," managed Vimes, desperate to tell them what he knew, but not wanting to curtail their eagerness.

And so they recounted the tale on the old tattered scroll about the death of the boy and the supposed miracles taking place in the villages all at the right time of year in Malaysia. Maintaining a stoic and calm demeanour, inside the *tor* was thrilled to pieces because their story very much coincided with what he'd found out. After they'd finished and had stopped to take a breath, he filled them in. Apparently there were logs going back centuries about unusually high amounts of magic pertaining to that particular area of Malaysia all at around that time of year, something that no one had either bothered or thought to look into.

All four of them utterly gobsmacked about how the information they'd gained supported the theory that something was going on, or at least had been in that part of the world, Peter was the one who bravely, at least for him, asked the question.

"What should we do now?"

Running his delicate, spindly little hands across the scales on his chin, Vimes considered their next course of action carefully. Thirty seconds later, he had it.

"I think it's time for a little field trip, students," he proposed. "What do you say?"

And so it was that twelve hours later, Vimes and his three students marched through the main entrance to the nursery ring, out into the cobbled streets of the second oldest dragon enclave in Britain, Purbeck Peninsula and, carrying huge backpacks that would hopefully contain everything they needed not only to survive, but to discover the truth of what had gone on, slowly headed towards the centre and, of course, the monorail station.

Based beneath the south of England in a region that covers the area from the east of Bournemouth through to the west of Swanage, as far south as the southern tip of the

Isle of Wight and as far north as Wimborne Minster, the modern day incarnation of Purbeck Peninsula dates back over three thousand years and incorporates a huge amount of not only dragon businesses, but houses as well. Drawing its name from the beautiful Isle of Purbeck up above on the surface which it lies directly underneath, the immediate area surrounding this cosy underground dragon community is encompassed by unusually dense layers of molten lava, thick and dangerous even by dragon standards, making it almost inaccessible from other communities across the domain. Although there is only one main point of access for the rest of the prehistoric society from the north, just like most of the secretive world of the dragons across the rest of the planet, there are many hundreds of individual access points, almost all magical in nature, none of course available or known to humans.

Treading the cobbles, all three friends took great pleasure from the occasional giant crack or fissure that crossed their path, through which brilliant bright orange and red could clearly be viewed, the intense heat given off almost pleasure personified, at least to a dragon. It was in their fifth year that they'd learnt about how the roiling magma that makes up a huge part of the planet now serves to keep a great deal of the domain's cities not only warm but lit as well. Invisible, magical filters drew out all the harmful elements of the lava, leaving just the heat and light, making everything look like something from a fairytale. Cool, or not as the case maybe, it most certainly was.

They passed fantastic shops selling everything from huge, colourful and exotic tasting sticks of charcoal, to laminium ball and sandskimming merchandise with almost anything relating to the favourite players of both these dragon sports, including clothes, grooming kits, temporary tattoos, to scaled down models of the famous arenas that the teams graced. This shop more than any of the others caught the eye of all three friends, and was one they often frequented on Sundays, the only day of the week they were allowed out into town on their own.

Following in the wake of Vimes' fast march, the three of them smiled at each other, excited to be on an outing and away from the nursery ring, Peter's stomach doing somersaults, that was how nervous he felt.

Two short minutes later, they turned a corner and strolled purposefully out onto the concourse of one of the busiest monorail stations dragon domain Great Britain had to offer. Massive, even by the domain's standards, the station itself was of course a terminus because of the limited access. But what a terminus it was. Overlooked by the huge silver office building that hung up high above everything else and effectively controlled all that it gazed down upon, from the huge LCD screens that constantly updated arrivals and departures down to the second, to controlling the points that so effortlessly allowed the massive silver bullet-like carriages to seamlessly glide in and out of the right platforms, it, like all the other underground stations across the dragon domain, was a marvel of technology, and the height of advancement for their race. With just two lines disappearing off into the shadowy, dark almighty tunnel that was cut into the rock face to the north, one for arrivals, the other for departures, on opening out into the station in a spider's web kind of fashion, eighteen branch lines spread out, two platforms serving each so that passengers could embark and disembark from different sides of the carriages simultaneously, so as to speed up the process, with each monorail only really at rest for a matter of moments before powering up and joining the short, orderly queue to shoot off through the gargantuan exit tunnel. Had humans tried to take in this sight, they would have come up short, with the monorails themselves moving so fast, even on the branch lines of the station, that only beings with magically enhanced senses were able to take in all the finer details.

Stopping momentarily in front of a huge LCD screen that constantly updated departures and arrivals down to the second, Vimes found the information he needed, 'P13

6.31.22 Pudding Lane, London', about the monorail that would take them to the intercontinental complex, and swiftly headed off in the direction of platform thirteen, the three youngsters following his lead.

Sure enough, at exactly 6.31am and twenty two seconds, the round, bullet-like head of a glistening silver carriage, silently glided to a halt directly in front of them, its huge reflective, electric silver doors opening with a WHOOOSH, allowing passengers to board from this side, whilst all the time passengers were exiting from the other... orderly, efficient and most certainly dragon-like, just as it should be.

Once inside, the four of them took a seat on the garishly red, long sofa-like seats that ran down either side of the carriage, each guiding their tails through the holes in the rear, designed especially for that purpose. After that all they could do was wait for their journey to begin.

For the three friends, memories of field trips gone by raced through their minds. For Peter, thoughts of a trip to Bath Spa came rushing back, when he and Richie had only just become friends with Tank, on their way to the History Fest Face-Off, something that had started as a day out, and ended as an adventure he'd never forget. Their class had won, stopping the Bath nursery ring equalling the longest winning run in their history, mainly thanks to Tank, who'd helped sabotage the deceitful Cowl's cheating scheme, and of course Richie who'd stepped up at the last minute, defeated her opponent and in doing so, had earned her rightful name. What a day that had been.

For Richie, given the significance of that trip to Bath Spa, it did, momentarily, pop into her head as the monorail's doors WHOOOSHED closed, but it was soon trumped by another, more vivid memory. A class human social science trip up to the sprawling metropolis of the capital, London, taking in everything above and below ground, was what came back to her, the noise of her classmates echoing around what was left of the space inside the monorail carriage, rowdy and uncouth the words best used to describe the very beginning of their journey. Only in their twenty fifth year, it was in many ways a fond time to look back upon. Having mastered absolutely no magic at all, familiar only with the most rudimentary of mantras, all the youngsters were cocky and full of false confidence, including, much to her embarrassment, herself.

Arriving at Waterloo West, they had disembarked as one, their *tors* accompanying them to the concourse, trying to constrain their excitement, without much luck, it had to be said. A reminder of the rules, what to do in an emergency and a haughty talk about how they were representing the whole of the nursery ring followed, after which they were allowed to go their own separate ways, mostly in groups, one or two on their own, herself falling into the latter category. Having done her homework dutifully (something she did all the time, being probably the brightest student of the lot) on where she wanted to go and what she wanted to see, first off for her was a trip to the Buckingham area of the underground domain, keen to take in the much talked about, and in her opinion, hyped council building. Approaching from the busiest direction past tall, high rise, high end shops that sold mainly clothes, including specialist cloak and hat designers, it nearly took her breath away when she turned one particular corner and strode out onto the plaza adjacent to the council building itself. WRONG, that's how she could remember feeling about the ultramodern structure that was over thirty storeys high (and that's dragon storeys, not human, so about three times the size) rising into the shadows of what was hard to describe as the gigantic cavern that contained this part of the capital. It was mesmerising, from whichever angle you looked at it. The height, however, was not the most amazing aspect of the building. A litany of curves, there was not a right angle in sight, the construction totally and utterly seamless... no joins, gaps, nothing. And even she couldn't begin to take a guess at the material used in its construction, something that had been kept totally under wraps and was rumoured, at least, to be a combination of some newly engineered material and ancient dragon magic. Gleaming from every perspective, it resembled an ever changing oil slick, the colours within seeming to move of their own accord. It was nothing short of glorious, as she stood there mouth agog, unable to speak or even move. After the initial shock, she closed in for a better look, stomping up the huge giant steps to the entrance, dipping her tail into both the bubbling pools of lava on each side of them, revelling in the heat and the sumptuous feel of the roiling magma on her skin. Eventually though, she tore herself away, keen to transform into the human guise that she'd spent many, many years trying to perfect. Doing just that on her way to one of the more public entrances to the surface, a stairwell that arrived in one of the side streets not far from Trafalgar Square, the most powerful of perception pullers cast on it and the surrounding area to deter any and all human interaction, in her lithe, limber, long brown curly haired form, she slipped seamlessly into the humanity of London and continued on her merry little way. Even though having researched a dozen or so places she would have liked to have visited, her mood, as was its wont, had become more reflective and contemplative about once again being on the surface, although this time without any direct supervision from the *tors*. And so, wistfully, she just wandered, not having any destination in mind, sometimes following the humans, occasionally the landscape, seeking out little known alleys and lanes here, the cut through there, until at some point in her journey she found herself adjacent to a set of sports fields some way from the centre of the metropolis that she'd started out in. Still deep in thought, chiefly about what the future held in store for her, she continued to watch as a group of humans got kitted out for some kind of match. Only when they'd finished and grabbed their sticks and a ball, did it occur to her exactly what they were doing.

'Lacrosse,' she thought, remembering having studied this for part of her homework an awfully long time ago, which didn't really matter given, as a dragon, she, like all the others of her race, possessed a nearly eidetic memory. With the sun warming her pale arms and a light breeze tickling her long curly brown hair, she found a spot on the daisy ridden grass to sit down, and continued to watch, intrigued. From the off, the skill, commitment, courage, bravery and speed of the humans battling it out against one another became obvious, pulling her in, leaving her unable to think of anything else. Sticks clashed, the ball zipped through the air, keepers at both ends used their highly honed reactions to save with almost every part of their bodies, compelled to do so through instinct and it appeared, much to her bemusement, utter joy.

'How odd,' she could remember thinking. But that didn't last, because you see, even just sitting there, not involved, whiling away the time all on her own, she'd become hooked, fascinated by everything about the fast and furious, utterly compelling sport.

As the halftime whistle blew, startling her out of her thoughts, she realised that it was almost time to meet back up for the journey home. Vowing there and then that she would one day try the dangerous and tricky looking sport in her human form without any magic being involved, she hightailed it back to the nearest domain entrance and caught the next monorail to Waterloo West. To this day, that was one of the most fascinating and pivotal experiences of her very short (in dragon terms anyway) life. That vow to take up playing lacrosse still remained somewhere towards the top of her 'things to do on the surface' list, even to this day.

Tank reflected back on his first trip to dragon domain New York, one to the famed botanical gardens and the world renowned zoo. Being allowed to roam freely amongst all the wild animals and the deadly plants had been the biggest thrill of his life up until that point, because you see, plants and animals were his thing. He knew everything about them, sometimes surprising even himself, but regularly surpassing the knowledge of the *tors* on these two subjects, much to their annoyance, it has to be said. That trip had also inspired his education choices and the path they'd led him on, that and a school visit by a knowledgeable dragon from Gee Tee's Mantra Emporium by the name of Cat. All he'd wanted to do was work there, hopefully studying not only magic, but flora and fauna as well. With only ten years to go until he graduated, he most certainly was on track to do just that.

Just over fifteen minutes, that's how long it took to reach Pudding Lane station, not bad given that it was almost in central London. After that, the four of them crossed over to the middle of the three intercontinental platforms and patiently waited for their monorail carriage to arrive. Twenty minutes later, and to the second displayed on the screen, it did. And so they hopped on the direct monorail service to Perth, Australia, the three youngsters now more excited than ever at taking the express carriage.

Travelling beneath Europe, Turkey, Afghanistan, most of India, underneath the Bay of Bengal, finally at Singapore, eleven hours after boarding, all four of them alighted. On doing so, they quickly jumped onto a local carriage that headed north towards Terengganu, getting off about halfway, underneath the human city of Pahang. Slowly, they were closing in.

Bound, gagged, covered in hardened splodges of thick brown chocolate as well as some sickly sweet red concoction, sitting in one filthy, rancid corner of the room, Polkinghorne could only watch wide-eyed at the spectacle playing out before her, terrified on every level, not least by what was going on, but at the thought of not fulfilling her responsibilities and letting down all the humans that counted on her year round to bolster their hopes, dreams and wishes. Feeling as much of a failure as she ever had, with little choice she continued watching the freaky circus show, hoping against hope that this was some sort of nightmare and that any second now she would wake up in what passed for normality. Fat chance!

Delight and glee couldn't begin to describe the happiness of the three beings sharing the room with our very own Santa, as they laughed and revelled, sang and shouted, amused by everything, even the sound of their own voices.

"Again, again!" shouted the one with the bow and an unlimited supply of arrows.

MUNCH, MUNCH, chewed the furry fella next to him, up for some more fun.

"Okay, once more. But I'm not wasting all my good ones just for your target practice."

"BOO!" they both replied simultaneously, much to the hilarity of all three of them.

Pulling a slender white arm back across her shoulder, the smallest of them all hefted the shining, mighty white object, and reluctantly let it fly with all the gusto she had, which given her job, was not inconsiderable. Zinging through the air in all but a blur, the twang of a bowstring thundered off all four walls, followed closely by a thick wet SPLAT!

A CRACK and a THUNK later, the distinctive white object, zipping through the air like a comet, exploded into hundreds of pieces right before their very eyes, pierced straight through its heart (gives you a clue) by the unstoppable arrow that continued on its trajectory, unbroken. Before the tiny chunks had a chance to disperse, they were all contained by a thick, gooey layer of magical milk chocolatey brown, destroying their momentum, forcing them to fall to the ground with a loud, disgusting SQUELCH, which in turn was greeted by resounding howls of terrifying laughter, some of it more animal-like than anything else.

Trying to ignore the sick game going on in front of her, without much success, tiny tears weaved their way down Polkinghorne's face, dripping relentlessly to the floor when they reached the drop off of her chin, mixing seamlessly with the red and brown mess that was already there.

Having stayed the night in their human guises in a guest house in the city of Pahang, on the surface, in the eastern part of Malaysia, wanting to get a feel for things and become acquainted with the local customs, just after dawn all four dragons, the *tor* and his three students, set out in an easterly direction and, after a short taxi ride to the outlying region of Jaya Gading, found themselves very much in the middle of some dense jungle only two hours after having left the city. Little did they know that an apex predator had caught their scent and was well and truly on their trail.

Ninety minutes later, all four of them stood alone at the bottom of the most spectacular array of waterfalls that any of them had ever seen in the Sungai Pandan nature preserve, taking in all the beauty around them, especially Tank who was revelling in his natural element. About to retrieve something to eat from their backpacks that had transformed from the dragon sized ones they'd left the nursery ring with into much more appropriate human dimensions, but still carrying the same load, with the help of more than a little dragon magic, all four of them were suddenly aware of something coming out of the dense jungle from where they'd just emerged. It was a singular being. I say being, because although it looked like a lone human male, well built with short blondish hair, a sweat stained tee shirt with the name of some rock band or other faded through use, light brown all weather trousers that were zippered just above the knees and a tactical belt that every conceivable item in the world seemed to dangle from, it immediately became clear that this was one of their own, and an experienced one at that.

"Uh... good morning," was all that Vimes could think to utter, carefully placing himself between this newcomer and his charges.

"What are you doing here?" asked the rogue individual,

menacingly.

"Just, uh, just uh... taking in the delight of the waterfalls," Vimes replied as best he could.

"Don't give me that," declared the hunter, "there's something more going on. Spill it," he ordered.

Terrified, with as much fear as he'd ever felt coursing through him, which was quite something given some of the bullying he'd been on the end of during his time in the nursery ring, not from Richie and Tank of course, but one or two others that went out of their way to make his life hell, Peter thought there and then that both of his legs might give way.

Giving Tank a knowing look, Richie raided her mind for what little offensive mantras it contained, (year forty onwards was when attacking magic was covered in intricate detail... typical) and readied the most powerful, hoping it wouldn't come to that.

Tank, always full of wonder at absolutely everything, watched the female of his two best friends ready some magic and wondered where the hell this was all going. Surely it couldn't come to this, he thought. Yes, this newcomer that had clearly been following them looked pretty scary and downright shady, but you really should never judge a book by its cover as the humans like to say, something he believed in wholeheartedly. And so really not wanting to see any violence at all, and to the surprise of all his allies, he marched out in front of Vimes and to the amazement of everyone there, offered out his hand in a gesture of friendship in the direction of the recent arrival.

"Tank," he said softly.

Two steps behind the youngster, the *tor's* eyes nearly leapt out of his head at what his student had just done.

Suspicious beyond belief, but sensing no deceit or betrayal with his excellent, timeworn senses, the blonde haired apparent male reached out and shook the proffered appendage.

"Dendrik Ridge, but you can call me... FLASH!"

"Nice to meet you," replied Tank disarmingly. "Can I ask why you were following us?"

"I think before I answer that, you'd better answer my question. I need to know what you're all doing out here. It's important."

Looking over his shoulder, Tank's eyes locked with those of Vimes, who, as well as giving him a look, shook his head almost imperceptibly. Of course, that was never going to slip past Flash, was it, not with everything he was capable of.

"Listen right now," announced the Crimson Guard, not taking his eyes off any of them for even a second, especially not the girl because he recognised trouble and an attitude when he saw it and for him, looking over at her, it was like glancing in the mirror, on that much the senses within him that kept him safe, all agreed. "I'm a Crimson Guard here at the request of the dragon king himself, looking into something of the utmost importance. If you do not comply with me, I will have to assume you have something to hide, and will have no choice but to have you arrested for hindering an investigation, something that I'm sure none of you want, and that I only see as a last resort."

"I'd like to see you try," ventured Richie, choosing that moment exactly to get involved.

Peter closed his eyes and shook his head.

"Stand down Miss Rump, that's an order," stated Vimes, an unmistakeable no-nonsense tone to his voice.

"But..."

"NOW!"

None too happily, she complied, sure that it wasn't the right thing to do.

"I'm sorry Den... Flash," observed Vimes, stuck between a rock and a hard place, "but I'm afraid we can't tell you why we're here."

"RIGHT!" announced the Crimson Guard, reaching the end of his tether, "THAT'S IT!"

"Whoa," mouthed Tank, lengthening his arm, holding

his palm out flat, "please, just hang on a second, uhh... Flash. It's not that we don't want to tell you why we're here, it's as Vimes here has just stated... we can't. And I promise you with all my heart, that really is the case."

"I don't like others trying to pull the wool over my eyes," announced the Crimson Guard, using one of his favourite human sayings.

"I can understand that, I wouldn't either," assured Tank, taking the lead in whatever complicated negotiations these were turning into. "It's just that..."

Again, he turned around to the others, who all in response, including the *tor,* just shrugged their shoulders, which wasn't much help at all.

"It's just that," he continued, "we've all taken a vow, a supernatural one with quite serious consequences. If we reveal to you the reason that we're here, the magic will kick in and do its thing, and that will very much be that. Life for all four of us will never be the same again which I can assure you is something of an understatement."

Again the Crimson Guard sensed no deception or betrayal. Odd!

"That doesn't help my mission at all, does it?"

"I'm sorry no, it doesn't."

"I find it strange that you're all out here in the arse end of nowhere at this time of day, avoiding all the tourists, heading east of all places. There can't be many reasons why this would be the case. Can you not at least give me a hint as to why you're here?"

They all shook their heads in unison.

"Even the slightest hint that we've broken the vow and the magic that we're bound to it by will be unleashed. In all honesty, I think we've already said too much."

And then Tank had it.

"What about if we do to him, what you did to us?" he said, turning to face Vimes.

Flash very much did not like the sound of that, something that came across from the downright scary glare on his face.

"No, no, wait," started Tank getting in a muddle. "All I mean is that we could share the vow with you, and then you'd know what we were doing here, but you just wouldn't be able to tell anyone. Where's the harm in that?"

"Hmmm..."

"While I ponder that, why don't you tell me where you're all from?"

It was Vimes that rightly spoke up, not wanting to hold anything back from the Crimson Guard.

"The Purbeck Peninsula nursery ring, on the southern coast of England."

"I'm familiar with it."

"I'm a *tor* there, and these three are year forty students."

"Really?"

"Yep."

"How on earth did you get the head of the nursery ring to agree to let you bring your students out this far?"

Vimes swallowed nervously, aware that by now he'd probably lost the job and career that he almost loved above all else... ALMOST!

"I always find that it's not so much what you know, or who you know, but more, what you know about who you know, if you get my drift."

"Excellent," replied Flash, all the time chuckling, more impressed and inclined to trust the four by the minute. "You have some dirt on the top dragon. Well... good for you, good for you."

It was then that the most reserved amongst them spoke up against the background noise of colourful parrots squawking in the surrounding treetops.

"What's a Crimson Guard?" asked Peter inquisitively, a question the other two youngsters were keen to know the answer to.

Vimes and Flash shared a look, one that said something along the lines of, 'you can tell them, but do not go into graphic detail,' something that the lone dragon agent chose to respect.

"I report, answer to and go on missions of the utmost importance for the king himself, showing my face where he is unable to, carrying out some of the so called 'dirty work' that would sully his good name, but is always necessary in the background, whether diplomatic or otherwise. I take any number of roles depending very much on the situation. There are others like me. Mostly we work alone, but sometimes, in times of crisis, we pull together, team up if you like, and take on the world."

"Wow," mouthed Peter, more than a little in awe.

WOW indeed.

"Okay," announced Flash very matter-of-factly, "I'm in. Share the vow with me."

"Are you sure?" asked Vimes nervously.

"I am," replied the Crimson Guard, "unless of course you've been spinning me a yarn."

"No, it's not that. It's just that, the consequences of breaking the magical bond are quite severe. If that's the cost, how will you report back to the king?"

'A good question,' thought Flash and one he'd deal with when the time came.

"It'll be okay. Deal me in."

And so Vimes did, in exactly the same way that he had with the three youngsters, blowing the Crimson Guard's mind in the process, something not easily achievable.

"Well... that's something of a surprise," declared Flash, stunned threefold... one at Santa's current incarnation being female, two at the fact that they now knew her true identity. And three, that they were all working the same case, albeit from opposite ends.

There and then, he decided to come clean with the three of them. After all, they had been forthcoming with him. And so very much against protocol, he shared what he knew, how he was looking for some magical creatures gone rogue who were determined to ruin not just this year's Christmas, but to prevent it from ever happening again, something the king considered would have a detrimental effect across the surface of the planet and set the human race back decades, if not more. As a matter of urgency they had to find Polkinghorne in an effort to save Christmas and prevent total and utter mayhem on the surface, something they immediately all agreed on. And so pooling their resources, with Flash very much in charge, they set off into the jungle, continuing eastwards to the area where the dragon that had befriended the boy had supposedly lived. They had a long trek ahead, but with the sun's rays beating down on them, they could all at least take solace from the heat and the fact that they were now greater in number, hopefully giving them a better chance of finding the needle in the haystack they were searching for.

Spreading out across the jungle in a line, Peter jumping at the first sign of anything moving, much to the others' amusement, and with Flash at the centre, the five continued on, searching for the most minute amount of magical residue, no matter how old or degraded, using a complex mantra that the Crimson Guard had taught them, much to the delight of Tank who, like the others remained in total and utter awe of the dragon agent. Thoughts of becoming friends with someone like him at some point in the future had jumped high up on his list of things to accomplish by the time he reached the ripe old age of one hundred.

Minutes turned into hours amongst the same lush greenery, the fantastic background noise of all the tropical animals not so much of a novelty now, more an annoying distraction, something to be ignored, if that were at all possible. It wasn't for one of their troop, who had taken to multitasking to keep his wit sharp and his mind focused, something of a contradiction it would seem, but that was how he rolled. Naming butterflies, caterpillars, birds, spiders, monkeys and even tiny rodents, it felt very much like a night in the dorm for him, revising for any number of his exams. And when I say name, I don't just mean the English name for whatever it was that he'd spotted... NO!

The full on Latin name as well, all from memory, just one of the things he was born to be able to do.

Unsurprisingly it was the female of the bunch, Richie, who found the first hint of the supernatural in the form of half a dozen or so tiny remnants of magic that were at least decades old, dripping across a set of intricate tree roots, heading off in an easterly direction. Encouraged, they continued on, until two hours later, they reached... something.

An overgrown clearing covered in toppled trees and twisting sharp vines. If you were a human, you'd avoid this place like the plague because it positively reeked of evil. And that was probably the point. Slowly the group of four skirted around the edges, prodding and probing with their magic, well... Flash mainly, selectively using specialised mantras to check any number of different properties within the dense and overrun glade. The others, exhausted from their trek, took time out to rest and recover, eat and drink. Sometime later, the Crimson Guard joined them, frustrated to say the least.

"How's it going?" asked Vimes.

"Slowly," replied Flash, taking a swig from the water bottle attached to his belt, the one that remained replenished at all times thanks to some rather potent and powerful magic.

"What seems to be the problem?" enquired Tank, looking back over his shoulder from his outstretched arms that had brightly coloured butterflies drinking off each of his sausage like fingers.

"There's a reasonable amount of old ethereal energy kicking about the place, but nothing recent, which I find odd. If this is Polkinghorne's lair, there should at least be some indication of fresh mana, no matter how small. But for whatever reason, I just can't find it. And I've tried everything that I know."

"Wiped clean?" suggested the *tor*.

"Almost certainly."

"What does that all mean?" ventured Peter.

"That there's probably something here, and that our band of rogue magic users have been, and might still be, close by."

"Oh good," Richie chipped in.

"So what do we do next?" enquired Tank, still enthralled by his winged friends.

"I say we go in, but with extreme caution," urged the Crimson Guard, getting to his feet.

"What can we do to help?" Vimes put in.

"Nothing!" exclaimed Flash. "Stand back and watch."

Strolling over to what he considered the outer edges of the clearing, the Crimson Guard looked out across the mass of plants, huge fallen trees and just the nature overload before him. Cutting through all that would have been a challenge for most to say the least, but for him, it was child's play.

Opening out his arms, eyes closed, slowly the index fingers on both of his hands circled, almost imperceptibly slowly. Finding his focus, along with the words that he needed, he grabbed both with his will and flooded the combination with his inherent magic. What happened next was a sight to behold.

Against the backdrop of nature scattering in every direction, plants both dead and alive rose into the air. Not very much, only a metre or so, but it was enough to startle into action all the animals that had made this place their home, sending them skittering back into the jungle from whence they originally came. And then, throwing his arms open wide, Flash's supernatural power flung every single thing in the dell off to the sides. The sounds of clashing tree trunks and the harsh rustling of plants landing en masse had birds half a mile away leaving their nests, heading for the safety of the open air.

Collectively, the three students and their *tor* gasped at what had been revealed by their friend's supernatural efforts. Before them lay a huge rocky outcrop that surrounded a dark and mysterious fifty metre wide hole, clearly the entrance to some sort of cave system. It was a remarkable discovery for sure and one that, no doubt, they were simply not supposed to find.

"Shall we?" ventured the Crimson Guard, striding purposefully towards the edge of the shadowy dark depths.

"Is it safe?" enquired Peter, barely able to contain his fear.

"I do hope not," replied Flash, grinning inanely. "Where would be the fun in that?"

Facing them, his back to the hole, as casually as possible the newcomer to their tight knit group leaned backwards and without a care in the world, disappeared over the side into the darkness.

"Oh my," Vimes cried out, unsure of just how wise their interim leader's actions were.

"Should we follow him?" Richie asked eagerly, ready at least in her own mind for any eventuality.

"I think for now we wait," observed Vimes. "Let him scout ahead. I'm sure once it's safe he'll come back and find us."

Peter was very pleased with this, more than anything not wanting to go down into the hole. And then Tank piped up.

"What happens if he doesn't come back?"

'That,' thought the extremely shaken up *tor*, 'is a very good question.'

Appearing mid-air from out of the inky blackness of the hole, up shot Flash's dragon form about ten minutes later, taking just a moment to bathe in the sunlight once again.

"You should change back into your prehistoric forms and join me," he announced. "Don't worry," he assured, noticing the dire look on Peter's face, "I've checked that it's safe. Come on down, and I'll show you around."

After reverting back, but not before they'd gathered up their still intact human clothes and put them in their human sized backpacks, after having ventured into the edge of the jungle, each not wanting Vimes to see them getting naked in their human guises so that they could change without ruining their outfits, all four of them followed the Crimson Guard down into the dark labyrinth, astounded at the magnitude of twisting and turning tunnels, amazed that anything at all lived down there. Not only did something live there, but from the apparent look of things on entering one giant, well lit cavern, it thrived.

Extraordinary was one of the few words fit to describe what they'd flown into... a massive wide open cave, full to the brim with chairs and workstations, all human size, most of which had ancient maps rolled out upon them, with pins stuck in to mark precise locations. Dozens of shelves lay across each wall, running off into the distance as far as the eye could see, sculpted from the rock itself, containing hundreds... no, thousands, maybe even more, books, scrolls, tatty old tomes and one off mantras. Across the occasional wall that didn't have any sort of shelf, scribbled notes in a scrawl that was hard to decipher were glued, sometimes with huge unmistakable exclamation marks next to them, sometimes with the odd word underlined. Experiments of many different kinds seemed to have taken place there. It was mesmerising, astounding even. Sparkling captured magic zinged in every different shade around thick, transparent bottles, occasionally making them wobble, rumble and shake. Running around the edge, up the walls and on occasion up across the ceiling in every direction were a variety of trees, all of which Tank easily recognised. Different variations of apple and lime trees stood out, as well as crab apple and hawthorn, all with one thing in common, that of a smooth edged, bright evergreen plant with waxy white berries intertwining its way in and around all their branches and fruit... mistletoe! Attached by means of a structure known as a haustorium, Tank knew, the parasitic nature of the plant most associated with Christmas used host trees to extract water and nutrients. Dotted between all these were a series of miniature evergreen spruces, pines and firs. At first the youngster was puzzled as to how the fruit plants were being kept alive, but on waving his wing across a band of streaming beams of sunlight this far down, he followed their course back to the source and discovered several tiny holes over a hundred metres above their head, clearly on the surface, specifically designed to channel in sunlight. After that, a series of mirrors reflected the light throughout the cavern in the direction of the plants... fabulous and utterly ingenious, he thought, already forming a bond with the missing Polkinghorne and her love of nature. And as if that wasn't fantastic enough, in the middle of everything, highlighted from above by some kind of magical downlighter, sat one singular object that nearly every child in the world would recognise instantly... Santa's sleigh!

Gleaming bright red, so much so that you could see your reflection in it, looking as though it had come straight off the lot, it appeared empty apart from the leather reins for eight reindeer taking up much of the front row and an abandoned, flattened empty red sack with a white lining, flung across the back seat. It was total and utter proof (not that they needed it given everything else here) that this was Polkinghorne's secret lair.

"I would suggest," spoke Flash, "that we all change back into our human alter egos as this place appears to be best set up for such a thing."

They did so, with all three of the youngsters scattering off in different directions so they could change privately, much to the amusement of the Crimson Guard and *tor*.

"You did well finding this place," said Vimes.

"It would have taken much longer without all four of you. No doubt I would have found it eventually. Hopefully saving all that time will pay dividends at some point in the future."

"Talons crossed."

All huffing and puffing, Peter lagging behind, the three friends returned, throwing their backpacks into a pile next to one of the lime trees. Vimes gave Flash a look that just said, 'What can you do? Dragonlings eh!'

After the brief interruption, it was back to business.

"Spread out," the Crimson Guard ordered. "Try not to touch too much, but see if you can find anything relevant, and no, I don't know what we're looking for, so use that dragon initiative which I see engrained within all of you. Open your minds and let's join the dots."

And so they did, Tank resisting the temptation for a better look at all the plant life, heading straight, instead towards all the magic contained within the many hundreds of bottles that sat on some of the shelves, desks and significant parts of the floor.

A keen study, Richie started to peruse row after row of books, looking for anything unusual, whatever that may have been, starting up high, working her way down low.

Not left with much choice, Peter ventured over to the nearest desk, before pulling out the chair and sitting down, scraping its four metal feet across the stone flooring as he did so, much to the ire of the others.

Flash and Vimes tried to take in the bigger picture, investigating the sleigh and its contents for any clues, as well as everything the youngsters were so carefully studying.

Eventually, after it had gotten dark, the giveaway being the light for the plants gently subsiding, the group, led by the Crimson Guard, all pulled up some chairs around the exotic looking sleigh and tried to put together everything they had.

"Anyone find any obvious clues?" asked Flash, pretty sure of the answer since none of them had spoken out, up until that point anyway.

All of them shook their heads dejectedly.

"Any leads at all?"

"I might have something," announced Tank, making all of them turn to face in his direction. "Not about where Polkinghorne is, I'm afraid."

"Then what?" demanded the Crimson Guard, tetchily.

"The magic contained in the glass bottles, I think it

relates to her Santa duties."

"Really?" said Vimes sceptically.

"I'm sure of it in fact. I've tested as much of it as I can in such a short time and without the right equipment, and there's some remarkable stuff in there."

"Such as?"

"Well," continued the youngster, "without all the right equipment, it's hard to narrow down exactly, but there's definitely magic that slows time, by quite a considerable factor."

"Okay," mused the *tor*, encouraging his young charge to continue.

"Plus there's something the likes of which I've never seen that would most certainly speed things up. When I focus on that, I'm immediately drawn to the sleigh, but I'm not sure why."

"Excellent!" voiced Flash, his tetchiness having completely disappeared, pleased that the young dragon was losing himself totally in the magic. "Anything else?"

"Two more things of note," added Tank. "There's something very similar to the mantras that turn our dragon backpacks into human ones, but maintain the same volume. It's a bit different but close enough."

"And?"

"Last but by no means least, there's something I don't quite understand, but would, by the looks of things, appear quite important."

"How so?"

"The magic within the mantras is complicated, like nothing I've ever seen before."

"That's not too much of a surprise," voiced the Crimson Guard.

"No, you don't understand. I've studied complex, quantum, quadratic variables and can easily cast higher plane mantras with an integrity factor of fifty or above," announced Tank nonchalantly, much to Flash's astonishment and Vimes' pride. "But this is on a whole new level again. Its molecular makeup and regenerating architecture alone make it something absolutely amazing, the likes of which I struggle to imagine even in my wildest dreams."

"And boy," chipped in Richie, smiling, "that's what he dreams of."

WOW! That took away their breaths, momentarily at least. But the Crimson Guard had been around enough to recognise pure, unadulterated talent when he saw it, and unbelievably, it was on display here in abundance. So he deigned to utilise it as best he could.

"Go on then," Flash urged.

"Go on then what?" Tank replied.

"Use the powerful imagination that I sense resides within you and tell us all about it."

"I... I... I... I'm not sure how."

"Close your eyes, picture everything that you know about it and have seen, and expand your thinking out from there."

"You mean like brainstorming?"

"Exactly!"

"Okay, I can't imagine in what way, shape or form this is going to be of any help, but here goes."

Drawing in a big, deep breath, Tank closed his eyes and walling off his mind to anything even remotely outside his body, he pictured that particular magic and delved right in. Strangely, the first thing that occurred to him was an odd taste, something that ran rife across his tongue and the back of his throat.

'Bizarre,' he thought... 'kind of sickly sweet and yet savoury at the same time, with just a hint of... of what?' If he didn't know better, he'd have sworn it was alcohol with just a smidgen of carrot. Shaking his head, not on the outside you understand, but deep within his psyche, he ploughed on, determined to do as the Crimson Guard had asked.

Picturing molecules and atoms now, he tried to compare

them to all the magic he'd ever experienced up to this point, with absolutely no match at all. After that he delved deep into the supernatural repository of his mind, the one provided by his eidetic memory, the one that stored everything he'd ever read, and believe you me, that was quite something. Trying to find a match, or at least some combination that was even close, was like a supercomputer running a test, with tens of thousands of computations and comparisons taking place every split second, millions of results considered and discarded in only a few moments. It took close to sixty seconds before he opened his eyes and returned to some semblance of normality.

"Well...?" enquired Flash.

"If I had to guess, and that's all it would be, I would say there are three very different types of mantra all rolled into one, that all do very different things... a disentanglement spell that will break down a physical object nearby and then rebuild it further away. If it's not that, it's very, very close to that. There's also something that works in directly the opposite way, breaking down something further away, and then reassembling it close by," said the youngster, sweat pouring off his forehead by now, his mind was working so hard.

"And the last one?"

Swallowing hard, he searched for the words to describe what he'd found, no... not found, but imagined. Not feeling very confident at all, unlike his usual self, he was reluctant to utter the words he had to offer up, because, even in his head, they sounded bat shit crazy. With all eyes on him, and little choice but to continue, he did just that.

"Yearning... there was a deep sense of yearning. And yes I know, it makes me sound mad. But it's more than that, a... desire, a want... no, perhaps more a need to... please. NO. That's not it. All of those wrapped up in something else, something the magic is able to retrieve, but from where or the purpose of which, I really can't begin to speculate. That particular part of the mantra is just so complex, and yet when you delve into its very base layer, you find that it broadens out, almost as if to change the magnitude and scope. Intricate, searching for something specific and individual, and yet sweeping broadly across an open area... it's mad. Yes I know how it sounds, but that's all that I have for you."

"Brilliant! I commend you on your thoroughness, strength of will, bravery to voice your thoughts and out of the box thinking. You, my young friend, will go a long, long way. Perhaps you should take a look at becoming a King's Guard after you leave the nursery ring. Although not my favourite class of dragon, mainly because of the rivalry between our two factions, that's the way to go if you want to become a Crimson Guard. I'd be more than willing, from what I've seen, to put in a good word for you."

Both friends and their *tor* looked on in utter disbelief at the genuine offer that had just been made. Had their friend really just been presented with the chance of a lifetime?

Back to the matter at hand.

"What do you think it all means?" observed Vimes, watching magic of different shapes, sizes and colours ping around inside the array of individual glass bottles.

"I would have thought it's quite clear," suggested Flash, still mulling over the supernatural components to the last one. "They're all used to make Christmas happen."

'Of course,' thought Tank, berating himself for not having seen it sooner. But that realisation still didn't bring into focus what the very last mantra was, how it worked and the results of its actions, something that the Crimson Guard noticed not only him struggling with, but the others as well.

"If I had to guess," he said, attempting to put them all out of their misery, "I would say that the ethereal energy contained within that particular bottle, because of its complex nature, has been designed and re-fabricated over hundreds of years, if not longer, in an effort to perfect the intentions of whoever dreamt it up originally. Having researched Christmas thoroughly on the way here, I can think of only one purpose of such supernatural power."

"And what would that be?" asked Peter after the long, dramatic pause.

"To reveal a being's wishes."

"Rubbish!" spat Richie instantly, sure that no magic on the planet could do that.

Vimes, about to follow suit, suddenly found his mind holding back his tongue, as something deep inside him screamed out that it was true, and that a much cruder version of this must have been used on the very first villagers, the ones who had inadvertently caused the death of the boy that had befriended the dragon, in the tale that Peter had discovered. Catching the Crimson Guard's eyes, subtly he nodded his agreement.

"I understand your hesitation young dragon," Flash remarked calmly, "but I've seen other spells very much like this, and I assure you, it is at least possible."

"Really?" she questioned meekly, deferring to his experience and better judgement, which wasn't something that happened often, quite the turnaround.

"Really. As well, if you think about it, nearly all of it makes some kind of sense, in relation to Christmas at least."

"Where does this leave us?" asked Tank, still unsure of where to go from here.

"That's a good question, and if I'm totally honest, I really don't know. It doesn't get us any closer to finding Polkinghorne or the psychopaths that have taken her. And since there was nothing even remotely supernatural left behind for us to follow or analyse, we seem to have hit a dead end."

"That's it!" announced Richie cheerfully, all thoughts of her little outburst forgotten.

"What do you mean?" replied the Crimson Guard, confused.

"Whoever took Polkinghorne was careful and sensible enough not to leave any magical clues behind, but perhaps that's not where we should be focusing our efforts."

"Go on," urged Vimes, knowing how brilliant the young female dragon actually was, once she got going.

"If they spent all their time concealing any magical tracks that they left, then perhaps they were too busy doing that to cover just the normal physical traces. I don't know if this is possible, or even if you have the stature and power to do such a thing, but perhaps we could see if there's any satellite data from overhead in the human world. If there is, and they were lax on that side of things, might it not offer up a chance to see where they went?"

'Oh I like her,' thought Flash, keeping his face entirely neutral. 'Why didn't I think of that?'

"If I can get a message back to London, we might be able to do just that," said Flash, pulling out a chunky, dark black Nokia phone from one pocket of his utility belt. "Good thinking!"

"There's a communications console tied directly into the crystal node system up the far end," announced Richie smugly, pretty sure the others there hadn't spotted it yet.

"Really?" declared the Crimson Guard. "Show me!"

With everyone else following behind her, she marched to the furthest end of the gigantic elongated cavern they were in, and pulling some of the lime and apple tree branches in front of her, ones that appeared to have become overgrown and unruly, out of the way, slipped effortlessly through the tiny gap she'd created, drawing up against quite a big desk, two computer consoles, all connected to a pulsing white crystal that sat between them. This was part of a worldwide network of intricate crystals that enhanced both the range and connectivity of telepathic communication, allowing dragons to send messages in many different forms to the furthest reaches of the planet.

'I'd completely missed this,' thought Flash, one of the best of his kind and clearly not fully recovered from his exertions in Scotland. 'At this rate they'll all have to join the Crimson Guards! Wouldn't that be something?'

"It looks like you're right," Flash said, after a minute or

so of checking that everything was in order. "I'll get a message back to London and see if they can check for the satellite intelligence, should there be any."

"What do we do in the meantime?" asked Vimes this time.

"I think we all need to rack our brains and try and come up with a way forward. Since all three of you," he said, indicating the three students with just the flick of his head, "work so well together, why don't you sit down, look at all the different angles and see what you can come up with. Okay?"

It was, and so slipping back past the overrun and unkempt miniature trees, they found a workstation that the three of them could all sit around, and got on with it.

The sickly, spiteful games had taken another twisted turn. Still gagged and bound to her chair, the tiniest character of the lot now hovered briefly behind her, before placing a number of small, but quite weighty items atop her head. With a high pitched buzzing, the sweet and innocent looking monster fluttered out of the way as the other two, some way off, took aim.

Eyes as wide as they would go in absolute terror, Polkinghorne, or Santa as most on the surface would know her, could do little else but watch as an arrow was nocked, and the bowstring pulled back. TWANG! Even with her magical senses, the tied up captive couldn't begin to see the projectile cut through the air, that's how fast it travelled, only knowing that it had reached her when one of the objects above exploded out in all directions, sending shrapnel in the form of tiny white enamel shards in all directions, including into her head, something that hurt like hell and caused her to gasp and wince in pain. The sound of the arrow embedding itself in the wall behind her, and its subsequent fluctuation, sent a shiver of fear down her spine, causing her to wonder just how long she'd last in the company of these totally changed characters. Once they would have been... WHAT? Friends... not quite, but colleagues, co-workers almost, others that like her, shared a common goal, but not now. Something drastic had changed within all of them, causing them to act irrationally and irresponsibly. And of all the times, it would have to be now, wouldn't it, her busiest time of year, and one where she was needed the most. How she'd get out of this, she just couldn't fathom.

As another arrow pierced yet one more target balanced precariously on her thick, matted, sweat soaked hair, causing her to rally as much as she could against her restraints, her thoughts turned to Christmas itself, wondering if the previous year would be the last one forever. She knew that if it was cancelled just once for any reason, then the magic would be lost, perhaps never to return.

"You might want to all come and gather around," announced Flash to all the exhausted dragons from the nursery ring in Purbeck. "They're just about to send over the imagery from the satellite."

Not needing to be told twice, they all scampered to their feet and sped off in the direction of the communications console at the far end of the chamber. As Flash slipped back into the chair at the station's keyboard, the monitor directly in front of him flickered before resolving itself again, a huge map of Malaysia and the surrounding regions now appearing on it. Expertly using the mouse, the Crimson Guard zoomed in. Dragons disguised as humans in the United States military had already scanned through all the data, and using the coordinates given to them by Flash, had determined the exact time that Santa had been taken. (They hadn't been told any more than they needed to know, so nothing about Polkinghorne, well... the Crimson Guard couldn't anyway, could he, not even if he wanted to, because of the magical vow that now bound them all together.) Sure enough, as the picture on the screen grew larger, the surrounding countryside becoming recognisable, four figures resolved into focus, one much smaller than the other three. One of the others, although about human sized looked almost as though it might have dragon properties with the way in which its ears stood out, the other carrying some sort of weapon, all three marching their prisoner... WHERE? Rolling the recording forward five hours, it was then that they discovered it... THE VEHICLE!

"They've got a car!" mumbled Peter, stating the absolutely obvious.

"That makes things harder," uttered Flash, not taking his eyes off the screen for a moment.

After that, it got quite boring as the Crimson Guard attempted to use the telemetry from the satellite to track the vehicle, which from the information they could garner, had been stolen over a week ago from a garage in Pahang. After bundling Santa into the boot of the vehicle, it proceeded to travel north on a series of bumpy, harsh and hidden roads, appearing to do everything it could to avoid company, which under the circumstances seemed very sensible. Eventually it crossed into Thailand, which complicated things a great deal, as the coverage from that particular satellite didn't cover it. And so it was that Flash had to request information from what became a combination of two more satellites, much to the disappointment of the dragon disguised as a military general in the American army, but in the end he'd had little choice but to concede because guess what...? Flash outranked him, at least in dragon terms. It took three more hours, but eventually they were able to get back on the hunt.

It had, however, all been worth it because they found the final destination of the vehicle, deep within a mountain range in western Thailand, near a beauty spot called the Huai Mae Khamin waterfall in Khuean Srinagarindra National Park.

"Brilliant!" exclaimed Flash, pumping his fist. "All we

need to do is get there."

"How are we going to do that, and aren't you forgetting the elephant, or should I say... reindeer in the room?" quipped Vimes.

"And just what's that?"

"CHRISTMAS!" pointed out the *tor*, wondering where the poor wretch of a Crimson Guard had been educated. "We need to sort out Christmas!"

"We've got forty eight hours yet," put in Flash, wondering what all the fuss was about, more concerned with apprehending the kidnappers rather than the humans on the surface. But then he remembered his little chat with the king, and supposed that the *tor* was right, they should at least try to do something.

Mind ablaze with wanting to plough straight in and take off after the deranged magical creatures, he put that to one side for a moment and turned to face all three of the youngsters.

"Did you come up with anything?"

"As a matter of fact we did," replied Richie, comfortably taking charge. "We think that between us, we can get Christmas back on track."

"WHAT?" yelled Vimes, startling them all. "Without Polkinghorne, and with just the stuff available here...? You're mad, the whole lot of you. I should never have brought you along!"

"I agree," replied the young female wholeheartedly. "You never should have brought us along. But now we're here, we're staying, and with Flash's permission we'll use everything we know to save one of the humans' most important holidays."

"What do you propose?" interjected the Crimson Guard, hoping to be able to cool things down a little.

"Tank will stay here and work on the magic. In the meantime, we'll get him some equipment from the nearest available nursery ring that will speed things up a great deal. Peter and I will head off back to England. I'm going to see the head of the nursery ring to... persuade him to do everything that I ask. With regard to that," she said, turning towards her *tor*, "you're going to have to dish the dirt you have on him, to me."

"Not a chance," replied Vimes, gobsmacked that the youngster would ask such a thing.

"I'm sorry, but you really need to if we're going to make things work. We don't have time to worry about morals and stuff. If you want to save Christmas, and I assume that's what Polkinghorne would want you to do, then you have to tell me, and quickly."

Mentioning her name made it a done deal, with Vimes vowing to tell Richie before she and Peter left for England.

"What are you going to do once you arrive in the United Kingdom?" asked the Crimson Guard.

"I'll use the head of the nursery ring to compel his counterparts at all the other nursery rings across the globe to help us."

"Help us do what?"

"Help us save Christmas."

"How?"

"Think of all the students above say... year twenty across the world. Millions and millions of them, and do you know what, we can use them to help make the dream come true across their local areas anyway, which will steadily become a global effort."

"But..."

"If we have to, we'll bind them all to the vow, if that's what needs to happen, but if Tank can figure out all the magic, replicate it and pass it on to those in charge of the nursery rings, then the students in say... groups of nine or ten, can carry out what we have planned. With roughly a million groups all doing their bit, talons crossed that we should come up trumps. And yes, I know it depends on the big fella there understanding the magic and getting it to work seamlessly, but if anyone can, he can, I assure you."

Flash didn't doubt a word of it. He did, though, have

one... suggestion.

"Before you pass on the magical vow to the students across the planet, please speak to me. I have a little smidgen of the supernatural that should be added to it, that... if applied correctly, will help with all the after effects."

"Sure thing," replied Richie.

"And what's Peter's part in all this?"

"He's off to London to see the king with a request directly from you."

"A request to do what?" stammered the Crimson Guard.

"A request to hand over his ring."

"NO WAY! NO WAY! There's simply no way that he'll let you have it!"

"You said that you work directly for him and that your work is of the utmost importance. He has to let you have it. How on earth can we possibly power everything we have planned without that ring? It just isn't possible. You will have to convince him to let Peter bring it back here."

Burying his head in his hands, the Crimson Guard's mind ran amuck. This was bad, he thought, really, really bad. That said though, part of him admired the youngsters' determination and ingenuity. What an idea, what a plan. Could it come off? It seemed unlikely, but since he'd always been taught to 'reach for the stars', he could hardly stop doing so now. And so with a heavy heart and wanting nothing more than to capture and contain the kidnappers, he said that he'd record a message on a crystal for Peter to take to the king and make arrangements for the nearest nursery ring to provide Tank with whatever he needed. Then they were all ready, except that they weren't.

"I'm coming with you," Vimes told Flash in no uncertain terms.

"You can't I'm afraid. It's going to be exceptionally dangerous."

"That's simply not good enough. I'M COMING!" screamed the *tor*.

'More time wasted,' thought the Crimson Guard. 'I'm

getting sick of this. There's a reason that I work solely on my own.'

"And you've yet to tell us exactly what it is we're facing," observed Tank, keen to know why it was too dangerous for their *tor* to go with the Crimson Guard and save his friend.

All four faces locked on his, Flash wondered what he should do. In these situations subterfuge normally served him well, but he was torn because they had all been quite open with him right from the very start, as well as their cunning and resourcefulness which had got them this far. Cursing his luck and longing to be back in the cold, frosty air of Scotland, he continued.

"From what little we can gather, the three beings in question seem to have almost lost their minds. Normally of sound judgement, good character, always looking to help the humans on the surface in any way they can, particularly given their magical servitude, to say they've gone off the rails is something of an understatement. And that's really all we've been able to gather apart, that is, from their names."

Looking more than a little downcast, the Crimson Guard was reluctant to continue, wondering if breaking the unwritten rule about sharing information with those outside the inner sanctum of the secret organisation he worked for, would cost him dearly much later on. Since he'd been in cahoots with the *tor* and his students for some time already, without which he'd probably still be hunting for this place, unusually for him he just blurted it out, figuring they should at least know what they were getting themselves into.

"Cupid seems to be their leader and to have co-opted the others, who are the Easter Bunny and the Tooth Fairy."

"WHAT?!" exclaimed Peter, absolutely astonished.

Likewise, the other three's minds were totally blown away.

"But these creatures," observed Vimes, "are totally benign, and forces for good. How the hell have they gone BAD?"

"Is it really them?" asked Richie concerned.

"I'm afraid so," said the Crimson Guard. "And to answer your question, none of us understand what has happened to them. But that's what I'm going to have to find out, as well as recover the hopefully unharmed Polkinghorne."

"I've told you, you're not going alone," reiterated the *tor*.

"Look, you can't come. I've already explained why, it's just too dangerous."

"I think you should take him with you," stated Tank, all businesslike.

"Rules are rules, and I work alone."

"But they outnumber you three to one. And yes, I don't doubt you're a formidable opponent with great knowledge and a wealth of supernatural power, but the beings you're up against are positively ancient, armed with goodness knows what and have centuries' worth of experience to draw on. You probably think it'll be easy. I'd be surprised if it's anything like that. To have an ally, even one that stays back and does what he's told, would no doubt be invaluable, even for you, and makes sense on every level. As well, you can see how much he wants to go and rescue his friend. If for no other reason, you should do it for that."

Taking it all in, Flash knew that the youngster was right, pretty much about everything.

"Take him to aid you, and we'll set everything in motion here in an attempt to get Christmas going again," suggested Tank, having wandered over to where most of the magic in the glass jars resided, taking particular note of the pink and purple hued sparkling molecules, ones that he knew substantially slowed the effect of time in a localised area.

With that, there seemed little more to be said. As swiftly as possible, plans were put into motion.

As Vimes stood talking to Richie and Peter before they all departed, Flash pulled Tank to one side, as it had been decided that he would bind all the students across the world to Polkinghorne's vow of secrecy via the communications array situated here, for convenience and practicality once all the magic had been properly dissected and the king's ring, hooked up, should the monarch deign it so.

"Tank," whispered Flash so that only the two of them could hear. "There are a few words I'd like you to add to the vow, when you bind the students."

"Okay. Can I ask why?"

"Things are getting out of hand. Too many beings already know the Santa secret. Even if it just remained between all of us, that would still be about four too many. Do you understand?"

He did.

"What will these words do?"

"If you add them to the end of magic, they'll make everyone forget the last forty eight hours. That should be long enough to rescue the holidays, return Polkinghorne and for things to get back to normal. Every being bound to the vow will have no recollection of what has happened once Christmas day proper has arrived, which let me assure you is the best thing for everyone."

"I'll do it," declared Tank reluctantly, knowing that if millions of dragon students worldwide knew the secret of Christmas, there would no doubt be a shed load of trouble at some point further down the line.

And with that, the Crimson Guard shared telepathically the words that the young dragon needed to change at least part of the vow he hoped to bind half the students of the world with.

Off in a far flung corner, Vimes stood talking to the other two.

"Now listen carefully to what I have to say."

"Okay," mumbled Peter and Richie simultaneously.

"You are to head back exactly the way we've come, understand?"

"We both do."

"Then tell me how."

"Back to Pahang and into the domain, after which we take the monorail south to Singapore, before taking the intercontinental line back to London, and from there back to the nursery ring."

"Good," said Vimes. "And I want no mucking about. Straight back to Purbeck, there's a lot depending on you both."

"We know," they both said, looking anywhere but at the *tor*, in a typical teenage manner.

"Well... good luck. Do your best, that's all that we ask of you. And just to let you know, Polkinghorne would be proud. Finer dragons to have helping out, I just can't imagine."

Those words made both the students start to blush.

"Right, it's time to leave," announced Flash, marching on over. "You ready?"

"I am," Vimes answered, his things packed.

"Good, then let's go."

Three hours later, Tank's equipment had turned up, Flash and Vimes had appropriated a vehicle and Richie and Peter were on the intercontinental monorail heading swiftly towards London. Events were in motion.

Across the world in cities such as New York, Sydney, Montreal, Paris, Berlin, London, Madrid and Rome, there were Christmassy things going on. Lights and decorations whistled in the cold wind, festive music played, mince pies were served, turkeys bought and presents were wrapped, but it was somehow... subdued, almost as if a big cloud hung over everything, sucking out not so much the life, but the spirit of the holidays, with the adults still going about their daily business, despite the day, or the hour, being so close at hand. Only the young children were unaffected, still crazy mad about all the things on their lists, still pointing and overexcited at brightly glowing trees and the odd house (although not nearly as many as usual) decorated to the hilt, lit up like a... CHRISTMAS TREE! And so they, unknowingly, carried the burden, the weight, or lack of it, in terms of expectation anyway. Slowly, and through no fault of anyone, well... perhaps our scheming psychos that had kidnapped the unwitting Polkinghorne... Christmas and everything related to it, instead of standing out like a shining bright star, very gradually began to fade into the background, its essence waning, the thought, passion and magic behind it teetering on the edge of collapse. If Santa didn't arrive, if wishes weren't fulfilled, there would be nothing for young and old alike to hold on to, this time of year would become an expansive hole, forgotten against the mists of time, only really any note due to the start of the upcoming new year. How all of this played out was important, and would have consequences for decades, if not centuries to come.

Inside the warm comfort of Michael and Caroline's terraced house a short walk from the city centre of Salisbridge in southern England, two tiny minds were absorbed by the Christmas spirit, more than making up for their parents' lack of it. For the baby, Rhianne, lying back in a soft, blue, boat shaped cushion on the living room floor, her wide eyes ignored the precariously balanced, brightly coloured objects spinning on the mobile above her head, instead choosing to focus on the ever moving, ever twinkling lights of the Christmas tree itself which she could just make out from the corner of her eye. Too young to do anything really, on some basic level, almost certainly because of the magic related to this time of year, she did at least just about manage to grasp that there was something special about the garishly decorated pretend plant that now took up quite a lot of their very small and elongated living room. For Meghan it was much the same, and although busy colouring pictures from the Christmas book that had seen her occupied for hours this week alone, she occasionally took the time to not only check in with her cute and spirited sister, but often glanced across at the tree, the standout highlight of the decorations, admiring the way the light bounced off the bright shades of tinsel and the myriad of baubles that she knew not to touch, the ones that if she got close enough would reflect her own image back at her.

Sitting contentedly back in her rocking chair, moving backward and forward in time with the strokes of her knitting, Caroline sat watching over the two angels, lost temporarily in a world of arts and crafts, pleased at not having to return to work until the New Year, delighted at being able to spend some quality time with her family.

Able to see the whole of his tribe from his position at the computer, Michael continued with his work, or at least gave the impression that he was trying to, his fierce imagination having deserted him, not for the first time today, making putting the words down on paper, or in this case onto the facsimile of such in the form of a computer program, all but impossible. His real thoughts focused on something far, far away from the imaginary, real life biting him on the butt crack, bringing him back to reality with a CRASH, the here and now disappointing him no end. And as you've probably already guessed, his mind had turned once again to the issue of not having the funds to buy his wife the boots that she would have liked. Staring glassy eyed at the screen, he ran through all the different ways that he could get his hands on what was really not very much money at all. But given how tight things were, his chances of doing so were practically zero, with everything he'd tried so far coming up a bust. Selling some of his comics... a bust! Some of his computer games... the same. That just left his collection of books that were almost sacred to him, having instantly dismissed that thought, not because he wouldn't do that for his beautiful wife, but because there was no way he'd get the kind of money that he needed. Second hand books were just too easy to come by. And that left him... out of options. Feeling very much like a failure, that changed immediately on taking in his happy and relaxed kids. Proud of providing a warm, loving and safe environment for them, something of a far cry from his own upbringing, a steely determination to do better next year rose up inside him...

but would he have the chance with everything that's going on? Momentarily, he did at least take some solace from all that. All thoughts of Christmas forgotten, he tried to discover his mojo and the words associated with it in an attempt to conjure them up on the computer generated page in front of him.

Breaking into a garage in the middle of the night using dragon magic as their friend, stealing a second hand Land Rover that Flash had inspected before deciding it was the vehicle of choice from the lot, the Crimson Guard and the *tor* set off north, keen to get to Polkinghorne as soon as possible. Unfortunately for them, the rest of the journey would have to mirror that of the humans on the surface, something there was simply no way to negate, not where they were going, as there was no monorail and no way to fly in their natural forms without being spotted. And so all they could do was be as prepared as possible and drive through the mud encrusted, dangerous as hell, off road tracks through the jungle and hope that their enhanced senses and supernatural perception gave them as much of an edge as they could.

Using just a touch of his inexperienced, but ultimately quite powerful magic to put the perception puller around the huge hole on the surface, as well as a great deal of the foliage and toppled trees that they'd already uncovered back into place, Tank waited patiently, his mind ablaze with possibilities over what they'd all gotten caught up in. Santa... unbelievable, who'd have thought, and all three of them learning her secret, something that was almost too much in itself. But now they really were going down the rabbit hole, in an attempt to try and understand the ancient magic Polkinghorne used to make the whole charade possible. Would they, should they, could they do it? These were all questions the kind, caring, intelligent and friendly dragon asked himself as he stood off to one side of the overgrown glade waiting for some dragons from the nearest nursery ring in Pahang to turn up with the equipment that he'd requested.

Sure enough, just like ninety nine percent of all the monorails travelling beneath the planet, the twelve strong group all in their human guises arrived exactly to the second, astounded to see just one ape-like figure standing there waiting for them. Having been told by the director of their particular nursery ring not to ask questions and to keep it brief, the orders for the borrowed equipment having come down very much from on high, the new jungle arrivals did just that.

"We've got everything requested," said one stunning dark skinned female dressed in an array of brilliant red fabric.

"Thanks," replied Tank looking on as if this elicit jungle liaison was the most normal thing in the world. "I can take it from here."

"It's just you?" enquired another brightly dressed female, this time all shades of blue showing, totally gobsmacked.

"It's fine," reiterated the Purbeck student, knowing that it was going to take him at least ten trips to get all the necessary goodies down into the cave system.

"Whatever you say," observed one of the males wearing an all orange sarong, putting his crate on the ground. "But you do need to sign for all this. Director's orders, I'm afraid."

"No problem," said the youngster, grabbing the proffered pen and signing his human name.

After that, and without looking back, the twelve of them left, the soft falls of their footsteps barely noticeable as they disappeared into the jumble of trees in the direction that they'd appeared from.

It did in fact take Richie and Peter's friend twelve

journeys, each enhanced by quite a considerable amount of magic to transfer all of the equipment down there. Once done, he covered the glade hiding the secretive entrance to the cave system back up and started to unpack everything, constantly monitoring the communication system for any word from his friends.

Arriving in London, Peter had decided that instead of accompanying Richie back to Purbeck and then returning to the capital for his own part in the plan, that it made much more sense to just go directly from the monorail once they arrived. Alright, it didn't make that much difference as the journey to the south coast of Dorset was only a matter of minutes, it just seemed more appropriate, especially given that time was of the essence, with maybe even the odd minute or two being crucial. So the friends said their goodbyes on the platform of Pudding Lane station, and as the sleek silver doors of the bullet-resembling carriage to Purbeck WHOOSHED shut, Peter smiled and waved, despite feeling anything but cheerful, wanting his friend not to fret and worry, because currently he was doing enough of that for the both of them.

Regaining his composure and focus, he hopped over two platforms and boarded the monorail that arrived immediately, heading in the direction of Buckingham itself, the location of the council building and the king's private residence, something all dragons knew about, as that was drilled into them during year one.

Fiddling nervously with the backpack on his lap, he barely had time to put his tail through the hole in the back of his seat before the carriage reached his destination. Alighting quickly and orderly, he paused for a moment on the platform, watching the shining silver projectile shoot off through the dark, shadow filled gaping maw of a tunnel that looked out from the gigantic cliff side facing him.

All alone on the platform, briefly he wondered in what

form he should go and see the king. Logically, it should have been his natural form, the one he currently maintained, as that's what most dragons would do. But he'd heard tales and had read stories in almost all the papers about how the king favoured his human guise, supposedly some throwback to being a knight on the surface of the planet, hundreds of years ago. If he turned up in his dragon form, might the king be disappointed? It was difficult to know and almost too much to worry about. Vimes, Flash, Richie and Tank hadn't offered up any advice in this area, which just made him more nervous, as if such a thing were possible. Gambling, he slipped into the toilets for about thirty seconds, before returning in his chosen human outfit, his backpack slung over his shoulders, feeling, very stupidly, much more confident. How did that work, he thought, feeling better looking like this rather than his original, prehistoric incarnation.

He knew from one of his field trips to the renowned area of the capital that his destination was only short walk away, and it took just a few minutes for him to be standing at the bottom of the giant steps, taking everything in once again, still bowled over by the bubbling orange and red pools of exotic molten magma on either side, about halfway up.

Heart in his mouth at just the thought of meeting the king, briefly he wondered how the monarch would react to the request that he was carrying. And that was when it started... legs trembling just slightly, something inside his stomach bounding about, trying to get out, alongside an almost waterfall of sweat rushing down his forehead.

'Stop it,' he berated himself. 'Your friends need you to pull this off. You can do it. As well, all the humans are counting on you to do this. They need Christmas, so get on with it,' he told himself.

Swallowing nervously, ignoring his body's momentary misbehaviour, Peter strode purposefully up the giant steps, revelled in the extra heat washing over him as he passed the lava pools, and as casually as possible walked through the main entrance, all the time under the watchful eye of some carefully concealed King's Guards, tucked away on either side in strange little hideaways. Trying to be as brave as possible, he wandered straight up to the front desk and ignoring all the high-tech LCD screens with a litany of information on them, waited to speak to the reception dragon.

Long grey hair running down past his shoulders, dangling against the back of the human shaped wooden chair, George, the dragon king, sat at his desk in his preferred human form, rummaging through the usual daily paperwork, something there seemed to be more and more of lately, a chore that made his fantastic life almost intolerable, almost but not quite. Oh how he longed for the days when he had been just a knight, riding across the different lands on fabulously fast steeds, occasionally flying up high in the bright, clear blue skies, basking in the rays of the sun when, of course, the opportunity presented itself, putting out fires, fighting the occasional dragon that had decided not to fall in line with the rest of the planet, banishing villainy, putting tyrants in their place, helping the humans with natural disasters, in general, doing good against a background of shadowy evil. It had been easily the best time of his life. In some ways, looking back, it was a shame that politics had started to consume all of that adventure. That was when things had changed, swapping a sword and a fast horse for the council chambers and the sordid goings on associated with it. And then there was his best friend Fredric, the one single being on the planet who he considered family. They'd met in the aftermath of his encounter with the dragon, the one that had done so much damage to the city of Salisbridge all that time ago, winning by a hair's breadth, or as his friend liked to put it, a gnat's genitals. That made him smile, just thinking of the dragon he thought of as a brother. As per normal though, it didn't last, not after what had happened to him.

On becoming king, much, much later on, he'd sent Fredric, by then the founder of the Crimson Guards, on a mission, not a particularly dangerous one by the standards of some of the things they got up to, more suited to his cunning and guile rather than any all out fight to the death. That had been over fifty years ago, and nothing had been heard of him since. Missing, presumed dead. It was the lowest point of George, the dragon king's life, and his biggest regret. If he could go back and change things, he would, even if it meant laying down his life for his friend, something he'd do in a heartbeat. Alone, ignoring the work he was supposed to be getting on with, suddenly a familiar telepathic tickle nibbled at his psyche. Brushing away the past, he reached out.

"Madeline?" he queried.

"Your Majesty."

"What is it you want? I'm rather busy with all of this week's paperwork you know."

"I'm sorry sire, but there's someone at the front desk of the council building demanding to speak to you."

"Really?"

"Yes, a young dragon from the Purbeck Peninsula nursery ring. He says that he has a message and is absolutely insistent that he brings it to you personally."

A chill ran down his false human back on hearing the words Purbeck Peninsula nursery ring because not only was he familiar with it, but would quite often pay the odd illicit visit. It couldn't be, could it? Surely that just wasn't possible.

"Does this dragon have a name?"

"Peter Bentwhistle, Majesty."

'Oh crap,' thought the king. 'Has he discovered the secret? Will I have to confess all?' It hardly seemed possible given the lengths that he'd gone to in an effort to cover his trail. But for Peter to be here, now, was nothing short of a disaster. Swallowing awkwardly, considering the best course of action, quickly the king came to a conclusion.

"Send him up Madeline. And I do not wish to be disturbed, under any circumstances. Do you understand?"

"Yes Sire," she replied, before cutting off the telepathic connection.

Still reeling from the visit of the one being he'd hoped to conceal his identity from, the king swept aside all the paperwork and hurriedly transformed back into his true dragon identity, unlocking the magical bonds of his DNA, feeling the ethereal energy sweep across him, causing the prehistoric monster inside to take effect. Less than two seconds, that's how long it took for him to change into his dragon persona. Why the rush, I hear you ask. Because Peter was totally familiar with his human guise, the mysterious old man with long grey hair, a haggard and worn, unshaven face, despite which usually housed a smile, whatever he was doing. For him to be here now was nothing short of miraculous, but it was dangerous too. So by transforming back into his dinosaur-like, original form, he hoped to be able to throw the youngster off the trail of truth he appeared to be on.

Eight minutes later, Madeline appeared at the entrance to his private residence, guiding the human shaped young student who looked more than a little uncomfortable to say the least, hopping about on both feet, his face white as a sheet, looking almost as if he were about to throw up.

'Hmmm,' thought the king. 'I wonder just how much he knows.'

Absolutely nothing as it turns out.

"Thank you Madeline."

"Majesty," she replied, turning and wandering back the way she'd come, leaving just the two of them surrounded by marble, mainly white, from the stunning staircase that looked as though it wouldn't be out of place in the grandest of ballrooms, to the intricately decorated balustrades which covered the length of every floor, to the whole of the massive arena-like room that they now found themselves in, containing a stunning stone plinth set dead centre, with delicately decorative blue text running throughout the dazzling floor, a marvel to behold, one that very few beings ever get to see.

Noting the clear discomfort of the young dragon, the king decided, against his very nature, to play it tough.

"What is it you want youngster? Are you lost?"

Barely able to look the monarch in the eyes, Peter, afraid and as nervous as hell, thought about everything that he'd gotten caught up in over the last few days, pictured his friends, and for their sakes forced himself to continue.

"Uhhhh... no I'm not lost, Your Majesty. I have a message from Flash, uh... I mean Dendrik, Flash... your Crimson Guard," he stuttered, pulling out the crystal from his backpack and offering it out towards the king, who didn't show it on the outside, but on the inside was absolutely flabbergasted.

'How on earth are you mixed up with what Flash is doing?' was his first thought, quickly followed by, 'Is it just a coincidence that you're here?'

Snatching the proffered crystal, he beckoned the young dragon to follow him. Which he did, through a neatly concealed door and into what appeared to be a living room about the size of a football pitch, a fabulous bright red sofa the focal point right in the middle of the room. Marvelling at the tapestries that hung high around the walls, ignoring the pictures on display, which was a good job because the dragon monarch hadn't in his haste thought to hide or turn over any of those, which would have been the ultimate giveaway considering that most showed the monarch with some of the most recognisable human faces on the planet... rock and pop stars, as well as famous movie faces beamed down, all with him in his human guise. The list was almost endless.

Strolling over to a plain wooden, human sized desk with a monitor in the far corner, the king opened up the top right hand side drawer with his tiny dragon hands and slipped the crystal into the designated hole. Immediately the monitor sprang to life, Flash's recognisable face swimming into view. Both watched as the Crimson Guard spoke.

"Sire," said the recording. "I've done as you've asked and remain solidly on the trail of the crazy criminals. More than that, I've found Santa's lair with a little help from some unexpected allies, one of which has been dispatched to bring this crystal to you. I hope to catch up with the magical monsters that have Father Christmas soon, but it might be as much as a couple of days yet, which very much means the holiday season itself is in jeopardy. That said, my cunning new friends have come up with a plan to save Christmas itself, which is bold and brave enough to work, if Lady Luck is on our side. I assume that you'll approve of all of this, given the importance this plays in the physical and mental wellbeing of the humans and the hope that it brings to those across the world."

Shaking his head against a jungle backdrop, Flash, sweat pouring off him, looked as though he was reluctant to continue, thought the king, raising not only his hackles but alarm bells as well.

"The reason for this message and the messenger is that we need to ask a favour, one that I wouldn't do lightly. Getting Christmas back on track is no easy feat without Santa. The allies I've found believe it can be done by sharing the load around and involving students from every nursery ring across the planet. Not bad I grant you, but the magic, which is being studied right at this very moment, is both strong and complex, and without something of legendary magnitude to power it there's just no way it'll get off the ground."

It was then that the king cottoned on to what he was supposed to do, and to say he wasn't happy was an understatement. But before he could vent that fury, the Crimson Guard on the screen continued.

"I know that it's a big ask, Sire, and if I could find any other solution then I would, but we really need your ring. You know me, and you said you know my makeup. Please, trust me now and give the young dragon in front of you the enigmatic band. It will only be for a few days, I assure you. And you'll have it straight back when it's finished with. Thank you, Majesty. Flash out!"

Red in the face, steam almost venting from his ears, the ruler of everything on this planet in his extreme prehistoric form looked more than a little unhappy, with smoke and dribbles of flame exiting his nose and licks of bright yellow fire lighting up his bright white, razor sharp incisors. Turning to the youngster, as angry as he'd been in decades, he spoke his mind.

"There's simply no way in hell that this is happening. Involving hundreds of thousands of nursery ring students in this is just ridiculous, and as for having access to this amount of magical energy, you'll have to prise this ring off my cold dead body (that's the way in which the powerful magical artefact is normally passed down from dragon monarch to dragon monarch) and even then, it won't be easy."

Slowly backing away, the sheer terror in Peter's face gave the king cause for concern, suddenly realising that this was nothing to do with him, he'd only delivered the message. And then a sharp beep from the monitor caused both of them to turn and face it. Abruptly, a swathe of jumbled up symbols and icons that the young nursery ring student couldn't make head nor tail of very quickly scrolled down the screen. Whist Peter, even with all his language skills, which were modest by dragon standards but not much more than that, couldn't ascertain a single thing from what was clearly a message, it was obvious that George could, the tiny motion of his prehistoric head flicking side to side, reading it as you or I would devour a book. One of many secret ancient languages that allowed the monarch to communicate with his most trusted agents with little chance of it being intercepted or understood, this time it had served both parties well, the king pleased with what Flash had in mind to contain the situation and wrap things up after the whole sorry episode had ended. Moments later the monarch reached the end of the text. Peter waited for the continuation of the irritation and rage. It never came.

If it were any other beings on the planet, the answer would instantly be no, and not just a very leisurely no, but a great big **** off NO! But these two were different. The Crimson Guard, Dendrik Ridge, had proved his worth fifty times over, once having very directly saved his life during an underwater skirmish off the coast of Turkey, against some rather dastardly mer-folk that had found themselves under the influence of some rather dark, shadowy magic. Only Flash's quick thinking had stopped him taking a trident to the chest, a moment that he relived, right here, right now. Yet one more brush with the Grim Reaper, thought the king, having had a career of doing just that.

Snapping back to normality, he gazed across at the dragon in boy's clothing. Of all the beings to turn up here and now, it would have to be him. Bowled over at the turn of events, especially because they'd already met on dozens of occasions, something the youngster would have known had the king stayed in his human guise, the monarch had to wonder whether or not Fate was once again giving him a nudge in a certain direction. It wouldn't be a surprise if it was, at least not to him, because that had happened before, he was sure. Confusion reigned, at least momentarily. After that, everything became clear. It was a gamble, that's for sure. If the ring, and more importantly the great power within it fell into the wrong hands, the fate of the world could very well be at stake, that's how much pressure there was on making the right decision. But with Christmas itself on the line, the consequences of that not happening were equally diabolic, something he was acutely aware of. Ruling over the dragon and human worlds was never going to be easy, of that he'd been promised on taking up the role, but times like these really shone a spotlight on the difficulty he faced, not just during a crisis but on regular days as well. There was so much to fight for, so much to do, even with his extended lifespan. But he knew better than most that he could only deal with one thing at a time, whatever fate threw up in front of him next. And so he did, much to the young dragon's surprise.

"Is this wise?" echoed a voice throughout his mind, realising exactly what he was about to do.

"I trust Flash implicitly," replied the king, once again, only across his psyche.

"What happens if there's a crisis here? You won't have access to my array of powers and supply of mana. Would you be able to manage?"

A small smile wriggled itself across the king's browbeaten and weathered face, causing the stubble on his chin and cheeks to move ever so slightly as he considered the questions.

"I haven't always been the king, and I did manage to stumble my way through life up until the point at which I was crowned and our paths crossed. While your talents, mana, experience and advice are always very welcome, I think most beings that have met me in the past would describe me as an accomplished warrior. Go with the youngster, help them out if you can, but try not to give away any unnecessary clues as to who and what you are. I understand that you might have to if it comes down to it, but chose carefully those with whom you share your secret. I'll create a false story about some catastrophic damage to the crystal node network somewhere and have traffic limited which should help with the plan. As well, if you can disguise yourself as something totally and utterly plain so that this one can wear you on his journey across the planet, that would be great."

"No problem."

"Do you think it a coincidence that his grandson is standing here before you now?"

Letting out a breath, the king shook his primeval head ever so slightly before answering the ring's question.

"It seems unlikely at best. The odds of our paths crossing outside of what has already been going on are astronomical. I would think that Fate herself has something in mind, perhaps a taster of what's to come."

If ever any being in the history of the universe could be

right on the money, it was the dragon monarch, right here, right now.

"Right," said the king before slipping the enigmatic band off his finger. *"Stay out of trouble, look out for all of them, and I'll see you in a few days."*

No reply in words came, only a recognisable, to him at least, sort of mental nod.

"Hold out your hand," ordered the king.

Instantly Peter did as he was told, well... you would, wouldn't you, for the king of everything on the planet, dragon and otherwise? Carefully, with his spindly little hands the king pulled off the most famous piece of jewellery in the dragon domain, and much to Peter's astonishment, slid it carefully onto the index finger of his right hand. Wondering what the hell was going on, expecting to carry it back to Tank in Malaysia in the backpack that he remained wearing, he couldn't see how he was supposed to keep it on his finger because it was much too large. In an instant, that all changed. In a smidgen of brilliant purple light that just enveloped the ring itself, abruptly instead of feeling loose and waggling about all over the place, the band suddenly appeared to fit perfectly. Not only that, but it had changed from the most stunning piece of jewellery, made up of a blue, shimmering crystalline structure, the likes of which he'd never seen before, to a flat smooth band rounded out of oak. Polished and plain, it just looked ordinary and of no value at all.

"Keep it on you at all times youngster," urged the king, glancing into the face he knew only too well. "If things get tough, and I know this sounds a little ridiculous, ask it what you should do. You'd be surprised at just how much help you might receive."

"Uhhhh... thanks, I think," replied Peter, barely able to get his head around everything going on.

Out of the blue, the last thing the young dragon expected happened.

"How are you getting on with your studies, Peter?"

asked the monarch, the red, orange and yellow flame in and around his prehistoric mouth and nostrils having all but disappeared, setting the youngster much more at ease.

"Uhhh... fine thanks," he uttered, shocked that the king would take an interest in lowly old him, a being so far from anything spectacular that it just wasn't true. If only he knew the truth.

"I was under the impression that you'd been struggling with some of your maths classes... quantum algebra if I'm not mistaken."

'What the hell?' thought the student, his mind whirring about just how the king could possibly know. Once again, if he could have seen the monarch's human form, everything would have become clear and obvious. But he couldn't, and being as naive as he was, there was little chance of him seeing through the deception.

Pleased at keeping him a little off balance, despite part of him thinking it a little cruel, it was then that George remembered all the pictures on the shelves on the way into the room. Thanking his lucky stars that the young dragon had been too preoccupied with being in his presence on the way in, with just a touch of his ancient magic, he changed them into something else, breathtaking views of some of the dragon domain's most magnificent natural wonders, for the journey out. Inside he let out a huge sigh of relief.

"I've been having catch-up classes during some of the lunch times," Peter offered up nervously.

"And have they helped?"

Nodding his head, the young dragon answered as honestly as he could.

"Yes, they have thanks. I don't struggle anything like I did, and feel much more comfortable in those lessons."

"Excellent! Keep up the good work youngster. It's never a sign of weakness to ask for help. Every being on the planet does it at some point no matter who they are... even me," admitted the king, giving him a sly wink.

And that was enough to set him totally at ease. But it

mattered not, because their meeting had drawn to an end.

Telepathically, the king called for Madeline to come and get Peter to escort him out, which she duly did. After that, the two of them said goodbye, the student vowing to take care of the ring.

And that was yet one more meeting between the two of them, something that had occurred dozens of times before, but never here and never with the king in his natural prehistoric form. Unfortunately it had to be that way, with the monarch fulfilling the vow he'd made to the missing best friend he thought of as a brother.

After returning to her dorm to change out all of the things in her backpack, mainly the human set of clothes, she was determined to get on with things. Despite the relatively late hour she purposefully strode down the cool dark stone corridors in the direction of the office belonging to the nursery ring's head, quite a puny dragon compared with most of those in charge, bright red in colour and a stickler for the rules, who went by the name of Grover.

'Well,' she thought as she continued on her way, 'this should be nothing if not... interesting.'

Able to see the office door in the distance, Richie could just make out the light inside. Clearly the head was burning the midnight oil. Boy was he in for a surprise. Deciding on a rebellious course of action, on reaching the door, instead of knocking which would have been the appropriate thing to do, she just opened it up and barged straight in. Whipping around from the chalk board he was working on, Grover glared in her direction, about to open his mouth, almost too shocked to do so, when she slammed the door behind her and to his astonishment, took a seat.

"What on earth do you think you're doing, MISS RUMP?!" he roared, his temper clearly disproportionate to his diminutive size. "I thought you were on a field trip with Vimes?"

Allowing the tip of her tail to slide effortlessly through the hole in the back of the chair, it brushed against the polished floor as she wriggled around trying to get comfortable. This made the already tempestuous dragon even more riled up.

"Explain yourself, NOW!" he demanded.

Turning to face him, a smug smile etched into her dinosaur-like jaw line, knowing that she was about to turn the tables on him made her feel powerful, invincible and downright devious.

Looking up into the absolute fury flooding his face, she decided that she'd had her fill of fun and games and would put him out of his misery in short order.

"I need your help with an urgent matter. I wouldn't normally come straight to you, but it's important and needs to be dealt with quickly," she stressed.

"What in God's name makes you think that I'll help you, particularly after the rudeness you've just shown?"

Narrowing her eyes, the smile swapped for something far more serious, she glanced directly at him, both of them locking looks, Grover sure that he had more authority and power, the young dragon about to prove otherwise.

"You will help me. And you will do it now!" she stated firmly, her voice measured and calm, a no nonsense tone carrying across the room.

"I don't know what's got into you Miss Rump, but your behaviour will simply not be tolerated. From this moment on, you will find yourself suspended from your studies until a board of review can look into this matter. Now, get out of my office and stay in your dormitory until such time as you're told to do otherwise," he ordered.

Unwavering, she just sat there, eyes firmly locked on him, causing him to swallow nervously.

"Did you hear what I said?"

"I did," she replied. "When the board review this matter, would you like me to explain to them how you've been fiddling the exam results of this nursery ring so as to make it look much more productive to the council than it actually is?"

'Oh crap,' was Grover's first thought. Swiftly followed by just one word... 'VIMES!'

Temper under control, well... just barely, Grover pulled back his chair and sat down, his demeanour very different now.

"What is it you want, Miss Rump?"

"Nothing that should be too much trouble," she declared, leaning back in her chair and smiling.

"Why am I not so sure that's the case?"

"You need to get in touch with every other nursery ring on the planet. We need the help of every single student, year twenty five plus. You need to do this immediately."

"WHAT!" he exclaimed. "You're kidding, right?"

"What do you think?" she quipped.

"It can't be done, not straight away. Something like that could take days... weeks even."

"Well that's a shame, because if it isn't done within the next two hours, the message I've sent will reach the chairdragon of the oversight committee and then they'll all know what you've been up to. And given just how much they all have at stake in this, I'm guessing they will not take it well. If I were you I'd get moving, time's ticking."

"What am I supposed to say to them all?" he asked, the pent up fury in his voice from earlier having changed to fear at the thought of losing his position of power.

"You need to tell those in charge that their students will be helping to save Christmas. Without them, it will not happen and may be gone forever. They can expect to be on a conference call across the crystal node network explaining all the details at say... 9am GMT tomorrow. Their co-operation in this venture will be mandatory, each and every one of them."

"The students themselves will never go for that, and there's no way you can force them to comply."

This had her thinking.

"What about if it counted towards part of their exams?"

"I don't understand."

"We incorporate what we're going to do into their curriculum. They all play their part, which in turn goes towards say, fifty percent of their final year human studies module... can't say fairer than that."

"That'll never work, the *tors* and the exam boards will never go for such a thing."

"They will if the king orders it!"

"And will he?"

"Let's see, shall we?"

Forty minutes and half a dozen phone calls later it was done, with Flash having got hold of the king, who was not particularly pleased at having to intervene yet again on the Crimson Guard's behalf, but who reluctantly did what was asked of him. And so the exam boards were informed, along with the heads of all the nursery rings across the planet who, as one, all waited with baited breath for the conference call that would explain all this. All that was left was for Tank to get his brilliant mind around all the magic used in creating the Santa Claus legend so that he could apply it to what they had planned. No pressure there then!

As two beings used to dropping vertically at speed, pulling high G turns and having the forces of gravity assault their bodies on a regular basis, both Flash and Vimes were having a difficult time coping with the car journey they currently found themselves on. Disguised with just a hint of magic, the vehicle that they'd stolen, despite being four wheel drive, mostly found itself up past the bottom of the doors in mud, sliding around all over the place and, more often than not, stuck in the thick sticky goo that the rain had turned the earth all around into. Every so often, the Crimson Guard cursed himself for travelling the back routes towards their destination. Logically, at the time, it had seemed like the right decision, avoiding the most densely populated human roads, raising less suspicion and generally staying out of the way. What he didn't know and hadn't bothered to research was the fact that they were back roads for a reason, chiefly the weather and the treachery caused by it. Even with a relatively new and high-tech car, the going was tough and more importantly slow. The longer the journey took, the more danger Polkinghorne would find herself in, something the two of them were both acutely aware of, with Vimes slipping that particular subject into what little conversation they often shared. Tense didn't begin to cover not only their journey, but the dynamic between the two dragons.

Exhausted from the multitude of trips to get the loaned equipment down to the cave system all on his own, only the singular determination to do his part in an effort to save Santa from a deeply despicable fate spurred on the young dragon. Foregoing any sort of sleep, he regularly used the magic that has been his since birth to replenish his energy and refresh his tired and aching muscles. So far, all on his own and all things considered, he was doing a fantastic job.

Putting the finishing touches to the magical containment cube, one of the cruder pieces of equipment on loan (he was used to something much more state of the art back at Purbeck) briefly he wondered how his friends were getting on with their own missions and whether Peter had managed to procure the king's powerful ring. Just the thought of that had goose bumps racing up and down his false human arms, forcing the hairs on them to stand to attention.

'Imagine that,' he thought. 'I might actually not only get to see the king's ring, but get to use the ethereal energy associated with it... brilliant!'

Testing the cube's integrity with a spell he knew well, Tank watched as crimson coloured energy assaulted every single surface, even the one that sat on the floor of the cavern. Delighted that he'd set it up correctly, he knew it was time to get on with the complicated and stressful business of dissecting the supernatural elements contained within the glass bottles stacked throughout the cavern. Wishing momentarily that he had some help, even if it was just Peter, who would have fussed over everything and made the whole process slower, he knew, just to have a sounding board, someone to share ideas as how to best proceed, would more than have made up for everything else. Hopefully he would be here soon. And so without further ado, he grabbed the first bottle off the shelf, the one that seemed to his naked eye to distort or slow time in some way, shape or form, opened up a gap in the cube, slipped the bottle in and closed up the hole. Watching intently, his equipment set to scan, at least he thought it was, as once again it was unfamiliar and more than a little dilapidated, with his mind he pulled off the stopper and waited to see what would happen.

Shooting at speeds of up to six hundred and fifty miles an hour beneath the Bay of Bengal, worn and weathered backpack perched atop the chair beside him, Peter sat fiddling with the plain wooden ring on his index finger. He pondered the king's words, wondering just where the supposed stock of ethereal energy resided, how the intricate band could disguise itself like that and whether or not it would be enough to power what they had in mind and save the holiday season. It certainly didn't look as though it could accomplish all that, but as the humans say, never judge a hook by its colour, at least, that's what he thought the saying was, but it didn't sound quite right. As the dark walls, occasionally interspersed by pockets of luminous molten magma, zipped by on the outside of the carriage, he wondered how both his friends were doing and just how Richie's meeting with the head of the nursery ring had gone. He was a tough one, that Grover, he thought, but then so was his friend. If he'd been a betting dragon, he'd have put his money on her all day long. And he'd have been right to do so.

"I've done as you've asked," Grover told Richie, deeply unhappy at having had little choice but to comply with her... not so much a request, as an order.

Not bothered at what the head of the nursery ring thought, not giving any consideration to how the future might play out and what this might mean in terms of her stay here, Richie focused only on what was to come... saving Christmas for those above that so heavily relied upon it, as their hopes, wishes and dreams were so deeply entangled with that one single event.

"And?"

"They'll all be online across the network, waiting for the transmission. Whatever it is you have in mind, it had better be good. Otherwise my career is over, one way or the other."

"Don't worry," she said to him, "You'll be just fine, I won't say a thing, neither will Vimes... but from now on, no cheating, no forging papers or marks. This will be your one and only chance. From what little I know, you're good at your job, but if I catch you doing this again, I will reveal it to everyone, and when I say EVERYONE, I mean just that. Do you understand?"

"I do," he replied, in little doubt that she was good for her word, more than a little put out that he'd been caught and that the information about what he'd been doing had been shared. "How do you intend to use the other nursery ring students to save Christmas?"

"Ahh... well that's for me to know, and you to find out during tomorrow's transmission."

Satisfied that everything was in hand, as much as it could be, she scarpered out of his office and as quickly as she could, with her backpack slung over her giant prehistoric shoulder, headed directly for the Purbeck monorail station, hoping to join her friends back in Malaysia before the next phase of their plan started.

Using his mind to remove a tiny little section of the roof of the cube as the time altering magic zipped and zinged about the much larger space it had been released into, Tank watched as the half dozen or so leaves he'd procured from some of the miniature trees growing in Santa's lair dropped slowly towards the floor of the box, wondering what would happen. As three of them appeared to abruptly stop their downward journey altogether, hanging softly still in mid-air, the young dragon's disguised human mouth hung wide open as his eyes tried to register the truth before him. Ordering his mind to switch through the different types of vision available to him (something all dragons are taught to do during year eight of their nursery ring education) eventually he arrived at what he liked to think of as his mantra vision, something that detected everything supernatural going on, right down to the very last atom. Watching through the transparent protection barriers, now he could see that the leaves themselves were actually moving, only incredibly slowly, their fall curtailed by magic, not so much resisting gravity, as resisting time... fascinating!

And that was how Tank started off investigating the unfamiliar ethereal energy of Santa Claus herself.

Having retraced their steps exactly, due in no small part to his eidetic dragon memory, Peter strode out between a pair of huge trees into the glade that he knew beyond any doubt contained the huge shadowy hole that dropped down into the cave system where Polkinghorne's lair resided. However, at the moment it was all covered up with plants, fallen tree trunks and numerous animals, or at least that's how it appeared. Remembering that Flash had literally picked everything up with his mind and cast it aside, Peter stood there unsure of what to do, that is until a familiar voice rang out inside his mind.

'It's an illusion Pete,' declared Tank, 'created to stop any unwelcome attention. Walk straight on through the scrub and you'll reach the hole... careful not to fall in now.'

Doing as instructed, after a dozen or so steps through a mass of made up mayhem, the gaping dark opening did once again reveal itself. Climbing down, remaining in his human guise, ten minutes or so later Peter wandered in on his friend, who, by the looks of things, was up to his eyes in everything supernatural, with experiments set up and running on numerous different workstations around the confines of the main cave, as well as in the cube itself which sat smack bang in the middle, directly next to the iconic sleigh.

"How you doin' buddy?" asked Tank, thrilled to see his friend.

"Much better now that I know it's just an illusion up there. Thanks for the save. I might have been pondering what to do for hours."

That caused his friend to chuckle.

"How's it going here?"

"Slowly! I seem to have figured out about half of the magic and have found a way to successfully duplicate it, which should help when the time comes. There are just a few more mantras that I just can't wrap my head around. If I can't get to grips with them, then I can't see how we can proceed."

"Oh," was all that Peter could reply.

And then Tank remembered the whole point of his friend's mission.

"Did you get it?" he asked excitedly.

"Uh?"

"The ring... did the king let you have it?"

"Oh yeah," answered his friend, nodding his head vigorously.

"Come on then... let's see it!" Tank demanded.

Peter held out his hand proudly displaying the smooth, plain wooden band wrapped around his finger.

"That's not it!" stated Tank, certain that he knew exactly what the monarch's ring really looked like, the tiniest tint of anger hidden within his words.

"It is... I promise."

"ENOUGH!" he chided. "We don't have time to muck about Pete. Show me the real ring."

More than a little confused and disappointed at his friend's reaction, not knowing what else to do, he brought his hand with the ring on it up to his face, and glaring at the ordinary wooden band, ordered it to reveal itself.

Only then did his friend believe him.

"That's really the king's ring?"

"Yes," replied Peter. "It transformed when I put it on at the king's behest, so that I could travel here safely with it."

"WOW!" was all that his friend could come up with. "Can you feel the power? Did the king tell you how to use it?"

Both good questions, neither of which Peter could answer.

"All he said was that if times got tough, I should ask it what to do."

"Really?"

"Yep."

"Go on then. Ask it what to do."

"Um... can you do it, please?"

"Okay... give it here."

Slipping off the ring, he passed it across to his friend, who wondered how he was going to slip it onto his much bigger, sausage-like fingers. Holding the plain wooden band next to the tip of his enormous index finger, abruptly the loop expanded in size, making itself just slightly bigger than the digit itself. Sliding it down as far as it would go, Tank was gobsmacked when all by itself it tightened ever so slightly, leaving it fitting perfectly.

"That's what happened to me," his friend exclaimed.

"Please will you help us power all the magic we need across the world tomorrow night?" said Tank out loud, addressing the ordinary circle, feeling it had to be said, a bit like an idiot.

"I will assist you in any way possible as per the king's orders," whispered a silky smooth voice floating across the confines of his mind.

"How does it, I mean you, I mean... the whole thing. How does it work?" Tank replied softly amongst the confusion of his intelligence.

"You just have to ask and I'll bring forth what you need. I would suggest that before you do, you show me the magic that you're dealing with so that I can gain a better understanding of what it is comprised of and exactly what its stated purpose is. That way I'll be able to power and control it much more efficiently."

"Understood... D... d... d... do you have a name. How should I address you?"

For the first time in many decades, this really made the band's presence sit up and think. Should he tell him, or just make him call him ring or something? Not joined in any way, shape or form, unlike he was to the king, For'son, as that was the name he'd gone by long in the past, decided, on further inspection of the youngster, that he could indeed be trusted.

"When you address or call for me in your mind, you may refer to me as For'son. Please do not say my name out loud or tell your friends. I can't tell you why, but it's of great importance... I'm trusting you a great deal."

"Uhhh...sure thing," answered Tank, surprised and more than a little taken aback.

And so with Tank guarding the ring's secret, all three of them got back to work, even though only two physical bodies inhabited the cave system.

SMASH! The chair and its occupant crashed to the ground, a stifled groan just audible from behind the gag that was tied tightly over Polkinghorne's mouth, blood pooling on the floor from the impact of her head, dazing her greatly, eliciting pain across her body, the fruitless screams from the past hours having long since been given up on.

"Why did you do that?" demanded the Tooth Fairy, still faintly clinging on to some semblance of right or wrong despite the enthrallment with which she'd been bewitched, the enchantment dominating almost all of her.

"Because I can," replied the Easter Bunny, chomping in between licking thick milky chocolate from his paws and around his lips. "And, because it felt good. She deserves it!"

"How so?" enquired the Tooth Fairy, trying ever so hard to be the voice of reason.

"All she does is take them away."

"Who?"

"You know who... our followers. They all get pulled in and caught up in all the Christmassy stuff. 'Ow look, a tree that lights up. Ow... look, let's have a kiss under the mistletoe. Ow... look, presents for all the children that have been good. Ow... look, a brightly decorated human with matching sack and sleigh that can magically deliver gifts into one another's houses... how brilliant!' What an absolute load of rubbish! 'Whatever your wishes are, I can make them happen.' Bullshit!"

"So what?" queried the Tooth Fairy. "There's still no reason to go and hit her like that."

"Well I say there is, and if I want to do it again, there's simply no way you can stop me."

About to butt in, not really sure why, it was at that precise moment that Cupid appeared, an array of arrows stored in a quiver over his back, bow carried firmly in his left hand.

"If he feels like hitting her, then he can," offered up the god of love, twanging his bowstring for good measure. "She has over the years demeaned our positions in things, taken away devoted followers from all of us and because of the commercialisation of that abomination that she calls a holiday, has fooled so many of the humans into believing that Christmas should require all their care, love and attention. Well," he said turning to face the stricken Polkinghorne bound to the toppled chair, sprawled out across the floor, blood and tears flowing profusely, "I'm here to tell you no more. Christmas has been and gone, to be remembered no more. After tomorrow night, when nobody's dreams and wishes are fulfilled, you'll be vilified as the fake you are, with the humans turning to more trusted allies to accomplish their wishes. Once that happens... SANTA, you'll be of no more use and we'll take great pleasure in feeding you to the dogs. There's something for you to look forward to."

Not even bothering to pick up the chair or check her wounds, the three dastardly protagonists turned and began walking away, their laughter trailing off in the distance, the Tooth Fairy taking a quick glance over her shoulder as they did so. Lying in a pool of her own blood, tears and worse, Santa tried once again to bite through the gag, the constriction around her face driving her mad, but to no avail. Sniffling miserably, head ringing like a gong being struck by a strongman, black boots scuffed, her red and white suit a mess, covered from head to toe in sickly sweet goo and dark brown blobs of every type of chocolate, she felt lost and alone, even unsure whether or not her last gasp message had gotten out to Vimes, the best friend she missed with all her heart. Not a day had gone by during all the time she'd been doing the best job in the world, that she hadn't missed him. But that was the sacrifice she'd had to make. Why? She didn't know... it was just a long standing part of the tradition handed down across generations. That was supposed to help her understand. It didn't, normally just leaving her a confused mess, now more so then ever. Fearing that she might well die at the hands of these monstrous fiends, her thoughts remained firmly focused on her best friend, and what it was between them that she'd unduly sacrificed. Was it worth it? Could they have had the relationship that she'd dreamed of? And had there been any way to bend the rules so that she could have had both the things she'd wanted? All questions that presented themselves to her there and then, on the floor, covered in goodness knows what.

Not having planned to stop, the two of them and their battered and beaten Land Rover had little choice but to find some kind of civilisation on their way north, due in no small part to the fact that they'd had one puncture along the way, and the timing belt had splintered into a million pieces. Applying a degree of magic to it had kept it running, but not reliably, and certainly not well enough to get them to where they wanted to go in a hurry. And so it was that they found themselves in a small town called Surat Thani, some way north but probably only about halfway to their destination, grubbing around for parts for their car, a spare tyre and some much needed food, all the time wondering how the others were getting on in their attempt to rescue Christmas.

Guided by his new found friend, efforts back at Santa's lair were going great guns. The slowing of time in relatively small areas or bubbles, as For'son had kept explaining to Tank, was relatively easy for both the physical friends there to get their heads around. What was more complicated was extending it out further, something that the presence inside the ring told them couldn't be done, at least not on the scale they were looking for.

"Then what do we do?" asked Tank deep within his mind, knowing that the enigmatic band would pick up on it.

"It cannot be stretched out as far as you wish. You must localise the area around which you wish to use it."

"That means more groups of dragons going out into smaller areas," the youngster replied, *"and we're dangerously close to running out of the actual amount of students as it is, if we're going to cover the whole of the earth's surface."*

"Try altering your thinking young dragon," berated the band.

"You have a brilliant mind, but you need to expand your thoughts and use your imagination."

"How so?"

"So far," reflected the mysterious presence that was the king's constant companion, *"you have ten dragons in every group."*

"That's right. Eight who will disguise themselves as reindeer, and two who will do all the deliveries, one of whom will be Santa himself. But that can't be helped; it will take at least two to transport everything down, and the pies, sherry, carrots, etc, back up," replied Tank, more than a little irritable due to his lack of sleep and his exhaustion at having singlehandedly lugged all the equipment out of the jungle and back down into the cave.

"I agree, but that's not where I'm suggesting you can cut corners. Think about it... do you really need eight students each trying to be a reindeer?"

"Well..."

"Why not have one student onboard the sleigh on reindeer duty?"

"You mean..."

"One student pulling the sleigh along disguised as a reindeer, alongside seven projected others... think about the savings in dragonpower alone. You'll be able to more than double the amount of groups that you send out."

"Brilliant!" exclaimed Tank in his psyche.

"Thank you," replied For'son graciously.

Tank told Peter about the idea and, as agreed, left out any mention of For'son. His friend was ecstatic.

With only a couple of hours to go until the broadcast to all the nursery rings across the planet, something that had already been prearranged, an unexpected presence in her dragon form took them both by surprise... RICHIE!

Back from the nursery ring in Purbeck, she'd just about arrived in time for what would be absolute chaos and was able to lend a hand with the last of the experiments, something Peter was grateful for, as Magical Adaptation and Quantum Entanglement had never really been his strong points.

Ninety minutes later, Tank shouted across the main area of the cave they all occupied.

"What do you think, Rich?" he asked, more than a little concerned.

"Well... even though I don't understand exactly how it works, we can at least replicate it on an almost industrial scale with the huge amount of power available to us from the king's ring. And that should be enough, it really should. It... just makes me nervous. Dealing with the humans' hopes and wishes is something beyond all the magic we've had explained to us over the years. What if something goes wrong?" she said, voicing the concerns all three of them had. "Without Polkinghorne, we'd have absolutely no chance of diagnosing a fault, let alone getting close to fixing it."

"I know," replied Tank, sharing his friend's frustration.

"But what else are we supposed to do?" asked Peter rhetorically. "It's either this... or nothing!"

And he was right. They had absolutely nothing else.

"What do you think about all of it?" asked Tank of the ring, keen to hear his take on what they'd been doing.

"I've not seen anything quite like this, but it does all seem genuine and well put together. If you want my opinion on whether or not you should take the chance, the answer is most certainly yes, you should."

That was enough to convince Tank they should follow through on their plan and replicate Santa's magic in an attempt to keep Christmas alive across the planet. The others, following his lead, wholeheartedly agreed.

Having cleared some of the overgrown scrub from the assortment of trees that had gone wild, creating a superb hidey hole for the communications array, all three (or four, counting For'son) of them sat in front of the monitor waiting to connect to each and every one of the nursery rings on the planet. It didn't take long. Enhanced by more than a little exotic magic and power from the ring, it resembled the most populated zoom call ever to have been made, and this was fifteen or so years before that particular technology would be available to the humans on the surface.

"Welcome," started Richie, taking charge as was her wont, much to the happiness of her two friends, neither wanting to front up this part of the plan.

"You've been asked to join this call today because we need the help of all your students, year twenty-five and above," she continued.

Immediately there was much discussion, dragon nursery ring leaders and directors talking and shouting over each other, and you can imagine with this kind of system, alongside the infinitesimal delay, much mayhem ensued.

Giving them a few moments to get it out of their systems, hopefully letting them realise that this was getting them absolutely nowhere, abruptly, out of nowhere, she slammed one of her delicate, slim fists down on the table in front of her, adding just a touch of her ethereal energy to make the required amount of noise and garner the attention she required.

Having won their undivided interest she continued.

"This is not a request. You are required to comply by direct order of the king, and I'm here to tell you exactly what's going to happen. Make sure you understand that!" she stated with all the authority that she could. Across the world, dragons that had spent decades, sometimes even centuries reaching positions of power in all those nursery rings, bowed to her demands, despite the fact that she herself was a student. What a turnaround.

"You might all be aware of the small celebration coming up on the surface of the planet... that's right, Christmas. Well... without all of us, it simply isn't going to happen. To share the details of this, every single dragon to a being is going to have to accept being bound to a magical vow, and yes, our ruler has agreed to that as well. So without further ado, I suggest you open yourselves up telepathically to all your older students, who should be standing by. Once you've acknowledged that you're ready, we'll begin. It won't take long. After that, I'll explain everything that needs to be done. Let me assure you, if we all play our part and work together, we CAN get this done."

One hour later from their hidden away base in Malaysia, it was complete, dragon students across the world bound to the magical vow, the threat of having their memories wiped permanently hanging over all of them and of course the same applied to the *tors*.

Throughout nursery rings across the earth, dragon students below year twenty-five were quarantined on the false premise of a potential pandemic. For the most part it worked a treat, keeping the youngsters well out of the way of what was really happening, the most cunning of plans, combined of course with an astounding amount of ancient dragon magic. Carefully, students were split into three and allocated part of a local area. For some that might have been a series of out of the way villages in the midst of the English countryside, for others it would have been a suburb of one of the most famous cities in the world, such as New York, Sydney, Paris, Tokyo or London. Slowly the planet was being carved up into tiny little cake-like slices, the likes of which had never been seen before, all in preparation for the wonders that would hopefully be forthcoming in only a matter of hours now.

From Santa's lair Peter sent out the intricate specifications for the mantra that would conjure up the famous sleigh, knowing how important it was to get the details right. After that, it would be down to a specialised group of students and *tors* in each particular nursery ring to alter it just enough to fit in with local tradition. In some places the colours would be changed just enough to match the previous year's incarnations, in others writing on the side in the customary local language would be appropriate. It would all have to tally seamlessly with what Polkinghorne had achieved previously, all noted from her well kept records. Nothing would or could be left to chance.

Two out of the three students in every group practised fervently at applying the mantras they needed in an effort to keep the ruse from being discovered. Across the land, dragon forms in all shapes, colours and sizes briefly blurred before transforming into either magnificent looking reindeer, of course with a red nose... if you had to choose one to become yourself, all day long it was only ever going to be Rudolph. Whilst the change for others didn't resemble anything four legged, but a rotund human, dressed in brilliant bright red, edged with white that matched the colour of not only the hair on their head, but the fluffiest of beards, a pair of small round glasses the final touch. Almost perfection for all of them, all they had to do now was practice maintaining that form indefinitely, no easy feat for dragons so young.

Back in Malaysia, at For'son's insistence, Richie and Tank set about bolstering the communications array so that it could handle the ring sharing its almost unlimited amount of mana across the crystal node system. What they discovered in the process, was that the cave, and the communications array, were sitting almost directly on top of one of these renowned crystals, making the job that much easier, and the transfer of power that much safer... a stroke of luck if ever there was one.

Freshly watered and fed, having procured a brand new spare wheel and two new timing belts, the Land Rover in which Flash and Vimes sat continued on its way in the pitch black, slipping this way and that through thick, slick mud that in some places almost reached the height of the door handle... Almost! But through sheer perseverance and the occasional touch of magic, they were at least making headway towards their destination, something both of them silently considered right at this very moment.

What it would be like to be in her presence again, he just couldn't imagine. It had been so long, yet it only seemed like yesterday that they'd been playing with magic in the library, igniting everything in the grounds and staying up all night discussing their hopes and dreams. Only now did Vimes realise what they'd had. Only now did it occur to him exactly what he'd lost. Not so much a friend, more a... soul mate. It might sound corny, but it was no less true. During the few hours of sleep that he'd had since they'd left the others at the lair, dreams of her had haunted his unconscious mind. A life together, secrets shared, a family, contentment and happiness. After that the nightmares started, stray dark thoughts about what those loathsome characters were doing to his friend. As the ever spiralling feelings of despair threatened to take him, a bump in the road, one that nearly rolled the entire car, shocked him awake, startling him like never before. Despite their sticky situation, he was glad to have returned to reality, too afraid to even consider what was happening to the dragon that he... LOVED!

"Sorry!" shouted Flash over the noise of them traversing the road, slipping and sliding across the thick, dirty and deep mud that the rain had brought into being all around them.

"No problem," replied the *tor*, trying to shake off all thoughts of his friend.

"I have something to say," stated the Crimson Guard, all businesslike.

"Go on."

"When we get to our destination, you have to follow my lead and trust my decision making. It won't be easy for you, but we can't rush in, and I can't afford for those creatures to gain another hostage. Do you understand?"

"I do," mumbled Vimes. "But I want her back in one piece, and I'll do anything it takes to make that a reality. I know your priority centres around the monsters that have her, but my focus is on her and her alone. Please, don't sacrifice her life, she's just too..."

With the words hanging in the air, it was difficult for Flash to drive and find the appropriate response at the same time. Eventually he did, but it did take a while during which awkward silence reigned.

"In some regard you're correct, my mission is to capture

the crazed creatures and ideally bring all three of them into custody so that we can find out how this has happened and make sure that it doesn't occur again. That said, keeping Polkinghorne safe is right up there on my list of priorities. If I had to choose between her life and letting those monsters escape, I would choose to save her every time. We all, including the king, know how valuable she is, not just in terms of what she does, but the magic she wields as well. Whether or not there's a contingency in place should something bad happen to her is neither here nor there as far as I'm concerned. We go in to save her, capture those demonic beasts that are up to no good, and hope that our allies can turn things around on the surface. That's the plan, but you need to remember that I'm in charge. This isn't my first rodeo, and I assure you I'm more equipped than ever to deal with this."

Vimes didn't doubt it for a minute.

Those dragon students in their groups of three that didn't have to don a disguise were busy practising their own mantras, the ones that searched out a hidden space somewhere within a fifty metre radius, ascertained what was there and then deconstructed said item, before reconstituting it back at the sleigh. This was awkward, unusual and complicated magic that required the utmost concentration and a huge dab of willpower, something the students of varying ages were only just getting to grips with. Food seemed to be the popular choice, giant sticks of multicoloured charcoal disappearing from one part of the floor only to rematerialise right at their feet, before being quickly chucked up into the air and swallowed down whole, the stomach rumbling reward for a job well done as well as an incentive to do the same again. And so it continued, and as you'd expect with students of any kind, they quickly became more masterful at it, which in turn led to... high jinks.

Picture huge open courtyards with young dragons all practising these spells, primarily with food, drink, but occasionally something else, their belongings littering the place, all knowing how important this was to get right, especially given the magical vow that they'd been bonded to. But being students, once they'd tasted a little success, they assumed a mastery had been attained and with their wandering minds, starting mixing up the mayhem... just a little, not in a malicious way, more in a kind, caring and friendly, tickling-their-friends-with-magic sort of way. Across the planet, charcoal imbued items of food were ceremoniously ripped away from grubby little dragon hands as they were about to be tossed down throats, only to materialise, much to the amusement of those all around, in the possession of one of their friends, and so on and so forth. Soon chaos ensued, something the *tors* had to deal with quickly and in such a way as to communicate the importance of what they were doing to their students, who, it has to be said, still didn't grasp the relevance of what they and the rest of the dragons across the planet were involved with. It was going to be a long night in more ways than one.

"When the time comes, how exactly are we going to do this?" asked Richie, wanting to nail down every detail, keen to avoid any unsuspected surprises.

"What do you mean?" replied Tank, with Peter in the background looking on.

"Someone needs to dish out instructions to those students across the world that'll be doing our bidding. Since you have the ring, does that mean you'll do that as well, or do you want one of us to do it?"

"I suppose it makes more sense if I do it," Tank answered, "since I'll be channelling the power from the ring across the crystal node network so that they'll be enough magic to slow down time and for everyone to weave their wizardry."

"And the fact that the king's had most of the network shut down for supposed maintenance will help," added For'son's silky smooth voice across the soft landscape of Tank's mind, something the young dragon acknowledged with a mental nod.

"In that case, Peter and I will monitor everything going on from the consoles back here," she indicated with her hand. "We should easily be able to track power consumption and the scale and success of the coverage."

"Don't forget wish fulfilment," observed Tank wandering over to his friend's position.

"Really?" the other two stated simultaneously.

"I think so," asserted Tank. "My best guess is that Polkinghorne uses this console to record the level of wish fulfilment throughout Christmas Eve and then is able to review it on her return, thus giving her some kind of accomplishment baseline. From what I can tell, it's mainly geared towards youngsters, say... thirteen and under. But there's definitely scope for adults to appear on it as well."

"Does that mean that none of the human adults get what they desire?" Peter asked.

"I'm not sure it's so much that, it appears that it's more to do with belief than anything else. Remember what we've been taught all along about belief, from those very first lessons in the nursery ring."

Peter just looked a little puzzled, while Richie almost certainly understood.

Deciding to put his friend out of his misery, Tank continued.

"What would happen, Pete, if you let rip with a mantra but put absolutely no belief behind it?"

"It would fail instantly or there might be some catastrophic side effects."

"Of course," replied his friend. "And this seems to be designed in very much the same way. No belief, no wishes. And just who are those that believe the most?"

"Children!" both Peter and Richie exclaimed in chorus.

"Exactly!

"So if there's the odd adult or two that still very much deep down believes, then they will show up, and maybe even have their wishes fulfilled?"

"Maybe," replied Tank, "but don't forget, it's not quite as simple as that. It's got to take into account the amount of mana required to power the magic, the intensity of the belief, and exactly what the wish is. There's not suddenly going to be a Ferrari in the drive or the deed to a small Caribbean Island."

That made all three of them laugh.

"So I'll map power consumption and coverage," announced Richie, "and Peter can keep an eye on wish fulfilment. That way we can gauge the success of our outrageous plan."

All three (well... four actually, including For'son who would be guiding Tank through how to channel his almost unlimited supply of mana, adding a few tweaks here and there) agreed that this was the best way to proceed.

Across the nursery rings of the world, things were progressing at pace. The final touches were being put to the sleighs, individual magic cast according to where they were, some to make them shimmer and sparkle in the night sky, others leaving a trail of frosty white snowflakes in their wake. In addition each was having two very specific mantras cast upon them, one to make them invisible to radar, not that in theory at least they should be going that high, and two, an intricate little spell that should render them practically silent as they cut through the night sky, helping the bold plan along at pace. Of course there would still be the odd child or eight that would be able to sense the magic and look out from behind steamed up glass to witness what was going on, but that was the point. How else does the legend of Santa spread? So all of that combined with just a smidgen of the time-slowing mantra should serve them well and allow them to at least cover for Father Christmas, for just one night, if the young dragon friend's hypothesis was correct. For that to be known, we'll just have to wait and see.

Stunning was how it could best be described. A towering mountain range off to their left, the lush green canopy of the jungle covering it like nature's tablecloth, a cool mist hiding the peaks, exotic brightly coloured birds just visible in the surrounding skies, the humidity still almost unbearable, well... for humans anyway. To the right, just past the beautiful, bright, tempting blue water, sat the Sinakharin hydro power plant almost watching over the body of water that this area was renowned for. Magnificence in all its splendour, both natural and manmade... it was quite a sight.

'Amazing what the humans are capable of when they put their minds to it,' thought Vimes, astounded at the huge artificial expanse of water, drawn to it in the heat, much as he assumed the humans would be in the surrounding settlements. Dragons do like a swim, not of course anywhere cold like so many of the seas encompassing the globe, but somewhere warm like this, most certainly. On another day, there'd be no stopping him. But apart from this brief distraction, his focus was firmly on his friend and her precarious predicament, well, that and one other thing... THE VOW! Worried more than a little, he wondered just how things had gotten this out of hand. Bonding the magic to Richie, Tank and Peter was one thing, even Flash, once they'd met him and teamed up, but now hundreds and thousands of beings were in on it. Of course the magic wouldn't let him down, with something like that having a mind of its own and being almost inexhaustible. It was more the sheer number that worried him. When does a secret no longer become a secret? What's the number? Two... ten... one hundred... one hundred thousand? It seemed like the right thing to do, to get Christmas back on track, and he was absolutely certain that SHE would have wanted him to do his utmost to save the holiday that humans valued the most, especially given just how much they benefited from it. Things had spun out of control unbelievably quickly though, with him having very little choice but to go along with the spur of the moment plan. But now it pained him to have done so, his thinking skewed and unclear. If they managed to rescue her, what would she say? Would she be pleased at the turn of events... not the rescue, of course she'd be pleased about that, more the 'everyone knowing' that she was the mystical Santa that spread happiness and joy throughout the land, at least on the surface at that very special time of year. As the jeep veered viciously to the left, he gripped the dashboard in front of him frantically, hanging on for dear life as Flash offered him up a cheeky smile. This was definitely not going the way he'd planned in his mind. Fearful of any number of outcomes when they reached the deranged mythical monster's hideout, the biggest terror within came from the thought that his friend (and secretive love) would despise him forever for what he'd done on behalf of her and the humans.

It was time... well, nearly. The transports were prepared, with specialised routes to the surface wide enough to accommodate the sleighs and the dragons pulling them, sorted out for each and every nursery ring, the *tors* had made sure of that. Across the planet deep within the dragon domain, thousands upon thousands of sleighs were rolled out, each passed to a group of three dragon students, all of whom supposedly knew what to do. Leaping in the back simultaneously, the two with the most technical of tasks double checked, they had everything they needed as the third member of the trio used the tried and tested mantra that they'd been given to transform, not into a human this time, something that the students had spent years perfecting, but a flawless incarnation of a reindeer, one who in most cases had a shining bright red nose. Some had opted not to be Rudolph, but you know most teenagers, vying for glory, wanting something to remember, something to tell all their classmates and friends. And so with the second most important form alteration completed and strapped firmly into the reins, it was time to add a few friends and go to some lengths in completing the deception. All around that one classic, brown and white coated iconic animal, abruptly seven others appeared as if from nowhere with just the slightest of POPs giving a clue to their ethereal existence. As antlers wriggled and jiggled against each other, sounding very much like the real deal, another more life confirming piece of magic, at least for the humans anyway, sprang into existence. And what might that be, I hear you ask? Santa Claus himself, well... not exactly, not given what we know about her, but you know what I mean. Perfect bright red suits of the most sumptuous material, outlined with the purest white, donned modified human forms that had to all look one hundred percent the same. Tank had given some guidance to the *tors* in charge of this part of the plan, with a little help from For'son, the age old presence trapped in the ring, so that a one size fits all mantra was designed for all of them, complete with a massive belly that wobbled like a huge bowl full of jelly, a majestic silver beard of the finest quality hair and smooth, round, gold rimmed glasses. It was all topped off with glistening black, almost knee length boots and a sack that could conjure up almost anything because it was directly connected through the supernatural to not only the king's ring's supply of mana, but to the ancient magic that sought out the wishes that only Polkinghorne really knew about. The falsehood forms across the planet were a marvel of ingenuity even by dragon standards, and that was saying quite something.

As Christmas Eve turned into Christmas Day across the planet, silent jetfighter-like blurs of brown and white followed by sumptuous red rocketed up from secret specially designed entrances, glistening magic trailing in their wake, each surrounded by a pocket of time-slowing ethereal energy and the wish fulfilment mantra that should, if working correctly, spread festive cheer across the tiny part of the land that those particular students were responsible for.

In a hidden control centre deep within his private residence, known only to a few, George the dragon king and mysterious ruler of the planet lounged back in a comfortable leather chair on coasters, his feet up on the desk, watching a huge monitor that he'd specifically set up to track and trace the student Santa task force as he'd like to think of it, enabled by the crystal node network and the essence of his friend, For'son's supernatural gift. Crossing his fingers, a habit picked up from his time spent on the surface in the guise of a gallivanting bold and courageous knight, all that time ago, silently he wished all the luck in the world to those trying to save Christmas, especially Flash, his Crimson Guard, who he knew would have a tough time facing off with those devilish monsters that had somehow gone rogue, and the young dragon student from Purbeck who much to his surprise had turned up here on Flash's behalf. Given the guarded nature of their relationship, it was odd that it should be him, thought the king. But Fate, fickle as she often was, in his experience anyway, was known to throw the odd curve ball or two, and so he shouldn't really have been surprised. Assuming that the youngster was back in Malaysia in the very heart of things, he wished him and his friends well. These holidays and the hope that they brought had to be maintained, it was vital, of that he was certain. For Christmas to be ruined, even once, could well spell disaster for the humans on the surface, the charges he regarded as his responsibility, and there was simply no way in hell that was happening on his watch. Taking a slow, smooth sip of the sherry out in front of him, in an effort to get into the

Christmas swing of things, he turned back to the monitor and settled down for a long night, intrigued as to how things would go. Just like most of the children across the world, he let his mind fill with ideas of Father Christmas, reindeer, mince pies, crunchy carrots, peace and goodwill.

Speaking of anything but goodwill...

"How goes our little experiment?" he asked, keen to get an understanding of just how much magic would be needed to advance his cause to an almost industrial level.

"The enthrallment took effect right from the very first moment he picked up the arrow," replied Red, a sick and twisted grin etched into the features of her beautiful, yet deadly face. "And we're sure that it's attached itself to the other two."

"But?"

"As far as we know, they haven't yet killed their nemesis, something that if the magic had worked as planned, should have already happened."

"Might it be a glitch, sort of a caster error or some kind of magical defence on their part?"

"Frankly, it could be any of the above, but I'm hopeful that it still might happen."

"Really?" he said a little sceptically.

"I am," replied the vicious vixen of evil that would have turned most beings on the planet into gibbering wrecks by just being in their presence. Not him though, never him. "From what we can tell, the Tooth Fairy seems to have some kind of natural immunity to at least part of the spell. She's the one best able to resist it at the moment. But that, in my opinion, can only last so long. Once it breaks down her defences, she'll join the other two, and then the focus of their ire will be... TOAST!"

Those words were enough to put a smile on his face for the first time in what seemed like weeks. That, however, didn't last as the sound of his father's footsteps pounding the floorboards in the adjacent room reminded him of the pressure they were all under to succeed and of the vile abuse that was only ever a moment or two away from filling him with fear. Nodding his head at her, desperate not to attract attention from next door, he whispered his thanks and told her to keep on monitoring the situation.

Having been hugging the coastline of the enormous body of water that was referred to as Sinakharin up until this point, Flash and Vimes, getting ever closer to their destination, ditched the Land Rover amongst the nearby dense jungle, just far enough in that none of the local population would find it, but close enough that they could get to it in an emergency and hopefully use it in an extraction if required. Cutting through the gorgeous leafy green lush and wondrous brush, they skirted their way through the dense undergrowth, using it as cover whilst staying parallel, at least for a time, to the shabby road that led up to the Huai Mae Khamin Waterfall deep inside Khuean Srinagarindra National Park. In their human guises, wary of using magic because it might alert their prey to their presence, it was hard going, so much so that after only a few minutes all their clothes had become soaked with sweat from the exertion. After an hour of back breaking work, nearing their target, both men/dragons stopped to take one last drink, dehydration threatening to overcome them. Catching their breath, it was the *tor* that started the whispered conversation that only the insects, birds and monkeys could hear.

"How far?"

"By my estimation, between five and seven hundred metres."

"How do you want to go in?"

"On my own," was what Flash wanted to say, but he'd long since come to the conclusion that the dedicated and pushy *tor* would not be denied the chance to risk himself for his friend, and so knowing that ordering him not to follow would just make him rebel and want to do it more, he tried to find the right sort of compromise that would let him do his job and keep Vimes at arm's length.

"I need to do a little scouting before we go in guns blazing," announced Flash all matter-of-factly, as quietly as he could, his cohort giving him a knowing look as he did so, "just to make sure that there are no other hostages or any unusual surprises in the form of reinforcements, human or otherwise."

That got the *tor's* attention, with Vimes admitting to himself that he hadn't considered any of that, instantly provoking two thoughts. One, that he was glad Flash was here leading the way. And two, that he'd never felt so far out of his depth. Anything teaching or worldly wise related he could cope with in the blink of an eye, but this... here and now had his stomach lurching up and down, his legs quivering more than a little, and thoughts of Polkinghorne's demise rushing around his brain. Never before had he felt so lost and scared, something that although he didn't know it, the Crimson Guard before him could sense.

"It'll be alright, we'll get her back," Flash urged the being he'd almost come to think of as a friend over the last day or so, which in itself was odd because he'd never considered any one being in that way before. "But we have to use our heads if we're to do so. Caution should be our watchword. All three of them are proficient magic users in their own right, and who knows just how amped up they are in there. As well, if they have allies of any kind, there's a good chance that we'll have to retreat and call for reinforcements... just so you know."

"Reinforcements? Is that really a thing?"

"It is, but it's not something done either lightly or that will happen any time soon. For help to get here, it could take many, many hours at best. Hopefully it won't come to that... okay?"

Vimes nodded, concern for his friend at the forefront of his mind.

Finishing his mouthful of water from the magically replenishing bottle at his hip, the Crimson Guard nodded back at his partner and, leading the way, stalked off into the lush foliage in the direction of his quarry.

With Rhianne long since having been tucked away for the night, which in itself was a miracle, the younger of the two siblings thankfully having not taken after her sister in actually sleeping through the night instead of waking up every couple of hours, now came the time for the ever inquisitive and intelligent Megan to go to bed. Given that it was Christmas Eve that would prove to be, as with most children across the planet, no easy feat. Four bedtime stories she'd had, two from each parent, the beautiful little girl twisting their arms, cajoling and even begging, much to her mum and dad's disbelief, even more so the fact that she was still awake despite copious amounts of yawning. Inside, Michael grinned, taken back to his youth, fully aware that he used to do the same thing. Perhaps not at quite such a young age, but certainly a little later on he could remember pretending to have his eyes closed when checked on, screwing them up really tight, because that's how he thought people slept, obviously a dead giveaway to any grownup ever. More often than not though, it just left him fatigued the following day, exhausted from having stayed awake until three, sometimes even four in the morning, desperately hoping to catch a glimpse of the one being that could grant not only hope, but wishes as well. As a youngster he never had, but that hadn't dimmed his belief. Even as an adult, some tiny part of him deep inside still believed in magic, especially after that one night and at this time of year.

One more story, this time made up, not from a book but by her mother, had the delightfully excited Megan fast asleep much to both her parents' amusement. Slipping the bedroom door silently closed behind them, mother and father wound their way down the tight, twisted staircase and headed for the living room for a much merited rest, flaking out in front of the television on the couch the order of the day, a well deserved glass of wine for the lady of the house and a bar of chocolate for her husband, both knowing that the well positioned baby monitor would alert them to any kind of child movement from either sibling upstairs.

With the biting cold outside nibbling at the meagre defences of what had once long ago been a small terraced railway cottage, the loving couple snuggled up ever more as was their wont, providing warmth and comfort in each other's arms. That is, until tiredness took over, and time slipped effortlessly onwards, heading steadily for the main event of this festive period, Christmas Day itself. Barely able to keep their eyes open any more, both skulked off to bed, checking on their beloved babes on the way as they did so, silently dropping off a huge red sack with Santa's face emblazoned on the outside on the bottom of Megan's bed with just a few small presents and treats inside for the morning that would hopefully keep her occupied when she awoke. As the darkness beneath their toasty warm duvet took them both, Michael couldn't help but feel a slight tinge of guilt about the presents under the tree downstairs. Not because there were none, that wasn't the case by a long shot. NO! But because they were all for the children, not one single one there was for the wife he so loved and adored. As his mind slithered off into oblivion, his last thought was of the boots in the shop window, the ones that his wife so coveted. Time ticked on, Christmas moved ever closer and somewhere close by a snort of flame licked Santa's nostril, nearly setting his sack on alight.

The world was on fire, or at least that's how it would have looked from above to any of the supernatural beings with the correct vision selected. Bright orange, red and yellow circled the globe but only across the major land masses and unlike in years gone by, this magic didn't belong to Christmas but to... DRAGONS!

Across the crystal node network, power in every size, colour and form abounded as well as tens of thousands of messages from those that still knew that it worked and wasn't under maintenance, as was the considered belief. *Tors* guided their young charges, making sure every last mile was covered and that no household was left untouched. A skill to be sure, but one they were easily adept enough to perform, particularly with all the available ethereal energy left. Of course the time-slowing mantra around the sleigh each group of three found themselves on helped. Most useful on high rises and apartment blocks, the Santa fakes had little trouble in doing a single skyscraper in all but a real time minute. Magic at work for the benefit of human kind, something often ascribed to Christmas itself in normal times, which these most certainly weren't.

Silently and surreptitiously tiny glasses of sherry disappeared, atom by atom, from carpets and floors in households across the planet, mince pies and half eaten carrots joining them, reconstructed almost immediately only a short way away, the air itself shimmering and sparkling briefly, a faint tang of the smoky supernatural the only hint that anything untoward had occurred.

As if all that wasn't enough, strands of subversive, enchanted, unexplained particles followed the path of belief, invading the minds of mainly the young, but the old as well, the tentacles grappling with tangled reflections, sorting thoughts from wishes, doing the magic's bidding, finding that which could sensibly be conjured into being. Powerful couldn't begin to describe what the humans found themselves inundated with.

As time slowed throughout the world (not by very much it had to be said, after all the dragons had an army of students numbering in the millions, but perhaps making the day thirty hours long in some places, rather than twenty four) the rush of magic fulfilling its purpose zinged and zipped around every different neighbourhood imaginable, not bound by ethnicity, standing, money, orientation or even as the lists suggest, good or bad. Of course, the supernatural stopped inherently bad people wishing for inherently bad things, whether that was to have an automatic gun instead of a revolver, a tank instead of a car or just plain and simple revenge. Ethereal ethics had been programmed in at the basest level and could not be circumvented either by the supernatural or sheer desire. Bikes, skateboards, scooters and even in the odd case, cars (beaten up old things, not the Ferrari types mentioned earlier, something a teen might appreciate when learning to drive) appeared out of absolutely nothing, some wrapped... I think you can guess which ones, others... not so much. There were dolls, action figures, board games, pens and colouring books as well as clothes, sports equipment and occasionally a sly ropey looking envelope full to the brim with money in all local denominations, enough for say... a couple of months' rent, just when it was needed most. If you could imagine it (and quite a few of the humans could) then there was the possibility of it turning up. But not everything, even the powerful prehistoric power of the planet's ruling race couldn't do that. Children wished for their sick parents to be cured of a variety of illnesses, ranging from the most simple things like broken limbs or twisted ankles all the way through to a myriad of incurable conditions such as cancer. Heartbreaking as it was, the magic involved could not perform miracles, certainly not on that kind of level, but there was a degree of compassion built into it which allowed for, shall we say, a few extra special gifts for those in that position, no consolation I know, but the best that could be done given the unusual circumstances. Wishes and desires were fulfilled as much as possible on an outstanding scale, in places even eclipsing what Polkinghorne would have been able to achieve, so great was the co-ordination and team work of the nursery ring students around the globe. Back in Malaysia, three of their kind looked on keenly, trying to get an overview of just how things were going.

"It's working," said Peter in wonder, watching what they'd achieved unfold on the monitor before him.

"You doubted it would?" asked Richie, with raised eyebrows.

"Well…"

"I think we all had our doubts," chipped in Tank, keen to rid the air of even the slightest bit of tension, "but I think we can agree that the students across the world are doing a grand job."

Silently his friends nodded their accord.

"I wonder how Flash and Vimes are getting on?" ventured Peter, pondering the fate of the real Father Christmas.

All three of the young dragon friends focused their thoughts in that direction, hoping that things were going just as well as the efforts to save Christmas.

And that was the million dollar question.

She swore… loudly in her head and behind the gag that prevented pretty much any noise from escaping, but if it had, it would have turned the air blue. What had caused one of the most benevolent, kind and caring dragons on the planet to do such a thing…? An arrow had hit her, straight through the calf of her false human form, spraying blood across the floor beneath the chair and up the wall beside her, much to the delight of Cupid and the Easter Bunny, the Tooth Fairy not so much.

"I think that's enough, don't you?" remarked the gatherer of teeth to the other two, trying to be as forceful as her gentle personality would allow.

But by now, the other two were well and truly lost and were having absolutely none of it.

Chuckling loudly, Cupid effortlessly pulled another

arrow from his quiver, this one a rainbow litany of fletching, looking like it had been made from a unicorn's tail, and after pulling back the bowstring, slipped it seamlessly into the nock of the multicoloured projectile. Lowering his head to get perfect line of sight, all the time cheered on by the Easter Bunny, from behind his infamous weapon, he uttered,

"We're only just getting started, my love," and with that, a whistling TWANG filled the air as yet one more of his arrows tore the atoms in front of it apart, closing in on its helpless target.

In that moment, right before it struck, the Tooth Fairy locked eyes with Polkinghorne, both magical entities sharing not only a look, but a thought as well. And that went something along the lines of, 'We need to end this... NOW!'

Ignoring the impatience he could feel radiating off the *tor* about one hundred metres away just beyond the tree line, as quiet as the tiniest of mice crossing a carpet in an extravagant set of slippers, Flash, flush to the wall of the strange structure that had been built into the side of the mountain, locked down the magical part inside him, scrunching it up into a ball, making it as small and hopefully undetectable as possible and, as alert as ever, tiptoed into the darkness beyond.

Almost drowning in sweat, crouched down on the jungle floor, peeking out from between the splintered gap in between two trees, mouth absolutely parched, more so than an overused tumble drier, Vimes watched the Crimson Guard disappear inside the entrance and couldn't help but worry. To be this tantalisingly close to finding his friend and be ordered to stay out of the way felt absolutely agonising. If only he could get a little nearer, he thought. Just maybe he could help out after all.

An almighty CRACK echoed around the chamber followed immediately by a muffled THWUMP and what sounded like wood bouncing off rock. As the brave and heroic being the world would have recognised as Santa rocked uncontrollably in the chair she was tied to, doing everything in her power to wash away the agony from the arrow that had just splintered her left knee into a dozen different pieces, a steady stream of teardrops meandered down her pale freckled face, as her long unkempt blonde hair waved precariously about behind her. Inside she was furious, the rage at what was being carried out here, against her, totally and utterly maddening, but that was tempered by the fact that her magic had been somehow curtailed, so much so that she was unable to do anything to heal her damaged knee, calf or palm, the injuries with the arrows remaining in them making her look like a cross between a giant pin cushion and a voodoo doll. Also, the cold didn't help. Despite where they were, deep within the jungle on the western fringes of Thailand, the underground chill from beneath the mountain nibbled at her skin, akin to a needle constantly pricking her all over, causing the tips of her fingers to burn and her lips to feel numb. For such a wondrous being it was a sad turn of events, that's for sure, something even the wickedly devious entity known as Fate could agree on, and that was saying something because she never normally had an opinion one way or the other, only ever interested in the delicious journey and not the outcome. Against the horrific sound of yet more laughter, some of which sounded very bunny-like, with the odd wet, chocolatey SPLAT thrown in for good measure, Polkinghorne's consciousness descended into the shadows, her mind shutting down, the only defence it had against the craziness and the all encompassing pain.

The splintering sound of a colossal CRACK had him searching around for targets in the concealed narrow corridor he found himself in, his Crimson Guard training now taking hold of his every action.

'Calm down,' he told himself, reining in everything

supernatural within, knowing that the element of surprise might well be his biggest advantage, something that he'd probably need, especially since he was outnumbered at least three to one. Up ahead his magically enhanced senses picked up a slight banging sound against the background of manic mockery. Not only did it raise the hairs on his sometimes cumbersome human guise, but his hackles as well. Whatever was going on had no right to be happening, he knew. There and then he vowed to put a stop to it, no matter what the cost.

Torn between keeping the promise he'd given to Flash and concern for his best friend, the battle between the two raged on for more than a few moments deep within Vimes. Never before had he found himself so conflicted. After that though it was clear, at least to him, about what he had to do. Skulking out from between the trees, he threw caution to the wind and headed straight for the gloominess of the entrance.

Tucked into a little recess a few metres back from a sharp corner that the resounding laughter appeared to be coming from, Flash swallowed sharply, more than a little concerned about what might be waiting for him beyond. If it was them, and he assumed that was the case, something that his training rallied against a little, knowing that the mother of all assumptions could well lead to a very sticky end, then the time had come to act. What was blatantly obvious was that he just had to know what he was dealing with. Searching his vast repository of exceptional knowledge, he came up with something that might just do the trick. Closing his eyes and taking a deep breath to calm down and focus his mind, all the time aware of his surroundings, the words he needed suddenly appeared at the forefront of his mind. Applying all of his extraneous will, he whispered them in his head, adding a considerable amount of his ethereal energy as he did so.

Abruptly, on the cool stone of the passageway that he stood in, right next to the wall about a metre in front of his right foot, a superbly sculpted scorpion shimmered into being, about the size of a small human hand, an ethereal blue glow surrounding its entirety. As his eyes shot open he marvelled at the magnificent creation for but a moment, before it skittered off around the corner heading towards the source of all the commotion, a tiny blue ghostly umbilical dragged in its wake that only he could see, connecting the both of them. Not something he'd used very often or at least very recently, this particular mantra had proved handy on a number of occasions in the past. A spirit animal, that's how the cool, calculating Crimson Guard thought of his ethereal companion, one that should, if things all went to plan, be able to act as his eyes and ears. Things were looking up.

Overwhelming amounts of magic continued to flow out across the crystal node network, perhaps more so now than at any other time in its history, extraordinary in itself. It allowed the hundreds of thousands of Santa wannabes to complete their missions, the humans' wishes to be extrapolated and children everywhere to wake up surprised and happy. But that wasn't all that was happening. Telepathic messages, the main purpose of the network and the very reason it had been created, were flying all over the place, mainly from the *tors* safely tucked away in their particular nursery rings, to some of the more mischievous dragons under their guidance.

A common one went something along the lines of,

'Do you really think it's appropriate to leave a steaming pile of reindeer poo outside that poor family's house?' Which garnered much merriment from all those that heard it.

Whenever encountering two mince pies at a house, some of the 'full of beans' and fun loving students decided to leave them there, arranged rather comically with the carrot, forming an unmentionable shape, designed to cause offence or much merriment depending on the personality of the humans that arrived downstairs on Christmas morning.

One or two, determined to make the most of being on the surface and having almost unlimited freedom, started using their magic to not only deliver presents and fulfil wishes, but to swap things around in the houses that they visited, such as coffee for gravy and salt for sugar, this being the highlight of their evening, much to the hilarity of those involved.

Another common theme was telling offs for leaving little calling cards with specially designed 'Santa Tips' that included: 'Don't eat yellow snow,' 'You never realise what you've got until it's gone... toilet paper is a good example of that,' 'Farting in a lift is wrong on so many levels,' and 'What did the pirate say when he turned eighty years old...? Aye matey,' all of which the young dragons found side-splitting.

All of this I suppose should have been slightly predictable given the diversity of the students involved, the sheer numbers, and the fact that almost every single one of them loved a good prank. What was surprising was that the magical vow that had been shared with them didn't keep them in line, either with a slight supernatural prod or just the threat of what would happen should they misbehave. They'd all been told of the dire consequences, but it seemed very much as though they didn't care if their memories were wiped, something those in charge found hard to comprehend. Just like teachers across the surface the *tors*, on occasion, still failed to understand fully what drives their charges onwards.

Using the magic of his birthright to scan the intricate and complex signals and ethereal energy bombarding the crystal node network across the planet, pleased that things were pretty much going as planned and that the humans' belief in their most important holiday remained very much intact, the dragon king, George, had also, as you would expect, encountered many of the messages from the *tors*, berating their students for what they considered poor behaviour. But having spent all the time that he had on the surface, albeit not so much nowadays apart from the odd 'holiday' here and there, disguised in his robust, inoffensive old man form, the monarch found most of the goings on amusing rather than anything else. He knew that a great sense of humour was just one of the things that made the humans so special, almost certainly contributing to the potential the dragon world had agreed to nurture and develop when it had signed up to the mysterious prophecy, many thousands of years ago. Sitting there monitoring everything going on, the king briefly wondered if 'The White Dragon' from said forecast would ever show up in this world or any other. He supposed that if it did, it would be far in the future because currently, both above and below ground, things seemed to be going pretty well. Little did he know what Fate had in store in that regard and just how his life was intertwined with some of the courageous beings best serving the world right at this very moment.

With a partial mind of its own, guided in some regard by the consciousness at the other end of the ethereal tether, the skittering scorpion had taken to using the wall in an effort to get closer to its goal, its eight legs finding purchase in the cracks and gaps between the hastily erected, uneven and mismatched bricks that made it up. Abruptly it drew to a halt, concerned for good reason. Just ahead, the shadows it had traversed in the darkened hallway to get this far suddenly disappeared, replaced by a much brighter artificial light which emanated from the much more expansive and spacious room that started to open out in front of it. Against its magical nature, for fear of being discovered given that it had some semblance of self preservation built in, despite not technically being alive, Flash urged it on, filling what basic intelligence it had with the urgency of the situation, knowing that he needed to get an understanding of what they were dealing with as quickly as dragonly possible. Unable to resist, slowly and very carefully it ventured out onto the brightly lit wall, almost able to sense that it was nearing its target. Two more minutes... that's how long it took for the relatively tiny creature to find itself in a position to see out into what looked very much like a grotto, ironic really given the most famous person to supposedly reside in one of those.

Aware that a pivotal point had been reached, Flash gave more of himself over to his spirit animal in an effort to ascertain the situation, looking to finally resolve the situation to the satisfaction of everybody, except that is, the diabolical creatures that had set all this in motion in the first place.

Through very unusual eyes, everything playing out in the room, from those present to the tortuous evil being carried out, swam slowly into view. Sitting off to one side, unable to move at all on a battered old chair was a stunning blonde haired human shaped being, tears gushing down her face for very good reason... An array of sickly arranged arrows stuck out from all parts of her body, brilliant thick, bright red blood running out of each wound, some of it pooling on the floor, the rest absorbed by her grubby suit that had seen better days, one which was instantly recognisable as the most famous on the surface of the planet, that of... FATHER CHRISTMAS!

Back down the corridor, a variety of emotions played out in the mind of the very sensible and pragmatic Crimson Guard.

"Hooray," shouted part of him, "I've found Polkinghorne," but the much more realistic and hard-nosed fraction of him screamed a warning that it was never going to be that easy, because to say the least, she looked in quite a state. And the only real conclusion he could draw from that, was that the three supernatural beings he was up against had somehow not only negated her magic, but had managed to withhold it altogether from her... no mean feat against a being of her quality.

In the confines of her mind, Santa, or as we now know her to be, Polkinghorne, was having a dreadful time, which was odd because you would have thought that things couldn't have got any worse than her actual reality. Possibly caused by the date itself or maybe as a direct result of the vicious torture that she'd suffered at the hands and paws of her assailants, her mind was a whirring blur of negativity and downright destructiveness, causing confusion and sending her thoughts into a downward spiral of darkness. Images of young children waking up on what was supposed to have been Christmas morning haunted her, their tiny footsteps padding downstairs, their gleeful smiles at what was to come ruined by the discovery that not only hadn't Santa visited, but what remained of the tree lay scattered across the room, baubles splintered into a hundred shiny pieces, tinsel torn and scattered everywhere, branches of the tree, dead and dying, torn apart, a pile of pine needles haphazardly built up in front of the hearth, the remnants of Christmas cards smouldering in the fire. It was everything she dreaded, all seemingly coming to life right before her eyes. In a burst of light, the scene changed to one of utter carnage, burnt out houses in what would once have been a delightful cul-de-sac, the charred remains of scorched buildings still smoking despite the heavy night-time drizzle. Families sitting on curbs by the roadside sobbing their hearts out, the adults using all their bravery to assure children that everything would be alright, their offspring not believing a word of it. And then the questions came, over and over again from any number of different children, to any number of different parents, like a dagger through her heart.

"WHERE WAS SANTA, MUMMY?" "WHY DIDN'T

FATHER CHRISTMAS STOP THE BUILDING BURNING DOWN, DADDY?" "IS CHRISTMAS REAL?" asked another small child in Polkinghorne's mind, his parents barely able to answer, so soul destroying was their ordeal. Amongst all the fiery wreckage and the piles of broken rubble her vision focused in on numerous broken toys: a blistered doll's head, the charred remains of a small bike, a teddy bear's singed arms and a punctured and deflated football. Psychologically, it was all too much; the pain of seeing her worst nightmare play out threatened to splinter her amazing dragon intellect, even if it was only contained in this fragile human form. Descending into chaos on the inside, outwardly the forged biped figure let out a high pitched squeal behind the gag that circled her head, squeezed out a few more tears and with no more fight left in her, exhaled her last breath.

Across the universe, throughout every different alternative reality... HOPE DIED!

Futures changed, the suffering of the human race intensified tenfold, the world as one delving irreparably into darkness. Fate gasped, shocked to her very core, sorry that she somehow hadn't intervened, not that it had been her place to do so. Children's lives became mired in sadness and despair, opportunities to grow up in a bright, optimistic and lively world diminished vastly as the cold harsh grip of terror, fear, anger and rage plagued what remained of the earth for generations to come. Wars broke out worldwide, not only between different countries, but internally as well. All thoughts of a greener, cleaner planet were forgotten instantly, selfishness the key ingredient now that Christmas had been lost. You might have thought that the beings who had been party to all this would have benefitted beyond belief, but not so. As the chaos and mayhem spread, Easter was the first to go, nobody now giving a rat's arse about chocolate eggs or the goodwill behind that particular gesture. Next, only by a hair's breadth was of course Cupid, all but made redundant from the position he'd made his own since the humans of this world had walked the earth. There would be no pension for him, only a decaying and rotten world to watch over, wondering just what could have been.

As for the Tooth Fairy, well... that was a different case altogether. Fighting was very much the name of the game in this modern day future without a future. Optimism and expectation had been well and truly replaced by greed and despair, with almost every human being doing their best to step on the neck of their neighbour to gain any kind of advantage and work their way up the ladder. Even the tiniest amount of kindness was hard to find in a world so awful and nasty. And given that the Tooth Fairy was so busy that she had to take on extra staff, what with all the brawling, battles and hostility, you'd have thought that she'd have been happy. But due to the extra supply of teeth in every shape and size, the value of each individual tooth at the magical exchange she dealt at, plummeted no end, forcing her and her new employees to work twenty four hours a day, every day of the year, with absolutely no respite, creating yet one more being with a whole host of regrets.

It wasn't just the humans that were affected. The dragon domain itself spiralled out of control, with the realisation that they'd failed their charges and more importantly, voided the prophecy which had guided their race for thousands of years. The king abdicated, a first in the history of the prehistoric flying giants, the council fought for decades over a suitable replacement, whilst in the meantime, the needs of ordinary dragon citizens were well and truly ignored. In truth, even after millennia, the planet was still reeling from the loss of one of its greatest unsung heroes, the source of hope and good for so many, most especially the young.

Watching through the eyes of the ethereal blue scorpion, his spirit creature, Flash's blood ran cold, the false, thick red human blood of course, not his normal, pale green dragon blood. A sinking feeling the likes of which he'd never known sucked the life out of him, threatening to pull him into an endless abyss of despair as he watched Polkinghorne's lips start to turn blue.

Exactly then, two things happened simultaneously. One, the Easter Bunny, normally a sweet and sensitive figure that wouldn't hurt a fly, started to become agitated and angry for no apparent reason. And two, a solitary figure from behind Flash, managed to take him by surprise.

Caught off guard initially, it took him a few extra moments to react, but react he did, instinctively and living up to his name. Severing contact with his spirit animal, in a whirling blur of athleticism the Crimson Guard ran up the wall, backflipped over on himself and, readying half a dozen offensive mantras at the forefront of his mind, came up fighting.

Scrambling back furiously, hands out in front of his face, afraid for his life, Vimes tried to reason with Flash who was angrier than he could ever have imagined. Dispelling the supernatural spells, the Crimson Guard grabbed the *tor* by the scruff of the neck and with his hand over his mouth, pulled him up against the wall off to one side of the corridor, signalling for him to be quiet. Reluctantly he complied, calming down in the process. Disappointed, Flash removed his hand.

"W... w... w... what's going on?" stammered the *tor*, desperate to help.

The Crimson Guard's mind shot back to the last thing he'd seen before breaking contact with the scorpion, Santa still bound to the chair, head slumped forward, broken, busted and... DEAD!

Gulping anxiously, he wondered just how he was going to break the news to her best friend. Just then, the need to do so disappeared.

"HA... SHE'S DEAD!" bellowed a happy go lucky voice from not that far up ahead, sounding absolutely ecstatic.

"SANTA'S DEAD! SANTA'S DEAD! SANTA'S DEAD!" sang one more, merrily, much to the horror of Vimes whose wide eyes stared deep into Flash's soul, not wanting to believe what he was hearing.

Whether in dragon or human form, the Crimson Guard wouldn't have lasted two seconds at a poker table, unable to disguise what he knew to be the truth of the matter, even to spare his new found friend's feelings.

Unbridled loss encompassed the *tor*, tearing at his very essence, ripping the fabric of his soul, destroying the dragon deep inside... for a moment anyway. And then, resounding down the corridor once again, came more jolly laughing and singing.

"SANTA'S DEAD! SANTA'S DEAD! WE DID IT, SANTA'S DEAD!"

And before Flash could stop him, Vimes, in an act powered by anger, rage, revenge and... LOVE, shrugged off the Crimson Guard, soaked up all his magic and tore off round the corner, his ancient inbuilt dragon need for unadulterated violence spiking off the chart, all the time looking for a target.

Too slow to stop the *tor*, which in itself was unusual, only then did the link to Flash's spirit animal flare back up, something that the ethereal beast itself could and had initiated, but only in times of dire emergency. In the blink of an eye, the scorpion shared with him what it had found.

"NOOOOOOOO!" Flash screamed, sprinting off after the *tor*, adding all his supernatural power to the mix, desperate to get his hands on his friend in an effort to stop him reaching the chamber. But as he turned the corner, it became obvious that it was too late, with Vimes' speeding blur just passing the threshold as he looked on. Without a thought for himself, the brave, fearless and inventive Crimson Guard added every ounce of magic he had to his speed, sucking power and mana out of the laminium necklace and ring that he wore just for emergencies like this, at the fastest rate possible in an effort to reach his pal.

Skidding to a halt on the slick stone floor just inside the well lit room, the nightmarish scene playing out in front of him momentarily froze the *tor* to the spot as he took everything in. Cupid and the Easter Bunny high fiving one another as the Tooth Fairy looked solemnly on was about as bad as he thought it could get, and then he turned to his left. That's when his heart shattered.

Job done, magic depleted, the ethereal blue scorpion, Flash's spirit creature, flickered out of existence, its disappointment at not knowing the outcome of what was about to happen almost palpable.

Instantly recognisable, to him anyway because that was the human form she'd always taken during her time at the nursery ring, the fact that the pale freckled skin of her gorgeous face had taken on a light blue tint told him everything he needed to know. She had indeed died. Noting her lifeless blonde hair draped deathly still down past her shoulders brought back memories of better times... each of them in their human guises riding the other in their dragon form, experiencing the rip roaring emotion of flight from a totally different point of view had been utterly exhilarating. Traversing the jungle canopy in Borneo by running and jumping from tree top to tree top during the warm humid nights on a field trip had been the biggest, best and most dangerous game of chase ever. And as for those nights in their dormitory rooms, sampling as much of the human food and drink as it was possible to, including vast quantities of alcohol, some of which certainly had an effect... Those had been by far the most amazing times of his life, and now they were gone, never to be relived, a realisation that dropped on him from a great height, very much like something else was about to.

You see, the information that Flash's spirit animal had conveyed back to him had been about the huge room the creatures currently occupied and how the entrance to it had been booby trapped by the Easter Bunny. So as Vimes stepped across the threshold, he triggered the trap which involved about a thousand litres of magically molten hot, thick, gooey, quick setting, brown, milk chocolate descending from a magical vat hidden above the doorway in plain sight. As the first of it threatened to splatter all over the hair on the *tor's* head, the rocketing blur that was Flash smashed into him, knocking him forward at speed, thereby avoiding the delicious and demonic sweet treat in liquid form. Unfortunately, the same could not be said of the Crimson Guard, who took the brunt of the chocolate shower, instantly looking as though he'd bathed in it, the supernatural properties imbued within it causing it to set instantly, his speed negated, turning him into a very disappointed looking brown statue. Cue more merriment from Cupid and the Easter Bunny at the sight of their cunning ambush working to perfection.

Despite missing out on all the chocolatey goodness Vimes froze, more in fear at the sight of the menacing looking creatures than anything else, wondering what the hell they were going to do to him. Even with all the pent up anger and rage inside him at what they'd done to his friend, his limbs just would not move, something the evil threesome, or more accurately, the evil twosome and one rather undecided other, took note of straight away, immediately deciding to press home their advantage.

Brilliant bright orange with a wriggling tail of green sliced through the air in the cool room beneath the mountain range in Thailand, looking to add one more victim to the tally.

'Unbelievable,' was his first thought as the supernatural chocolate hit his pretend body, setting and securing him in place. Instantly, that was quickly followed by, 'Think, think, think... I need to be free,' something his well trained and adept mind immediately took notice of and began searching for solutions, magical and otherwise.

With an outstanding TWANG and looking to better his cohort's best effort, Cupid let rip with yet another of his multitude of arrows, the dull grey, barbed, razor sharp edges of the head on this one closing all the time on the fast paced orange and green blur intended for the interloper not captured by their trap.

With both a diabolical arrow and one of the Easter Bunny's favourite treats closing at speed towards the *tor's* physical, rather than broken heart, it looked for all intents and purposes as though he'd be joining his best friend and secret crush in the afterlife in all but a matter of moments. But Fate, her best friend Fortune and more importantly, one of the best dragon agents on the planet, all had other ideas.

Razor sharp... no, not the arrow, well... it was, but I'm talking about Flash's intellect, and in an amount of time so small that it was almost immeasurable, he had exactly what he was looking for. Instinctively the words appeared in his mind and combined without any fuss with his indomitable will and a great deal of his outstanding magic.

With the tiniest of hums both projectiles shuddered to a halt, the sharp tipped carrot just hanging there all streamlined and orange, its huge green stems trailing out behind it, in some ways mirroring the stabilising vanes on the arrow, well... almost, because what the inventive Crimson Guard had done just made it look that way. Taking a leaf out of the books of Richie, Tank and Peter, Flash had thrown a version of Santa's time-slowing mantra out in front of him, just far enough to encase Vimes, Cupid, the Easter Bunny and of course the two projectiles, now moving at a snail's pace between them all in a pink and purple hued sparkling cloud, identical to the bottled magic back at Polkinghorne's lair.

'Job done,' he thought briefly before realising two things. One, he was still confined in the magical confectionary concoction and two, he'd only dealt with two of the three criminals that he was here to apprehend. The Tooth Fairy stood away from the other gang members, much, much closer to Polkinghorne's lifeless corpse. Locking eyes with the free member of the malicious trio through a tiny pinprick in the hard as concrete goo that had set him in place, it was only as she began to pace towards him that he really started to panic, knowing that no part of the magic he'd just cast lay between either of them. About to let rip with his most outlandish spells in an effort to break free, abruptly he was stopped in his stride by the words of the enchanted being before him.

"Hang tight, I'll have you out in a jiffy," exclaimed the Tooth Fairy, pulling a tiny little hammer out from somewhere at the back of the work belt that she wore.

Sensing no duplicity and a genuine sense of help from the pint-sized princess, Flash maintained a hold on all his supernatural power, part of him still fearing some sort of treachery. Thankfully it never came and she had him free in only a few moments.

"Thanks," he ventured, eyeing her up, wondering what the hell was going on, sure that she had been part of the kidnapping.

"You were sent by the dragon king, no doubt," she observed, putting the hammer back on her belt, noting the inquisitive look on the Crimson Guard's face. "Don't worry about that, I carry it with me all the time. It's the easiest way to test if a tooth is rotten at the core. A couple of gentle taps is normally all it takes."

"Ahh," sighed the dragon agent in understanding. "And yes, I was sent by the king, to take all three of you into custody. Now though, I'm not sure if that's what's required. I was under the impression that you were working with these goons?"

Puffing out her cheeks whist fighting off the mixture of emotion that had been threatening to consume her for some time now, made a thousand times worse in the last minute or so by the demise of the being known to the world as Santa, the Tooth Fairy tried her best to explain.

"The m... m... magic, I think it's all worn off now."

"Magic?" asked Flash. "What magic?"

"We'd all met up at a bar in dragon domain Singapore, something we do two or three times a year in various gin joints around the world. All was fine to start with, but one by one, we all started to feel... not so much ill, but... STRANGE! Odd in itself because as you'd expect, we're all very resilient and pretty much immune to everything supernatural, but, over the course of twenty minutes or so, our attitudes changed totally. For me, it was like having an out of body experience, my mind fully understanding what was going on, but not being in charge of either my body, or in particular, my mouth. And from where I was standing, it appeared exactly the same for the other two, although I can't be totally sure of that."

"I understand," said the Crimson Guard, nodding.

"Anyhow, the next thing I know there's all this talk of kidnapping Santa. At that point, I absolutely couldn't believe it... any of it. But not only did the talk continue, so did our actions. My body, much as I fought against it, went along with everything that was suggested, no matter how abhorrent I found it. I fought with everything I had, but nothing would respond, not my mouth, not my arms or legs... nothing. It was as if I were a passenger, just along for the ride. And I'm guessing you know the rest, which has unfortunately led us here. Oh and neat trick by the way, slowing down time. How'd you do that?"

"Ummm..." smiled the Crimson Guard, "I think that's for another... TIME! I do have to ask though, how did you find Santa's lair? My understanding was that she was very much a loner, her base of operations not known to anyone, even those closest to her."

"It was the strangest thing, the moment I lost control of all my faculties I just knew where she was. Not only could I see the local area amongst all that jungle, and feel the magic camouflaging the entrance, but on a worldwide scale I could pinpoint her exact location. If I didn't know it to be impossible, I would say that it was programmed into the magic that we were struck by."

"Why do you think you're free of it now, while your two mates still seem to be under its influence?"

"Honestly... I don't know. But if I had to guess, and that's all it would be, something tells me that whatever hex or spell we were hit by didn't quite have as much control over me as it did over them. All the time things were going on, I knew what we were doing was bad, tried my best to rally against it and felt, well, still feel, terrible. Those two," she said gesturing towards Cupid and the Easter Bunny, "seemed to lose all their inhibitions and drop even further down the rabbit hole, so to speak, no pun intended."

"Interesting..." whispered Flash, wondering what to do next.

"What's going to happen now? Am I going to jail?"

"I don't think so, but for the moment we'll have to take you into custody and almost certainly back to the capital."

"London?"

"Yep."

"A common stomping ground of mine. In fact I was just there the other week, ready to catch the crown that dropped out of the Prime Minister's mouth as he slept... got a great price for that one, set me up for a month that did."

"Lucky you."

"Oh there's nothing lucky about it, I assure you."

That Flash could believe.

"What's going to happen to...?" said the Tooth Fairy in a wobbly sort of voice, gesticulating in Polkinghorne's direction.

'A good question,' thought the Crimson Guard, 'a very good question.'

Throughout the world, dragon magic triumphed over what would normally be happening at this time of year, but only just, and only because of three factors. The first was the sheer number of students acting out this parody, the second, the unconquerable strength of will and almost infinite amount of magic belonging to For'son, the presence trapped inside the king's ring and thirdly, because quite frankly all the dragons, from Richie, Tank, Peter, the *tors*, right down to each year group of students themselves were all working together, acting as one big team. That was all that held back the chaos and mayhem.

And still the effort continued, now with fewer pranks and more focus. Despite being dragons, all those involved were becoming weary now, each having dedicated so much magic and focus to the effort, it had started taking its toll. Occasional mistakes were made, mainly with regard to presents in the right house etc, but there were others as well. In some of the bigger cities, Santa wannabes got confused about their routes and supposed areas; on one occasion in Berlin this led to an all out fight between two groups, with the youngsters reverting back to their original prehistoric forms, battling it out in the air, tossing fireball after fireball at each other, forgetting who, and more importantly, WHERE they were and the consequences of their actions. A clean up squad of King's Guards were immediately dispatched from the nearest barracks with a view to wiping the short term memories of the humans that had witnessed the goings on. Luckily for them, it only had to be this way for half a dozen or so of their charges on the surface, probably because of the late hour and the importance of the night itself.

Things were never easy, at least not when creatures with magic went bad, not in his experience anyway, and being a Crimson Guard, Flash had had a lot of occasions to dwell on exactly that. And so it came time to make a decision as to what happened next. Whilst pondering that, he'd already called for backup, not to help take down the Easter Bunny and Cupid, because given how they were now trapped in the cloud of slowed time, he could pretty much take them down whenever he wanted to. NO! It was more about extraction and getting both of them and the Tooth Fairy (who he was now one hundred percent certain had shaken off all effects of the magic she'd been afflicted by) back to the capital so they could all be assessed and tested to see what had caused the outbreak of... WHAT? Madness? Could be... An accident of some kind? Maybe... Or something else, something much more... subtle and insidious. It could be any of these or some combination of them all, he supposed. It wouldn't have been too much of a surprise. But whatever it was, it had to be prevented from happening again. Too much was at stake, he thought, looking across at the cadaver of the beautiful human shaped Polkinghorne, blue in the face and still bound and gagged. Which led him on to his next quandary... what to do with her? Something respectful for sure, although what he just didn't know. But he knew someone that did and that ate away at him more than a little. So far he hadn't revoked the time-slowing mantra, not because he wanted to leave Cupid and the Easter Bunny under its influence until a local contingent of King's Guards got here to escort them back to the capital... no, not that. It was more about the *tor*, the one whose company he'd begun to accept and enjoy over the course of the time they'd spent together. Pulling him out of there would break his heart, having to deal with the death of his friend, and so he wanted to leave it as long as possible to spare Vimes having to deal with THAT! Part of him though, knew this to be wrong and that one way or the other, the *tor* and the rest of the planet would have to face up to the death of the one being they all loved dearly... SANTA! With that in mind, he decided to bring his friend back to reality, despite the cost.

"Stand back," he said to the Tooth Fairy, circling the mantra that he'd cast only a short while ago, assessing how best to go about things.

"Do you want some help? I can block the projectiles so that your friend remains safe?"

"How are you going to do that?"

"Easy, I'll just toss a couple of teeth out in front of them. I always carry a few spares with me."

"Teeth are tiny and are never going to stop either of

those two things," argued Flash, wondering if the effects of whatever supernatural power she was suffering from had driven her a bit doolally.

"You silly boy," she chided, "not human teeth, that's never going to work. Dragon teeth!"

"And you carry those on you?" asked the dragon agent, now sure that she'd totally lost the plot.

"Of course," she said, reaching into her belt before pulling out two pristine white incisors that started quite wide before tapering off into deadly sharp points, in total about two centimetres long.

"What are they from, the smallest dragon in the world?"

"Watch and learn," she quipped, throwing one high up into the air off to Flash's left, away from the other three stuck in the time distorting pink and purple hued, ethereal energy.

Tumbling over upon itself, cutting through the cool brisk air of the chamber, the bright white tooth, clearly from an apex predator, albeit a tiny one, reached the top of the arc on its trajectory and in one giant POP became exactly what she'd said it was... a dragon tooth, about one hundred times the size it had previously been.

Flash was gobsmacked and stood there wide-eyed, that is until the loud CRASH of the, by now, huge tooth smashing into the cold hard floor startled him back to reality.

"How...?"

"You have your magical secrets, quite clearly," smiled the Tooth Fairy, nodding her head in the direction of the time-slowing cloud that still had the others in its grasp, "and I have mine."

'Good enough,' thought the Crimson Guard, finally coming to an understanding as to how it should be done.

"Okay, you block off the projectiles and I'll deal with the psycho twins."

That made her smile, despite everything.

"I'm at your command," she replied.

But before they could get on with things, she flapped her tiny wings and hovered right over to his false human shape and much to his surprise forced his mouth open wide with both her tiny hands. Then she had a good old rummage around inside.

"Aaarrghhggh, aarrghhgghh, aaarrrrhghhgh," was all that came out as he tried to protest.

Prodding and poking a bit more, much to his dismay, eventually she let go, leaving the Crimson Guard frantically rubbing his jaw, wondering what the hell was going on.

"You need to clean your teeth more regularly," she said in a voice that was more of an order than a request.

"This form is a disguise and doesn't need its teeth cleaning regularly," he replied, disappointed, sure that she would have known that.

"What did we just talk about? I'm not referring to your charming strong man masquerade. I'm talking about your big, bold, do or die natural prehistoric form... the dragon one, idiot!"

"How on earth can you look into my mouth like this and know what state my dragon teeth are in?" Flash retorted, slightly irritated now, more at the fact that she was right on the money than anything else.

"Who am I and what's my job?"

"Fair enough," he mumbled after a short, awkward silence.

"Good," she answered, "and don't forget to floss."

Turning away so that she couldn't see, he rolled his eyes. "Let's do this shall we?"

Slowly, the Crimson Guard strolled around the periphery of the very special Christmas mantra that he'd cast until he found himself behind Cupid, who was still poised behind his bow, and the Easter Bunny who was covered in thick, gooey patches of chocolate, his fur clumped together in places, a manic grin etched into his bunny face, his long white ears pricked up and standing tall, waiting to see just how much damage his magically flung carrot would do.

Nodding in the direction of the Tooth Fairy, once she'd returned the gesture, he dispelled the magic.

Within the pink and purple bubble, cloud, call it want you want, time resumed with a vengeance, the wicked projectiles both speeding blurs, both looking to finish off the frozen and terrified *tor*. Timing it to absolute perfection, a tooth in each hand, the enchanted and enchanting Tooth Fairy worked her tradecraft, throwing both tiny teeth like little hand grenades in the path of the arrow and the vegetable. Two simultaneous POPs later, and much to the surprise of the evil perpetrators, BOOM, both projectiles were intercepted by the full size dragon teeth that had materialised in mid-air, and Vimes was very much able to breathe a sigh of relief. But things didn't stop there. Wondering what the hell was going on, and rightly so, Cupid and the Bunny looked on in utter astonishment as, from their vantage point, the intruder that a mere moment ago had been covered from head to toe in chocolate and stuck in place by their ambush was now nowhere to be seen, the only sign that he'd been there at all being a smashed up pile of the sweet treat in his place, very much resembling a small mound of rubble. And that led the evil twins to both have the same thought simultaneously.

'Uh oh.'

They were right to think that because they were in a whole world of trouble. Two ancient words, a dollop of his ethereal birthright, emboldened by most of his willpower sent a series of zigzagging lines of pure bright green electrical energy scything through the air from his fingertips, crossing the ten metres between him and his quarry in about a thousandth of a second, giving his prey, (yes, that's now exactly what they were, oh how the tables had been turned) absolutely no chance to react. Burying itself deep in their backs, the noise from their agonising screams of pain as they dropped to their feet was terror inducing and beyond anything that the Crimson Guard had heard in a long, long time, especially from the bunny whose howls were high pitched enough to have shattered glass. Luckily, there was none. Saying that though, he didn't stop, well... not straight away, figuring that these two, despite probably being under some enthrallment or other, still needed to be taught a lesson, particularly given the consequences of their actions, the body of which sat lifeless off in the corner for all of them to see.

Although not affected by the crackling, hissing and wriggling lightning currently being drilled into the backs of the two psychopathic maniacs, the *tor* dropped to his knees, covering his ears with his hands as he did so, barely able to think, that's how bad it was, never having heard a sound like it. And then from his prone position on the floor, out of the corner of one eye, he caught sight of her, arrows protruding out of almost every body part, blood pooling around her wounds and on the floor, the slightly baggy red and white Santa suit dirty and stained, her elegant pale freckled face mired in teardrops and dried blood, having taken on a slightly blue trace. Mind in tatters, the ear splitting noise of Flash's magical assault in the background, all Vimes could think of was... HER! Their time together in the nursery ring... first friends, then best friends and then... WHAT? For him it was so much more, they always seemed to complement one another perfectly, to know what the other was thinking, down to the point that they could finish one another's sentences. And he was sure it was more than just him imagining things, that their regard (or no doubt as he probably meant, but was too caught up to either say, or think it... LOVE!) for each other had been there all the time, with each only having eyes for the other. Perhaps it had been the job, he wondered as tears raced down his much darker skinned cheeks, weaving in and out of the lightly grown stubble, the liquid sadness constantly looking for the path of least resistance.

As the harsh sound stopped and silence returned, apart from the excruciating groans of pain from the instigators in this whole sorry affair, ignoring the smell of not only spent magic but roasted bunny as well, the heartbroken and shattered *tor* stumbled to his feet and staggered across to the chair holding the cadaver that had been the love of his life. Body on autopilot, he quickly untied Polkinghorne's corpse, removed the blood soaked gag and all the time holding on to her, slid down to the cold hard floor, his back against the crumbling and uneven wall. Landing with a BUMP, he cradled her cool broken body in his lap, inundating her with his tears, whispering to her that he loved her and that he wished not only had he got there sooner, but that he'd revealed how he felt about her a long time ago. Rocking back and forth, it was the saddest sight you'll ever see on a day that should be filled with hope, optimism, potential and excitement.

Tough, steely, hard as nails were all suitable descriptions of the Crimson Guard, things that he had to be because of his occupation, honed over the course of decades by the most brutal and rigorous training regime possible. Death, destruction and shattered lives were almost part of his daily routine, so familiar was he with the lot of them. Here and now though, it almost broke his heart as he glanced across to the corner of the room to see Vimes cradling Polkinghorne's broken body, rocking back and forth, teardrops streaming from his eyes, uttering absolute nonsense, the pain evident, the *tor* totally and utterly destroyed. Keeping an eye on the prisoners, briefly Flash wondered what he could have done differently. Could they have got here quicker? He didn't see how, not without transforming and flying in their dragon forms, something that was forbidden because just too many of the humans would have caught sight of them, more than could have had their memories wiped. Then what? Should he have just come storming in here, all guns blazing in one all out gung-ho attack? With hindsight that might have been a possibility, but with no actual way to know just who, or how many of them were in here, it would have gone against every protocol he'd ever been taught, and that was something that he just couldn't have done. Aware that the king would be pissed at losing Santa on his watch and that over the course of time the humans would no doubt suffer the consequences, guilt and a profound sense of sadness bubbled up inside him at having failed on what, crucially, had probably turned out to be his most high profile mission ever. Strolling purposefully over to Cupid and the Easter Bunny, both currently face down on the cool, dirty floor, the Crimson Guard dispassionately pulled out a series of plastic binders from the belt around his waist, and attaching them to the magical monsters' wrists and ankles, used the last set to bind them together, leaving them hog tied on the floor, barely able to move, grumbling in agony from the magic he'd used against them, their minds still unable to come to terms with how he'd escaped their chocolatey ambush and thoroughly turned the tables on them.

Looking on, torn up inside at the part that she'd played in all this, despite it not being her fault, no doubt under the control of some seriously dark magic, sparkling tear drops with just a hint of pink plummeted to the ground from the Tooth Fairy's draped head, so disgusted with herself that she just couldn't look at the deceased body of a being she considered one of her own. Although they hadn't known each other because, as was rumoured, Santa always liked to keep herself to herself, in a great many ways their jobs and the magic used in them were very similar indeed. Of course Christmas was on a much greater scale, with it being the pinnacle of annual supernatural trickery, on the surface anyway, but as far as she was concerned, all magical creatures had to stick together, no matter who or what they were, hence one of the reasons for the reasonably regular meet ups with Cupid and the Easter Bunny in the first place. Here and now though, she felt as bad as she ever had, the consequences of her actions covered in red and soaked in blood in the corner of the room, so much so that there and then she considered her position, and I'm not talking about hovering mid-air off to one side.

'Perhaps,' she thought, 'the time has come for the Tooth Fairy to retire and let the humans deal with everything teeth related. It would be touch and go to start with, but they'd probably get the hang of it after a few years.' It wouldn't be the same, of that there could be little doubt, but after what had just happened, maybe her particular brand of the supernatural was best off just fading quietly into history. Right here, right now, deep inside that buried room, grief, sorrow and a despondency the likes of which had rarely been seen in the history of the planet, sucked away all hope, not just for those individuals there, but for the entire dragon and human races as well.

Deep below ground at the king's private residence in dragon domain London a cold dark shiver, which for any dragon was a painful experience to say the least, unexpectedly washed over George, the dragon monarch, dropping him back in his chair just as he rose to his feet in an effort to top up his drink. Curling up into a ball he attempted to stave off the shadowy taint that had him firmly in its grip, at first by rubbing his human shaped arms and legs vigorously, and then by applying all his magical mental barricades, which succeeded to some degree, but not fully. Awake now, whereas before he'd been a little dozy, his vast experience assured him of one thing, that the situation in Thailand must have very much gone south and that despite having his most courageous, inventive and loyal agent on hand, the death of Santa hadn't been prevented. In his mind he swore loudly, fully aware of the future ramifications for the human race. Turning this around, he knew, would be all but impossible. Shaking his head at the impossibility of it all, one singular teardrop plummeted from his left eye, creating the smallest splash in the world atop the stunning oak table that he sat at, next to his empty glass. Even here in this most optimistic of places, the home of a leader that always gave his all, used whatever resources were available to him to make the human way of life better in an attempt to not only guide them along the right path, but protect them from themselves and keep them safe as a race, faith, expectation and aspiration had been gobbled up by the darkness in an instant, snatched unexpectedly away, replaced by a hole that could never be filled. All thoughts of a new drink having disappeared, the dragon monarch closed his eyes, leant back in his chair and drifted off into nothingness, because... that's all that was left.

Upstairs Michael, Caroline, Meghan and Rhianne all slept soundly in the small terraced house not far from the centre of Salisbridge on the earth's surface, the biting cold outside stayed by thick, comfortable duvets and in the case of the children, cosy warm blankets all tucked in rigorously. The only illumination in the entire house were the twinkling Christmas lights on the tree downstairs in the living room, under which sat a myriad of lovingly wrapped presents for the girls. Abruptly and without anyone being there to see it happen, the lights dimmed by about half. That wasn't totally unusual in itself, but the fact that they didn't return to their normal state was. Unfortunately, it didn't end there. What should have been a one off occurrence was anything but, with lights on trees and festive illuminations in general, across the world, all following suit, almost as if the bulbs inside them knew what had happened, realising that this might very well be their last outing.

Dragon students across the land, with the vast majority of their work already completed, started to get lazy and complacent. Presents were delivered to the wrong houses, drinks were spilled on carpets, reindeer disappeared, Santa flying with far fewer than the preferred eight, and the wish mantra started to dry up, much to the youngsters' bemusement and concern. Back at the nursery rings, *tors* and those higher up started to panic, not knowing what to make of things. There had been no adjustments, no one had fooled around with any of the settings and the students themselves, all of them out there doing the hard work, had been checked to see if it was something they'd done. But that simply wasn't the case. Quickly the grumbles became rumbles, with one or two mentions that the power supply from the iconic ring belonging to the monarch must be at fault. It could be only that. With the levels of distress and anxiety in the nursery rings ramping up with every second that passed, these worries were communicated with the three friends (and of course For'son, the presence that defined the enigmatic band) in Malaysia, over and over again, from different parts of the planet.

"What's going on?" asked Tank with his consciousness, addressing the ring itself.

After a slight pause, For'son replied.

"It's not me. I've checked, double checked and then rechecked again. The power is still there, as much as it was, all available for them to use."

'If not that, then what?' the youngster wondered, as confused as he'd ever been.

It had been rhetorical that's for sure, but as Tank considered what he'd said only in his mind, there was a noticeable and concerning silence which stood out like a hippy at a wellington boot convention. And so he just had to ask.

"What is it?"

Silence!

"For'son, please, do you know what's happening?"

"No," replied the unfathomable band truthfully.

"But..."

"I can hazard a guess."

"And?"

"You won't like it or want to hear it."

"Please..."

Conceding defeat and really not wanting to voice his

concerns, with his magic spread out across the planet via the crystal node network he could already feel the ethereal tide of power across the vastness of the earth shift in ways that he didn't recognise. Only something totally and utterly monumental could cause such a thing. It didn't take a genius to guess exactly what that was.

"I think Santa, or Polkinghorne as we now know her to be, has... DIED!"

There, he'd said it and despite being stuck firmly in an inanimate object, it filled him with sadness and disappointed him no end to do so.

"WHAT?!" exclaimed Tank, his conscious will a conflicted mixture of emotions.

Surprise, anger, fear, dread, loss and devastation all ran riot, muddling his memory, causing him to cry out loud, which was surprising for his two dragon friends to hear because they hadn't been privy to the conversation with the king's private confidante.

"Are you okay?" asked Peter.

"Tank?" queried Richie.

Swallowing nervously, still torn up inside, his burly false human face unsure of how to react, choosing instead to try and display everything that he felt all at once, the biggest of all three of them by quite some margin when they were in their natural prehistoric guises searched for the words to convey what he'd just been told.

"That's not possible!" replied Richie, after her friend had relayed the information.

"I'm not buying it," babbled Peter, really not wanting it to be true.

And then to the complete and utter surprise of all three of them, the shock from which nearly knocked them all to the floor, the enigmatic band spoke up, this time not within Tank's psyche, but out loud so that they all could hear.

"ENOUGH! What I've told you is my best guess from twenty thousand years of experience, and yes, that's how old I am," stated For'son, as forensically as possible. "Santa dying isn't something that I'd even dare to suggest if I didn't believe it with all my being. But what's happening across the world is nothing short of historic and colossal in its nature. The cause of something of such magnitude can only be tied to the death of a legend, one that will hit the earth and her population hard. There is simply no other explanation."

With a thousand questions running around their minds, not least about the ring, its age and how it could speak out loud, the friends all attempted to comprehend what had happened and the effect it would have on the future. One of them was switched on enough to speak up.

"Is there anything we can do?" asked the brave and intelligent female amongst them.

"I would suggest," replied the ring, "that you choose a god, any god, and start praying to them, because as far as I can see that's the only thing that's going to save us now." And just so you know, dragons, for the most part, do not believe in any kind of deity or benevolent creator, so that's how desperate things were.

Across the globe as Christmas Eve came and went, turning into Christmas morning, the magic, started to fade and disperse, not of its own accord, even though the dragon students were still trying to use and apply it. Pockets of time drifted up into the atmosphere where they could do no harm, after all the chances of them hitting an aeroplane on this day of all of them was remote at best, something like lottery winning odds. Reindeer mantras sizzled and fizzled out, unable to be brought back into existence even though the students tried, and materialising anything became all but impossible.

With all that going on, through no fault of his own, For'son, the mysterious and ancient manifestation within the exquisite piece of jewellery that belonged to the rightful king of the dragon domain, reined in the power he was sending out across the network, knowing that now he could not do anything to change the course of events.

All that was left was the supernatural ethereal energy seeking out the wishes. It remained in small patches and swirls as was its wont, occasionally seeking out the mind of a human child if their desire and will was strong enough, but for the most part now it ignored the yearning that would previously have seen presents created out of thin air or fancies fulfilled on just a whim. Hope had taken a long, deep breath, and then just given up... but not quite everywhere.

Dragons had roamed the world for as long as time could remember, long before men lived in caves with crude paintings, able at that point to cut through the skies at will, fly anywhere they wanted, the apex predator of the planet, their only real match being others of their own kind. It was a primitive and much simpler age where disagreements were settled with aerial duels, blazing fireballs, the raking of talons and the snapping of jaws. Some would say it was a crude era, but others would describe it as much more straightforward. You knew where you stood, which today was sometimes hard to fathom. And then, over the centuries, the prehistoric flying monsters started to discover the magic of their birthright, bestowed upon them by the gods, or at least so some thought, which enabled them to bring their dreams to life, limited only by their imagination. Eventually and through much spilt blood, an age of cooperation and understanding began with the world, at around For'son's time, coming under one complete dragon banner, united for the good of all, at least in dragon terms anyway, and at a moment when mankind had taken the first baby step towards fulfilling its potential. Of course there was the prophecy agreement that allied many of the magical races, but it also left some feeling like outcasts, never a good thing. As well as securing the future of the ape-like humans and avoiding a bloody worldwide confrontation, it also did something from which the planet may well not have recovered. What does all this have to do with the present predicament our protagonists find themselves in, I hear you ask? Everything!

What I've been trying to tell you is that magic in all its shapes, forms, colours, sizes and potencies has been present for many tens of thousands of years. Dragons, the planet's de facto leaders, have been primarily responsible for most of it, but not all. Other ancient races exist in far away, hidden places that use their fair share of it, albeit with a slightly different taint and texture. Over the course of all that time, not one tiny part of the earth has remained free of its supernatural touch. Magic has been everywhere! And what most beings, including dragons (although there is one old and clever enough to at least suspect this might be the case... no names, shopkeeper) don't actually know, is that when a mantra, spell, hex, call it what you want, is cast, not all of the supernatural ethereal energy is consumed. An inordinate amount remains, intact and just floating about unseen, with some of it leeching into the ground while an unspecified quantity remains entangled around the molecules of the air, hanging vicariously, invisible to absolutely all, waiting for... WHAT? Perhaps to be put to good use.

Should hope just be allowed to flutter off into the distance, unhindered and undisturbed? Is it just supposed to be as easy as that? Surely a being as renowned as Santa deserves something more, a last hurrah maybe or a final farewell? And it wasn't as if the blood line continued, as Polkinghorne had no children or family of any sort left to pass the mantle on to, something that her very special Christmas magic might have allowed much later on in her life. It really did look well and truly like it was the end of Father Christmas.

A refusal to accept the inevitable, that's what was needed, just one tiny spark, one act of rebellion against the cold heart of the universe itself. If that could be found then, just maybe, hope could be reignited. But how and where would it start? Watch and learn.

Sobbing uncontrollably like a distraught baby longing for its mother, Vimes was as lost as it was possible to be, at least in his mind. Caught up in the past, he cursed himself for not being brave enough to act and confess his true feelings to Polkinghorne back then. Young and too afraid, it was a combination that had cost him dearly, with him only now paying the price of his mild and meek manner. But as that realisation metaphorically hit him square in the face, the tiniest inkling of insurgence bubbled up through the clouded mess of his psyche and asserted its authority, much to his surprise.

NO!

That's how it started, here in Thailand in the cool stone room buried into the side of the mountain, with the battered and broken *tor*, rising up against all that had happened.

What good is that I hear you ask? On its own, not much, but you see, it very much wasn't alone. There was more to come... much, much more.

The dreams of the two gorgeous sleeping girls in the darkened terrace house in the city of Salisbridge were abruptly interrupted by simply one word, something the elder knew to use wisely, with her sibling being far too young to understand. Nevertheless, it stood out in the middle of their minds.

NO!

In the room next door, Michael and Caroline lay fast asleep, one of them snoring but it was hard to say which one. Without barely a sound and remaining in the land of nod, the two of them simultaneously whispered, "NO!"

Deeply lost in the thoughts of his responsibilities in his private residence in the dragon domain's capital of London, suddenly George, the monarch of this planet, unbeknown to the humans, was startled awake, his eyes opening as wide as they'd go, instantly alert, magic sizzling just below the surface of his preferred human form. One word popped into the front of his mind. A compunction grabbed hold of him, like none he'd ever experienced before and forced him to say it out loud.

"NO!"

Inexplicably, back in Santa's hidden lair deep within the Malaysian jungle, the three dragon friends, Richie, Tank and Peter, all in chorus with one another, mouthed the word.

"NO!"

As if that in itself wasn't strange enough, unexpectedly a familiar voice that wasn't his own spoke in a very matter-of-fact way across the depths of Tank's psyche.

"NO!"

Tank, hugely surprised, wondered what the hell was going on, but not nearly as much as his current partner in crime, the ring's ancient and omnipotent presence, For'son who for once, hadn't a clue. Anything that could compel him to do something against his will was mighty powerful, of that you can be totally sure.

Back in the cool room buried beneath the mountain, the one with Vimes cradling what was left of Polkinghorne's body on the brutal stone floor in one corner, Flash and the Tooth Fairy locked eyes momentarily, looking on, both intrigued and alarmed, as both of them at once firmly said the word out loud.

"NO!"

And that was just the beginning, as that one word raced around the planet like a Mexican wave without the sombreros and tortilla chips. Children whispered it in their sleep, new born babies of course couldn't mouth it, but they thought it, much like Rhianne back in Salisbridge, giving what was going on that extra little bit of impetus. Adults everywhere whispered it, some in their sleep, others still hard at work in all sorts of trades. Bartenders answered their customers with it, truck drivers suddenly blurted it out in the middle of singing along to their favourite song on the radio, taxi drivers uttered it for no apparent reason, whether they had a fare or not, along with countless numbers of others.

But it didn't stop there, oh... well, I'm not going to say it this time. Just like their king, dragons below ground started, for no (there it is again) apparent reason saying the word, no matter where they were or what they were doing. Travellers on the monorail across the globe all belted it out simultaneously, much to their utter astonishment, the word piercing the ears of carriages full of the prehistoric monsters. It echoed throughout the totally modern and impeccably well run council building that didn't stop for anything and worked at full pace twenty four hours a day, three hundred and sixty five days a year. Security was called to see what the hell was going on. Flying dragons, working dragons, sleeping dragons, those at play and rest, all in the middle of what they were doing mouthed, spoke or in some cases, even shouted that word.

On the outskirts of the capital, deep below ground, a dragon with the snore of an elephant with sinusitis rolled over onto his back in a bed almost the size of a tennis court, sat up sharply, the stripy nightcap on his head nearly losing purchase, the thick plastic glasses that had been still attached to his face tumbling off to one side, and without knowing why, shouted at the top of his voice... "NO!" Awake, stunned, but more intrigued than anything, the most famed master mantra maker in the land headed for the stairs that would take him down to the Emporium floor and more importantly the workshop because, despite not knowing exactly what was going on, he understood it was something momentous.

Those in nursery rings across the planet and the disguised Santas and reindeer who were still trying to ply their trade, with little luck due to the fading of the mantras they'd been using, all yelled that one tiny little word, leaving it ringing in the air, threatening to wake the human contingent they were trying to serve.

NO, NO, NO, NO, NO! It was everywhere, on every different continent, hanging in the air, little by little making itself known, a rallying cry for not only all of humanity, but the dragons as well. But a rallying cry for what?

Imagine all that spent magic over tens of thousands of years, just hanging harmlessly around in the air. You breathe it, walk through it, tread it into your house, it attaches itself to your clothes, fills your car, inundates your hair, sits on the food that you eat, mixes with the fabulous concoctions that you drink and settles upon you when you sleep. It's everywhere, sitting benign, invisible to the naked eye or any kind of technology that the humans possess, waiting perhaps for exactly this moment.

As that singular word echoed around the atmosphere of the planet, gathering up speed and momentum, it shifted everything, scattering clouds and winds, arranging some of the residual mantras that all the dragon students had been using much earlier in the night. Unbelievably, nearly all of that was swept towards the unremarkable mountain range in Thailand, the one where all hope had been lost, inadvertently being drawn to the wishes of those inside, who all wanted the same thing, one so much more than the others.

Dragon magic is powerful, maybe even the most powerful there is, but as I've already said the residual ethereal energy left lying about is made up from every different ancient race and mythical creature that's ever stalked the earth. Nagas, manticores, mer-folk, ra-hoon, basilisks, the heretics of Antar and the Hydra Queen to name but a few have all left remnants of the ancient supernatural power that they consider their birthright. Right at this very moment all those stray molecules of magic were waking up, being nudged in the direction of a purpose, by who or what it was hard to say, but unmistakably, it was happening.

After having dulled for a short while, the illuminations and Christmas tree lights in every household, everywhere, were all startled into life, brightening up house by house, shop front by shop front, street sign by street sign, dazzling with their radiance, becoming far more intense than they'd originally been, all on hearing that word and recognising the mutiny that the world was staging against the being known as Fate and her friend Inevitability.

Flash, the brilliant, heroic and dedicated Crimson Guard, and the Tooth Fairy glanced across at each other, sharing a look, one that said something along the lines of, "Oh my, this is something special. What on earth is going on?" Feeling the taint of the supernatural filling the room, both beings knew that it was too late to act, not that they would probably have wanted to, had they known the true purpose of the rallying cry.

It started in the corner filled with sadness, the one where Vimes sat slumped on the floor, arms wrapped fully around his friend's cadaver. A pinprick of light blossomed into being from nothing. Instantly it grew and changed colour, appearing right next to the *tor's* salty, tear stained face, the little hint of green that it gave off more than a little eerie. Snuffling like a pig on the scent of truffles, Vimes turned towards the single dot of light, wondering what the hell was going on. And he wasn't the only one, as Flash and the Tooth Fairy stood dumbstruck only a short way away.

Staring at the emerald glow only a hand's width away from him, his mind just could not make sense of what was happening, not because he didn't know, but because he simply didn't care. Within not only his body but his psyche as well, there was absolutely nothing going on, no comprehension of any sort, no understanding, almost as if his intellect had gone into standby mode. The only thing happening across the whole of his false form was one single desire, all encompassing and all empowering. As you could have guessed, it was his wish to have his friend back.

Across the globe the air ignited, an orange and yellow fiery flame sparking into life for but a brief moment, using the dormant magical molecules as fuel before converting it into energy. Every molecule, everywhere... houses, cars, offices, shops, in the sea, on the land... EVERYWHERE awoke, burned brightly and then moved on, and on and on until nearly all the earth's surface had caught fire. Only this wasn't just any fire, this was the combination of all that magic, made up from all those different races. For starters, it wasn't combustible, meaning that it couldn't physically set fire to any real world item or property... thank goodness, otherwise the world would be done for. And as I've already said, each one only lasted a fraction of a second. But burn they did, causing an extreme amount of magical power to race around the globe in almost the blink of an eye, that, with the guidance from the rallying cry made by all those beings, focused the tip of all the generated ethereal energy on one specific spot. Yes, you've guessed it... that mountain range in Thailand, and in particular the wishes of one being above all others because his need stood out like the sun cutting through a misty dawn.

As the eerie emerald light reflected off the *tor's* tear

slicked face, suddenly a multitude of POP, POP, POP, POPPING echoed around the room as hundreds, no thousands, no, hundreds of thousands, by now millions of similar small, bright lights burst into existence, breaking not only the silence but the laws of physics as well.

Flash and the Tooth Fairy stood rooted to the spot, unable to believe what they were seeing. In Vimes' case it wasn't so much that he couldn't believe, it was just that he didn't care... not one damn bit.

As every possible free space within the room became filled with these mysterious, glowing green lights, outside something could be heard off in the distance. Starting as a faint rumble, slowly it gathered pace, causing the earth to shake ever so slightly, swaying the jungle canopy, causing animals in all their shapes and sizes to panic and flee. Inside the room buried into the side of the mountain, the hastily erected lights flickered uncontrollably before dying altogether as the walls themselves trembled. It didn't matter though, as the glow from the millions of tiny green embers allowed them all to see just fine. Dust and fragments of brick from the decaying walls scattered into what little space was left in the air. Cupid and the Easter Bunny, both hog tied face down on the floor, quivered and cowered, terrified of everything going on around them. The Crimson Guard, about to ignite his magic in the form of a magnificently powerful personal shield that would encompass all of him and offer a modicum of protection, instinctively reined back his action, keeping the words at the front of his mind, ready to be deployed in an instant should he need to, waiting to see exactly what was about to play out, sure for some reason that it would be nothing bad, even though he didn't know why.

In between the trees, houses, villages, the water, the land and of course the air, everything burned. Not in a combustible way, it was just the remaining magic giving itself up in billions of tiny fiery flashes so that it could be converted into energy. And that all encompassing, huge wave of power and blinking light was now converging on Santa's position, heading straight for what was left of her, guided by the unusual green luminescence beneath the mountain, powered on by the now thunderous roar of nearly the whole world rebelling against what Fate had in store for the legendary being. Bowing trees back over on themselves, almost to the point of the canopies touching the ground, scattering lizards, monkeys, birds and a variety of insects in every direction, the periphery of the wave struck the outside of the bolt hole beneath the mountain that all six beings found themselves trapped in.

With a deafening BOOM, the ground beneath them all shuddered, knocking Flash off his feet, dumping him unceremoniously on the floor, joining both the bunny and the cruel archer, both of whom had unwittingly set in motion the events that had led up to this moment. Hovering in the air, the Tooth Fairy was abruptly whipped around viciously... that being said she did just about manage to avoid the worst of it. Slumped in the corner, through wide eyes the devastated *tor* gripped the body of his friend for all he was worth as all around him things went straight to hell. Following hot on the heels of the preceding physical wave, an almighty wall of noise flooded the chamber, sounding something along the lines of Noooooooooooooooooo, embodying the will of all those across the world who'd joined forces in their outrage at what had happened to Christmas, forcing all the beings there (except Polkinghorne of course) to cry out in terror and cover their ears with their hands, even Vimes who really didn't want to relinquish the grip he had on his love.

As the brickwork shook and dust filled the air, the all-powerful rallying cry and the energy from the defunct magic across the world combined with the emerald ethereal magic inside the chamber in what can only be described as a once in a lifetime event. Much to Vimes' horror, every single one of the millions upon millions of tiny green supernatural embers, in one fell swoop, flooded into Polkinghorne's shattered and bloody corpse, piercing her skin, heading straight inside. If the *tor* could have shouted out, he would have, but he was done, everything going on enough to have finally crushed his will and decimate any fight he had left. From the floor, Flash looked on in awe, reasonably sure he knew what would happen next. Fluttering in mid-air the Tooth Fairy did the same, recognising something wondrous and enchanting when she saw it.

Splayed out across Vimes' lap, Polkinghorne's body suddenly started to get exceedingly hot whilst simultaneously glowing bright green. It would appear that whatever supernatural activity was taking place had reached critical mass. A brief bright flicker and a momentary sparkle preceded an all out explosion of emerald radiance, forcing all those present to squeeze their eyes shut. Even through their eyelids the light still burned, that's how harsh it was. And as abruptly as it had arrived, it was GONE, the chamber returning back to the way it had been, dust settling all around, the only sound the rabbit-like squeals of the Easter Bunny and the distressed wailing of the matchmaking sharpshooter. Shaking his head and blinking uncontrollably in an effort to get his eyesight to return to normal after the blinding wave of light, Flash bounded to his feet, eager to get to grips with exactly what had gone on. Still hovering, wings going ten to the dozen, the Tooth Fairy looked around, waiting for her vision to clear.

Sitting on the floor, back against the cold, harsh wall, distraught beyond belief, Vimes kept his eyes closed in the hope that everything would vanish and that the world would swallow him up whole. That is, until the tiniest hint of movement across his right knee scared the living daylights out of him. Frightened by the thought of whatever it was, his eyes shot wide open just as he was about to jump to his feet. There and then, the need to do so evaporated like dew on a summer's day. Impulsively, she brought her arm up to her, by now, rosy red face, dragging it across something hard on the way, not knowing that the surface in question was the leg of her best friend, the one that she dreamed about hooking up with. Mechanically she exhaled, a brand new breath on the dawn of a brand new day, her body, mind and soul not only intact, but reconstructed and better than ever. Only then was she startled by a huge GASP from directly above her. Having not yet opened her eyes, still feeling her way around the new yet familiar body she now found herself in, she did just that and much to her amazement, ended up gazing fondly into the face of the one being on the planet who meant more to her than any other ever could... VIMES! Without hesitation, she brought her arms up around his neck and in one swift move, much to his surprise, pulled his head down towards hers and kissed him passionately on the lips.

'What the...?' he thought, sure that he was caught up in a dream.

But it felt so real, and there was a reason for that, because of course, it was!

As the kiss lingered on, washing away all the sadness and despair inside the confused *tor*, a glimpse over the love of his life's shoulder confirmed that which he now knew. It wasn't a dream, it was very much reality, a smile from his friend the Crimson Guard and the Tooth Fairy confirming just that, as they stood side by side, both with the biggest grins in the world etched onto their faces. And with that, the lovers' lips parted, the feel of her exotic breath sweeping across his false human face.

"You came for me," she whispered, looking a little out of place wearing the blood stained Santa suit.

"Always!" he replied.

As the seconds ticked by, the two continued to embrace, love having not only found a way, but the perfect match for each other. Only then did it occur to her, hitting her like a smith's hammer pounding an overworked fiery forge. Bouncing up to her feet, she pulled him up with her, shaking off the dust and debris that had been brought down upon them during all the commotion.

"What's the date?" she asked frantically, something gnawing at her insides.

"Christmas Eve or Christmas Day, depending on where in the world you are," answered Flash coolly.

"And you are?"

"His name is Flash and he's a Crimson Guard, one of the king's special agents. As well, he's... my friend."

That surprised Polkinghorne more than she would have ever thought, because she knew just how hard it was for Vimes to get to know others.

'This one must be special,' she mused. And she'd have been right.

"Great to meet you, Flash," she said cheerfully, eyeing up the Tooth Fairy suspiciously, which didn't go unnoticed.

"It's okay," ventured the Crimson Guard, "she helped us apprehend these two," he said, nodding in the direction of the Easter Bunny and Cupid, still bound up on the floor, "and has fully earned my trust. Some sort of dark magic turned them against you, of that much I'm sure. It's not affecting her now, but still, from what I can tell, has the other two in its grip. I'm going to make sure they get taken back to London so that we can investigate things further and hopefully free them from its grasp."

Polkinghorne nodded in understanding, before addressing the Tooth Fairy.

"Thank you for the assistance that you've rendered, it's much appreciated."

Swallowing nervously, the Tooth Fairy, despite her apprehension, attempted a reply.

"I... I... I'm sorry for what I did to you and sorry that I couldn't stop them. I tried as hard as I could, but whatever supernatural influence had me under its control, for a time, I just couldn't defeat it. I hope that one day you'll find it in your heart to forgive me for my part in all this and that perhaps we could be friends."

As silence hung in the air, everyone waited to see what Polkinghorne's response would be. They didn't have to wait long, but boy were they surprised.

It started off as a murmur, which quickly turned into an all out chuckle. After a matter of moments, the legendary being, a female dragon in the form of a human, responded as only she, or HE could.

"You don't have to wait for forgiveness. I forgive you here and now. All of you should know, Santa doesn't bear grudges, not now, not ever. And to answer your question, of course we can be friends, and that extends to you too, Flash. Anyone that this stunning dragon," at this point she punched Vimes firmly on the shoulder, in a fun loving, affectionate kind of way, "regards as a friend, will always be one to me."

Both the Tooth Fairy and Flash smiled back.

"But we need to get back to business. I have an inordinate amount of work to do and have absolutely no idea how I'm going to get it all done," declared Polkinghorne, her mind now focused fully on the job that she not only loved but gave her true meaning and purpose.

But her best friend and soul mate interrupted her train of thought by telling her what they'd become involved in and how the dragon students, right at this very moment, were doing all that they could to keep Christmas alive. To say she was stunned was something of an understatement.

"And you say that your friends are back at my base monitoring things as we speak?"

"Yes," replied the Crimson Guard, proud to be part of such a coming together across the planet.

"We need to get back there," Polkinghorne announced without further ado.

"There's a car hidden in the jungle not far away. We could be back there in a day or so," observed the *tor*, without taking his eyes off the one he loved.

"That won't do," she said sharply. "I need to be there now to see exactly what's going on."

"That's simply not possible," stated Flash, unable to think of anything supernatural that would give them even a chance of doing that.

But when you are the legend that she was, very little was out of the question.

"I can take us there now," she announced firmly, "but what do we do about these two?"

"They need to be taken back to London," replied Flash.

"Whereabouts?"

Not even thinking about withholding the sensitive information from Santa, something he wouldn't normally divulge to anyone at all, he willingly shared the location.

"There's a secret facility adjacent to the council building."

"The one below the massage parlour and hot pool palace, that one?"

"How the...?"

"Don't forget who I am and just what I can do," she ventured, all the time smiling. "Is there any particular cell you'd like them to appear in?"

Totally blown away, hardly able to imagine how such a thing was possible, and given everything he was capable of, that was saying quite something, the Crimson Guard just shook his head and mumbled,

"No... whichever one you like."

With just a tiny little click of her fingers and without any fuss at all, her magic fully returned, the bodies of the two mythical creatures, both of whom had nearly changed the course of history more dramatically than any other event ever could, disappeared completely, reappearing, much to the shock of the Crimson Guards stationed there, exactly where she had said. To say the others were taken aback was something of an understatement. But she wasn't finished there. Smiling, showing off her red rosy cheeks to them all, Polkinghorne raised her right arm, winked and then very loudly, this time, clicked her fingers. In a blaze of light, all four of them disappeared from existence.

Meanwhile, somewhere deep in a remote part of South America:

"REPORT!" demanded a harsh voice, one not to be messed with under any circumstances, something he knew from firsthand experience, despite having been sired by the being in question. "DID IT WORK?"

Fearing every second of delivering bad news, recalling what some of the consequences of doing so had entailed in the past, he swallowed apprehensively and decided to just spit it out and get it over with.

"I'm sorry, it failed. She's still alive and stronger than ever."

"HOW IS THAT POSSIBLE? You assured me that the enthrallment would succeed and that they'd kill her in the most horrific of ways. Just how has it gone so wrong?"

Visibly gulping and utterly terrified of his father's renowned temper, the being known as Manson tried to find the words to justify the failure he'd been complicit in.

"They don't know why the enthrallment didn't fully take, but for absolute certain there was magic involved, powerful magic."

"We need it to be unbreakable," he screamed at his son, "if our plans are to come to fruition."

"I know, I know... we'll get it right, I promise."

"Do you now, do you now?" replied Troydenn stalking forward towards his son, his prehistoric eyes filled with anger and rage. "Let's see if I can give you a little motivation to help, shall we say... spur you on."

The echoing screams from their incentive driven chat could be heard over a mile away.

In the confines of the hidden cave system deep in the jungle of Malaysia, the three dragon friends, Peter, Richie and Tank were doing their best to stay positive as everything in front of them started to fall apart. Much like the king back in his private residence in London, they could see the results created by the struggling pretend Santas and their disguised reindeer. With the magic having dissipated and For'son having withdrawn the almost limitless supply of mana that he had at his disposal, things were going straight to hell and there was absolutely nothing they could do about it. Christmas was ruined because the students had only managed to successfully cover about two thirds of the planet, and with the magic having worn off, all they could do was crawl back to their nursery rings, knowing that they'd given it their best shot, even though it hadn't been good enough. With it over, and having failed spectacularly at the end, the three friends all sat back in their chairs, deflated, demoralised and utterly disheartened.

"There was nothing more we could have done," observed Peter, sad that they'd let down some of the human population on the surface.

"Absolute ********," yelled Richie in frustration, punching the trunk of the nearest lemon tree to her.

"THAT," said a voice from out of the blue, "is one of my favourite plants. Please don't do that again!"

All of them whirled around, Richie and Tank with their magic at hand, ready to fight in the most inexperienced way possible, Peter too surprised to be of much use.

Simultaneously all three gasped, unable to believe what they were seeing. There, standing right behind them in the centre of the cavern that doubled as Santa's lair, next to the shiny, bright red sleigh, stood the famed and legendary being herself, Polkinghorne as they now knew her to be, along with Vimes, Flash and a tiny winged human who they all assumed because of their lessons on the subject, was none other than the Tooth Fairy.

Open mouthed and wide eyed, the three dragons just stood there catching flies, that is until Vimes bounded up to them all and enveloped them in the biggest hug of their lives, pleased to see all three of his brightest students again.

Appropriate or not, it was just what the trio needed, especially after receiving that kind of shock.

Pushing past the group hug, Polkinghorne slipped seamlessly into the seat in front of the monitor and began to quickly take in what had been going on.

Released from Vimes' embrace, the three Purbeck students quickly rushed over to Flash, each shaking his hand vigorously, all stating how happy they were to see him safe, before introducing themselves to the Tooth Fairy. Vimes on the other hand had taken up a standing position behind his love.

"How bad is it?" he asked, knowing full well that she was fully focused on Christmas now rather than anything of a more personal nature.

"Not that bad at all," she replied, happier than he'd expected. "Surprisingly, they've all done rather a good job."

"Thanks," shouted Richie from out in the main part of the cavern.

"You're welcome, youngsters," answered the female dragon dressed like a filthy drunken tramp in an alley wearing a beer and sweat stained, poorly fitting, second hand Father Christmas outfit.

"Is there anything we can do about the rest of the world?" asked Tank, focusing solely on what could be done now that the myth herself had returned from the grave.

"Do you know what," she replied, all rainbows and smiles, "I do believe there is."

Getting up from the chair, strolling straight past the soul mate whose conscious will and longing had saved her, she strolled down the cavern they were all in, the others following in her wake to the sound of the Tooth Fairy's wings beating like a bat out of hell. Reaching the gleaming red sleigh, the one that had been replicated across the planet with magic throughout the previous hours, gently she rubbed her delicate, pale white fingers across its mirror glaze finish, for the very first time noting the state of her outfit. Not done there, she turned to face the others, and in doing so closed her eyes, remaining as still as possible. Out of nowhere a shower of ethereal energy washed over her, transforming her suit immediately, making it look not only brand new, but special as well. Not stopping there, the baggy loose fitting jacket and pants had suddenly filled out, much like the rosy red cheeks that were now accompanied by a tangle of grey beard below and a pair of perfectly fitting gold rimmed glasses up above. Just to top things off, the being before them jiggled its belly like a bowl full of jelly and in its loudest voice possible, let out the one thing the world was desperate to hear, the one noise all those No's longed for.

"HO, HO, HO!"

Rapturous applause, well... as much as was possible given that there were only six beings there, greeted her performance, with the three young dragons all whooping and hollering, absolutely delighted by what they'd just seen.

Inside the ring, the presence that hadn't been introduced to Santa because there'd been so much going on, For'son, the ancient dragon wisdom trapped inside the magnificent band, gave a mental shout out, pleased that normality had returned and that the humans, their charges for a reason, could have their hope reignited and their wishes fulfilled. It was an emotional moment, but that's all it was... a moment. After that, there was work to be done.

"Now, if you'll excuse me, I have to get out there and finish what you've all started. I won't be long. In fact, I'll be back in a jiffy."

Once again clicking her fingers, she disappeared in a blinding ball of light, this time the glistening red sleigh and all of its belongings accompanying her.

Half an hour, that's how long she was gone, much to the other beings' surprise, who were only about halfway through telling their tales of the adventures that had led them to this very point. Arriving with very little fuss or noise, her ride in tow so to speak, Polkinghorne threw the jingling hat into the sleigh for next year and headed over towards what had now become a small gaggle of friends. As she did so, the transformation into the human woman whose guise she'd held on to since her time in the nursery ring took place, the glasses and beard disappearing, the cute and gorgeous pale white freckled face appearing in their place, all bedecked by a mop of blonde, beautiful, shining long hair that any Disney princess would have been envious of.

About to stand up and offer his seat, Vimes was slightly taken aback when his friend and love slipped onto his lap and wrapped her slender arms all around him. As if it were the most normal thing in the world, once again she leaned in and passionately kissed him full on the lips. For him the world stopped turning, momentarily anyway, with a very different kind of magic than the one they were all used to taking over. Happy couldn't begin to describe how he felt, something that on this Christmas morning, was mirrored across the planet.

And so the celebrations began, with the brilliant Polkinghorne using her strange and unusual magic that had been passed down by generations before her to conjure up the most amazing food, drink, decorations and of course presents for all of them, much to their astonishment.

The Tooth Fairy got a new hammer, emblazoned with gold, her initials carved into the handle, something she was more than a little overwhelmed with given everything that had gone on. Flash, to his delight, unwrapped his present to find a pair of specially designed boots that fitted perfectly. Just when he thought it couldn't get any better, Polkinghorne showed him their party piece by getting him to tap the heel of the right one on the floor. Silently, out shot a ferocious dagger, the edges on both sides of its gleaming blade razor sharp. Hard to think what else he could have wished for, it was the ideal gift for the king's protector and he couldn't have been more grateful.

Two down, three to go.

Tank opened his brightly wrapped package first,

surprised as to how small it was but not disappointed in any way. On finding a tiny red velvet bag, he opened the drawstring and peeked inside to discover... SEEDS!

Looking over in wonder at the female Father Christmas, he just had to ask. But she beat him to it.

"Some of the rarest, most exotic and magical plants on the planet," she announced. "I'm sure once they take root, a talent like you will recognise them and know how to care for them."

The youngster's eyes lit up in pure wonder, eager to take them back to his dormitory and start growing them.

Approaching her present with more than a little anticipation especially given its size and shape, the cocky female dragon picked up the long thin package with a bulge at one end and started to tear at the paper.

'I wonder if it's a broomstick,' she thought, having heard about some races using those to travel around on, as that was very much the shape the packaging resembled. Of course it wasn't. It was, though, something she recognised, from the human world up top of all things.

'It's one of those lacrosse stick things,' she mused, both astounded and delighted at the same time, watching as the head of the stick revealed itself, and then out plopped the ball to go with it, bouncing down onto the hard cavern floor, rolling off towards the still steaming sleigh before settling against one of its shiny metal runners.

And that left Peter, only it didn't because there wasn't anything for him. Always the first to stand up for her friends, and never afraid to voice her concern, it was Richie that spoke up.

"Don't you have anything for him?" she enquired, with a little edge to her voice.

If Santa noticed she showed no sign of it, the full on stunning smile still chiselled into her face. Disentangling herself from Vimes, she stood and proceeded to walk across to the bereft youngster, giving the female of the trio a sly look as she strolled past. Invading his personal space, something Peter was almost horror struck by given just how shy he was, well... around strangers anyway, leaving him dumbfounded, Polkinghorne cupped both of his cheeks and closed her eyes as the others all looked on. Wondering what the hell was going on, the young dragon just stood there, too fearful to move. After a moment or two, Santa pulled away and turned to face the Crimson Guard.

"What you told me earlier about the magic you added to the vow, does it apply to these three?"

"Yes," answered Flash methodically. "It applies to every being that's had anything to do with this, from the *tors* to the students, to all of us and the king. The only one that it's not relevant to is Vimes, because he's bound by the original magic you shared with him."

"Hang on a minute," declared Richie, wondering, along with her friends, exactly what was going on.

Before the Crimson Guard had a chance to respond, Tank beat him to it.

"Flash added an extra twist of the supernatural to the magical vow that every dragon involved bound themselves to, with regard to the identity of Santa, something that translated back to us. I'm afraid in a very short time all the beings involved will forget any of it ever happened."

"WHAT!" exclaimed the youngster holding the lacrosse stick in her hand, ball cradled perfectly in its head.

"I'm sorry," said Flash, "but that's just the way it has to be. This is a secret that needs to be kept safe, and it's not because you can't be trusted, all three of you have already proved that you can be. It's about hope, a time honoured tradition and the importance of Santa to all the humans inhabiting the surface. You all witnessed with your own eyes what nearly happened. We really can't afford to take that risk ever again."

"Bravo," added Polkinghorne, "I couldn't have put it better myself."

"You do understand, right?" Flash queried, noting the look of dejection on all their faces.

"We do," replied Tank, speaking for all three of them.

"It's just that it would have been such an exciting tale to retell," ventured Peter softly.

"EXACTLY!" voiced the Crimson Guard.

And then they really did understand.

"So, Flash," said Polkinghorne, changing the subject just slightly, "how long until the magic kicks in?"

Glancing down at his fancy new watch that was just full of magical and all other kinds of surprises, straight from the technicians at headquarters, the Crimson Guard did the maths.

"Forty five minutes."

"Hmmm..." mused Santa, wondering if she dared.

But she was who she was and if anyone could, should or would, it was her.

Directly addressing Peter, she looked him straight in the eyes.

"You are one utterly conflicted youngster, my friend, the likes of which I can't ever remember encountering, and that in itself is unusual to say the least. The answers and the resolution that you seek are beyond my ability to gift to you, but I can give you, at least temporarily, a little... how shall we say... taste of what you're looking for."

Holding out her index finger, Polkinghorne thrust it directly against the young dragon's forehead and as was her wont, delved deep into her magic. The sliver of contact between their skins very gently started to glow.

Taken aback, about to shy away, as soon as the contact was made he was stuck fast against his free will. Panic started to flood through him, not an unusual sensation by any means especially in light of the bullying that for him was an almost daily occurrence back in the nursery ring, just as senses, feelings, emotions and images started to assault his open and naive young brain all at once.

Outstanding amounts of pain coupled with intense cold hammered at his mind, almost knocking him unconscious, but not quite. What he'd done to deserve such a thing as a

Christmas present, he just couldn't figure out. Blisteringly cold brilliant white threatened to overwhelm him... it was everywhere, coupled with an underlying sense of tragedy, the feeling of being shackled and the sadness from which felt like a gigantic black hole trying to gobble him up. Briefly he tried to fight it, but because it was in his mind and controlled by another's magic, there was little he could do to rebel against it. Immediately he conceded defeat and let whatever it was take him on the journey of his life, or in his case... existence.

War... the Nazis fighting the allied forces, he recognised it instantly from the thousands of hours of history lessons he'd studied, recalling just how shaken up he was at learning the sheer propensity of evil the humans were capable of. Most of his classmates remained quiet during all those discussions, just taking things for granted but he, and of course Tank, asked as many questions as possible, trying desperately to get their heads around what had happened and what had gone wrong. But there was no time to dwell on that now because things had swiftly moved on from the torture, monstrosities and the sickly smell of death that now assaulted his olfactory senses almost making him puke despite the fact that he knew he was still tucked safely away in Santa's hidden lair.

And then it all went dark, in his mind anyhow. But that didn't last long, as a pinprick of light accompanying two sets of footsteps ringing in the air shattered the peace as two unidentifiable dragons disguised as humans knocked against a massive door more than five times their size, between them carrying what looked like a giant, white as porcelain egg.

He didn't know, of course there was just no way that he could, but something, some sixth sense, some gut feeling screamed out at him, making the hairs on his arms stand to attention, setting his brain on fire, assuring him that what he was seeing being delivered was in fact...HIM!

Framed by the long, black, shoulder length hair of the

human shape he found himself in, tears streamed from his frozen open eyes back in reality, weaving their way through the vast array of his designer stubble before plummeting ungainly to the floor, like lemmings throwing themselves off a cliff face, landing with the tiniest splash in the world as he tried to get to grips with what he was being shown. Instantly both of his friends stepped forward to aid him. Immediately Polkinghorne waved them off. This had to be done and now that it had been instigated, there was simply no stopping it.

Unable to breathe, or at least that's how it felt, a raw nerve had been poked and prodded because you see it was indeed the egg that he had hatched from over forty years ago and these, he assumed were the parents that he'd never known, despite spending thousands of hours of research trying to find them or any information pertaining to them. Just watching the event itself unfold felt like a gift from the gods and although he couldn't see her entire face he could feel the love of his mother towards her valued cargo.

Questions burned the back of his eyeballs, the main one as you'd expect being... WHY? Why abandon him, why leave him in the care of strangers? Why leave, never to be heard from again? And that's when his mother's love started to twist and writhe, getting caught up in the shadows, replaced by a feeling of betrayal and deceit.

With his friends looking on, wanting to step in and stop whatever cruelty was playing out, Peter had almost exceeded his tolerance for emotion shattering revelations, despite the fact that it went some way to providing clarity on a subject on which he had none. But it didn't end there, because the all encompassing frosty white cold was back with a vengeance. Just when he thought he couldn't take any more, BOOM! Everything playing out in his psyche was shattered into a thousand pieces, debris scattering everywhere as one almighty, giant fist smashed through it all. As a feeling of awe and excitement raced up and down both of his legs, his jaw opened wide, so enthralled was he at what he'd seen. Glancing up from the scuffed, bruised and cut knuckles of the hand, his vision travelled up an arm that could have belonged to a gladiator straight out of Roman times, the huge shiny muscles resembling massive bumps in a road. Then the view pulled out somewhat, revealing the being to which they belonged, in all his glory. Unkempt and dishevelled, wearing the tattered remains of what he had to assume had once been clothes, a male human shape with matted dark hair and a torso to die for glanced directly back at him, the piercing gaze feeling as though it was staring straight into his soul. Bravely he fought past the sensation, although it was difficult to say the least. Only then did it get his attention, the blue markings across one side of his well muscled, exceptionally honed chest. A tree of some sort, he thought. How odd. And that's when he realised that the pain and the harshness of the cold had disappeared, replaced by a blossoming sense that he recognised immediately... LOVE! Relentless, unrequited, unconditional love, the one thing he'd been searching for over the last few decades of his life.

As all this played out, the most powerful amongst them (surprisingly it wasn't Santa, but the enigmatic presence tied to the exotic band Tank currently wore on his finger) experienced something that not only shattered the solitude he'd come to appreciate more with age, but his understanding of the universe. As Santa's magic ran riot across the dragon disguised as a human male, a distant memory of a great battle, one in which he recognised some of the protagonists flickered between his thoughts. Not so surprising you might think until that is, you learn that it's a memory from... THE FUTURE!

Outside his mind, his body exhaled as the tiniest of movements turned his lips into a smile, the joy he felt almost visible for his friends to see. Unfortunately for him, Santa could only do so much and the intensity of her magic had started to fade, as had the vision before his eyes. Instinctively his mind tried to hang on to it, to grasp it with both hands, but it wasn't to be, slipping through his fingers like grains of sand. But it was enough... more than enough in fact, to know that there was one being out there, somewhere, who loved him more than life itself. He didn't know who, why, or where he was, he was just out there. And here and now, learning exactly that was the best Christmas present he could ever have wished for, and so as everything reverted to darkness deep inside his brain, he applied all his concentration and instantly found himself back in the cavern with his friends and of course Polkinghorne standing directly in front of him. Slowly she removed her finger from his forehead, something he was immediately grateful for.

"I'm sorry it wasn't more," she whispered, aware of the rollercoaster ride that she'd just sent him on.

"Don't be," he said confidently, which was unusual in itself. "Knowing that I'm loved unconditionally by someone, somewhere, is more than I could ever have asked for, more in fact than I could have dreamed of."

She nodded, fully understanding.

"Can I ask," he said, hesitating just slightly, "was that a member of... my family?"

"What you've seen is for you only. That being said however, I do believe that was indeed someone that you're related to. If I'm not mistaken, it was your grandfather."

"But, but, but I thought he was dead," stressed Peter, almost blowing a gasket.

"Calm down youngster, you'll do yourself no end of harm otherwise."

Following her words of wisdom, he took a few deep breaths.

"I can only tell you what the magic tells me. What I would say is that what you witnessed and felt might be from any time period. It could well be from the past, the present or even potentially from the future. More than that, I'm afraid I just don't know. I'm sorry."

Wiping his face with the arm of his sleeve, Peter turned to face his friends, who both rushed forward to envelop him.

And then they were all done, at least for the next forty minutes or so, with Flash and the Tooth Fairy discussing everything magical, the three students sitting on the floor trying to make head or tail of what Peter had seen, and Santa and Vimes cuddled up together on one of the huge dragon chairs. It was in many ways the perfect Christmas for them all and not that they had noticed, but it felt very much like any tight knit and loving family would on this very special day. Unfortunately, it had to come to an end.

Not wanting to be the one to disrupt the idyllic scene they all found themselves in, but knowing that it was utterly necessary because time was against them and even she couldn't do anything about that, Polkinghorne stood, shaking off the love of her life and addressed all the others.

"It's time, I'm afraid."

All of them came together, apart from Vimes that is. He stayed right by her side, much to the puzzlement of his students, something he noted with a heavy heart.

"I'm sorry," reflected the conflicted *tor*, "but Santa's given me my gift and I'm staying here with Polks. I'll miss the three of you like crazy, but unlike all of you, I'll be able to look back on this with fond memories that will accompany me until the day I die, which I hope will be many hundreds of years away," he smiled.

"You have our thanks, all of you," added Polkinghorne, "for what you've done over the last few days. I assure you that Father Christmas will never forget your courage, bravery and ingenuity. There will always be something special for you on this of all days."

As one, the group of five all nodded before Santa continued.

"I'll transport you back to somewhere that you'll recognise. You'll probably recall what's happened for a couple of minutes longer, but after that, the magic Flash wove into the fabric of the vow should take over and wipe the last few days from your minds. And I'm afraid that includes you too... For'son!"

'What?!' thought the ring, utterly astounded that she knew he was here, as not one of the others had thought to tell her.

"I've known all along," she ventured, "and as always, I very much appreciate your assistance."

'As always?' he thought, absolutely gobsmacked and as confused as a dinosaur in a maze.

"That's right," she smiled, "our paths have crossed on a number of occasions, but more than that I can't possibly say."

And leaving him hanging, bidding them all farewell, she wrapped her slender pale arm around the *tor* that she loved more than words could express, and one last time, clicked her fingers. Instantly they were... GONE!

Sitting on the floor of her dormitory, back against the bed, very much in human form, the young female dragon pulled the head of the stick back for about the hundredth time, chose a particular spot on the wall once more, and let fly, the ball hitting the exact mark without even the faintest use of anything supernatural, before bouncing straight back to her... BRILLIANT! Abruptly, just as she was about to give it another go, far from being bored, the door to her room was flung open as two vastly out of breath human shapes came bursting in. Jumping to her feet, she wondered what the hell could be wrong.

"H... h... have you heard?" mouthed Peter, sounding like Darth Vader stuck halfway up a mountain.

"Heard what?" replied the youngster, wielding the lacrosse stick.

"Vimes," bellowed Tank. "He's only gone and resigned."

"What?!" she exclaimed.

"Went off on sabbatical somewhere and he's not coming back," Peter added.

"Well, that's no good. He was the best of the lot."

"Our thoughts exactly," replied the two males, marking the start of a very long conversation about the quality of their education.

Before it continued though, Tank had a question.

"Where did you get that?" he asked, nodding in the direction of the lacrosse stick.

"I've had it... hmmmm," she replied. "You know, I really can't remember."

'Odd,' they all thought briefly before the laughter, banter and teasing started, which, much to the annoyance of all those in the adjacent rooms, continued long into the night.

Lying back on his exceptionally plain bed, in the private room that his rank afforded him, in the secretive Crimson Guard barracks adjacent to the council building and the king's private residence in the Buckingham part of the capital, strangely still in his human incarnation, utterly exhausted, Flash tried to ponder the events of the last couple of days. Unsurprisingly, he couldn't focus. There was something important there, of that he was absolutely certain, but however hard he concentrated, nothing would come to him, his last memories only swimming back to the medical bed and his recovery after the fight in Scotland.

'Odd,' was all that he could think, slightly perturbed by losing that amount of time. Instinctively he kicked the heel of his brand new boots against the bottom of the huge wooden bed that he lay on, only to be greeted by the slightest of clicks, that his super sensitive, magically enhanced ears were never going to miss. Bringing his foot around, he marvelled at what he found. There, poking out of the heel of his boot, was the grip to a razor sharp blade that had just sprung out from within. Amazed and confounded in equal measure, Flash pulled out the weapon, twiddling it around in both hands before gently sliding it back in place. Needing to know exactly how it worked, he performed the same action again, and again and again. Over the course of the next few hours his surprise and wonder very much turned into gratitude for something that he could appreciate a great deal.

At a human sized wooden table in one corner of the living room in the king's private residence in the dragon domain capital, the monarch himself sat writing a letter of condolence in regard to a member of the King's Guard who'd died tragically whilst carrying out her duties. A sad, distressing and haunting task to be sure, but it wasn't his first, nor would it be his last. As the leader in question searched for the right words to express his gratitude and sympathy with the parents in question, his constant partner, the presence in the ring, For'son pondered his own problem. Well, not quite problem, but... oddity. Something had gone on, of that he was certain. Scouring his memory, there was a gap and a big one at that, nearly two days missing, which for him felt huge, despite the fact that he was over twenty thousand years old. And while everything appeared as normal as it ever got around here now, any magic that could wipe that amount of time from his memory was a concern to say the least, because it must have been robust, formidable and ultimately as potent as it gets. As the king found exactly the right words for his letter, the presence behind the enigmatic band wondered who or what could have done such a thing.

Less quietly than they would have liked, and much, much earlier, the sound of torn wrapping paper and excited little footsteps echoed down from the loft bedroom above them, pierced occasionally by light chuckles and the odd word or two of wonder deep within the small terraced house just outside the centre of the ancient city of Salisbridge. Under the thick, warm duvet a velvety smooth voice belonging to the beautiful Caroline whispered the words, "Happy

Christmas," to her husband. Shaking his head at the early hour, not that she could see, he returned the sentiment, before kissing her firmly on the lips, knowing exactly where they were in the inky blackness. Once again the tearing of paper cut through the air, this time followed immediately by the grizzling of a much smaller being. The older of the two children had woken up her much younger sibling, which could only mean one thing... it was time to get up. Flicking on the bedside lamp, the happy couple threw on some clothes and as dad climbed up the twisting narrow stairs with very little in the way of headroom, in an effort to find Megan, Caroline paced into Rhianne's room next door and extracted her from the compact wooden cot she lay wriggling about in, much to the child's delight. With all four of them meeting up on the first floor landing, Michael headed downstairs first, keen to switch on the room's lights, looking to brighten the mood and let the children see what they were doing, despite it only being five-fifty-five a.m.. Stretching his arms out and yawning, he punched the dimmer switch on, illuminating the entire room and the vast array of presents meant for the children.

'Odd,' he thought, taking in everything beneath the false fir, his attention caught by the bright, twinkling multicoloured lights of the tree. Amazingly, and he had to blink a few times just to check that he was actually awake and not dreaming, there was an extra present that hadn't been there when he'd gone off to bed last night.

'What the...?'

Now that at least some of the downstairs was illuminated, the trio of mum and the two kids clambered down the last of the stairs and joined him, the excited toddler rushing into the living room, sliding to a halt on the floor next to the tree.

"Look mummy, look," she cried eagerly, "there's a present there for you, this one's for you."

Giving her husband the eye, sure that no such thing had been there before she'd gone to bed, and a little disappointed that he'd broken their pact of not getting each other presents because money was so tight, holding the baby in one hand, the beautiful blonde mum reached down and extracted the intricately wrapped parcel. Sure enough, it had her name on. Ignoring the genuinely stunned look on Michael's face and with just one hand, sticky baby spittle everywhere, she tore off the paper and was utterly astounded to find... the pair of boots that she'd been longing for.

"You shouldn't have," she said smiling, leaning in and kissing the love of her life.

"But..." started Michael.

By then though it was just too late, with his wife having handed over the baby, already slipping the perfectly fitting and stunning looking boots onto her dainty little feet, much to Megan's delight.

Blown away at having his wish come true, Michael turned his attention to the bundle of joy that he was currently holding, gazing lovingly into her wondrous brown eyes. Exactly then, and he would have sworn on his life that it was so, she winked at him, before giving him a knowing smile. Christmas had worked his, or rather her magic, sprinkling it over this tiny little household, bringing hope, joy and just that extra little bit of love to a family that thoroughly deserved it.

THE END

Or is it? Want to find out more about some of the characters you've just read about? Catch up with their latest adventures in 'The White Dragon Saga' to discover more about the dragon world they live in and whether a malevolent threat from the past will bring the planet to its knees.

ABOUT THE AUTHOR

Paul Cude is a husband, father, field hockey player and aspiring photographer. Lost without his hockey stick, he can often be found in between writing and chauffeuring children, reading anything from comics to sci-fi, fantasy to thrillers. Too often found chained to his computer, it would be little surprise to find him, in his free time, somewhere on the Dorset coastline, chasing over rocks and sand in an effort to capture his wonderful wife and lovely kids with his camera. Paul Cude is also the author of the White Dragon Saga.

Thank you for reading...

If you could take a couple of moments to write an honest review on either Amazon or Goodreads, it would be much appreciated.

CONNECT WITH PAUL ONLINE
www.paulcude.com
Twitter: @paul_cude
Facebook: Paul Cude
Instagram: paulcude

BOOKS IN THE SERIES:
A Threat from the Past
A Chilling Revelation
A Twisted Prophecy
Earth's Custodians
A Fiery Farewell
Evil Endeavours
Frozen to the Core
A Selfless Sacrifice
Christmas in Crisis

Printed in the USA
CPSIA information can be obtained
at www.ICGtesting.com
LVHW041640311023
762676LV00002B/299